A RUSH OF BLOOD

A RUSH OF BLOOD

David Mark

This first world edition published 2019
in Great Britain and 2020 in the USA by
SEVERN HOUSE PUBLISHERS LTD of
Eardley House, 4 Uxbridge Street, London W8 7SY.
Trade paperback edition first published
in Great Britain and the USA 2020 by
SEVERN HOUSE PUBLISHERS LTD.

British Library Cataloguing in Publication Data
A CIP catalogue record for this title is available from the British Library.

ISBN-13: 978-0-7278-8905-8 (cased)
ISBN-13: 978-1-78029-648-7 (trade paper)
ISBN-13: 978-1-4483-0347-2 (e-book)

Typeset by Palimpsest Book Production Ltd.,
Falkirk, Stirlingshire, Scotland.

For Nicola.

'For the life of a creature is in the blood, and I have given it to you to make atonement for yourselves on the altar; it is the blood that makes atonement for one's life.'

– Leviticus, 17.11

PROLOGUE

Cecil Court, Central London

The book smelled of meat, as if its pages had once been used to line a butcher's block. It carried the whisper of old churches; of pork-fat candles and blotted blood. It was a slim volume. Fine calligraphy to the title and flyleaf. No missing pages. A sheen to the black ink. Some philistine had scrawled some spidery opinions over some of the pages, but if it was period graffiti then it could well add to the value. A quality item.

Mr Farkas raised his fingers to his mouth and sniffed them. Enjoyed them. He thought the aroma of old books unendingly pleasing. Warm, somehow. It made him think of clothes that had been left to dry in a snug kitchen.

He looked around him. The little bookshop in the handsome arcade was rarely busy but the teeming rain and thundery skies had today depleted the numbers even more. He had the little bookshop to himself. He lifted the book to his face, breathing deeply, as if trying to draw the fading whiff of carnality into the very centre of his being.

Behind closed eyes, he saw her. Saw his girl . . .

Mr Farkas had to bite down on his tongue to prevent himself from crying out. He reached forward, taking his weight upon his left hand. He realized he was trembling. He anchored himself; planting his sensible shoes on the scarred wooden floor. The years were catching up with him. The past months had leeched the last of his youth from his skin and he had taken on the grey pallor of somebody who spent too much time indoors.

'Focus, Mr Farkas,' he whispered, and the similarity of the two words suddenly struck him as amusing. 'Focus, Farkas, focus, Farkas . . .' He had to press his lips together to suppress the giggle that threatened to shoot forth from his lips. The woozy feeling was hovering around the horizon of his consciousness and there was that same stale sickness in his gut. He wondered if bitterness could metastasize. Whether unshed tears could become a tumour.

Relaxation time. That was what his wife had insisted he pursue. No work. No hospitals. No running around. *Go and do what helps you relax . . .*

He examined the book again, his pulse quickening. What a find! A first edition. A real Jean Denys! He knew of the existence of the book but never imagined he would stumble upon one in a stack of yellowing paper and medical guides at the little bookshop two minutes from Trafalgar Square. He pictured the faces of his rivals when they learned he'd found an original. He concentrated on dredging up what he knew about the tome. It had been controversial, he remembered that. Had there not been talk of blasphemy, of Pagan practices? Blood from pig to man; from lamb to dog; from adult to child. Denys had claimed to have discovered the secret of soul transference: a way to alter the personalities of madmen by filling them with the blood of meeker creatures. The transfusionist had seen it as the first step towards a kind of immortality, a way to keep blood flowing even when the original host vessel has long since perished. It had been sent to the Royal Society in 1665: born in a time of plague and fire. It was a significant artefact: a true collector's item. A bonanza of a find.

'Beautiful,' whispered Mr Farkas as he stroked the book's cover. The paper felt luxurious against his fingertips. Waxy. He was tempted to put the tip of his tongue against the page.

He leafed through the pages; fingers gentle, as if shushing a frightened bird. Two words, scrawled in reddish-brown, swam suddenly into his vision.

George Acton.

He felt himself start to shake.

Acton. Alchemist to the Royal Court. Royal Physician. A pioneer whose experiments in blood transfusion had led to some of the great discoveries of the age. A figure on the fringes of immortality who flared brightly then disappeared from history.

Excitement bloomed like a folded rose. He took a deep breath and felt a fresh twinge of pain. He realized he had been squatting for too long. He raised himself up, gingerly, still holding the pamphlet. He had to act calm. The bookseller might see his enthusiasm and claim there had been an error in the pricing. The thought of losing the book within moments of discovering it was too much to bear. He felt a sudden rush of light-headedness. He chided himself as he realized he had forgotten to eat again. He would be scolded when he got home.

Mr Farkas cuffed at his eyes as he felt a tear bubble up like blood from a pin prick. He raised his hands a moment too late. The droplet of salt water had tumbled on to the precious papers he held in his pale hands. He looked down through blurred vision. The teardrop sat reverentially on the 'A' of Acton. It held its form, pearlescent and perfect. Then it dissolved into the page.

The copper scrawl began to swell. To dissolve.

It was like watching blood seep from a corpse.

Mr Farkas started to feel unwell. He could no longer see what was written on the page. He began to shake. Spit gathered at the corner of his mouth. His pupils contracted: dead flies in rancid milk. He began to see things. Taste things. Felt something moving inside his skin. He jerked, suddenly, as if he had emerged from icy water. He was clutching the pamphlet in a fist. He had scored crescent moons into the page. They leered up at him like smiling mouths.

Mr Farkas smiled back.

HILDA

Her name was Meda, and people said she looked like me.

She wasn't much of a dancer. Always half a step behind, like a buffering download. She had a habit of throwing an extra 180 degrees into each pirouette. Finished up facing backwards, looking at the audience with her broad shoulders and big round backside and wondering where everybody had gone. Mum said she looked like a plucked goose in a sparkly leotard, which was a bit upsetting, considering how often she told me we looked alike.

She only came to Streetdance class on a Wednesday night so her mum could earn a few quid cleaning offices at the end of Coronation Road. She didn't hold out much hope of turning Meda into a star. Her little princess wasn't an athletic sort. Used to be shiny and damp and pink by the end of the warm-up. If you pressed her cheeks you could leave big white fingerprints on her skin.

She had a surname too. Stauskas, or something not far off. Lithuanian. I can see her now. A furry hood on her puffer jacket and baggy knees to her leggings. Tall for her age and ungainly in that pre-teen way. All arms and legs. You wouldn't have felt safe taking her for a look around an antique shop. Wouldn't have let her pour from your favourite vintage teapot, though she would have loved to be given the chance. Liked old things, did Meda. Could have spent forever stroking a pair of fox-fur cuffs or staring into the back of a carriage clock. Didn't suit modern clothes, though her Mum dressed her like a pop star. Hooped earrings and hair pulled back too tight. Flashes of make-up on her cheeks. It just gave her a haughty kind of face that made me think of old Victorian photographs: all high necks and cameo brooches and lap dogs snacking on Turkish delight.

Her family lived in a flat between Bethnal Green and

Stepney. Three brothers, a sister, her mum, dad and Uncle Steppen, squished together into five rooms on the second floor of a drab, grey-fronted old building with a rubbish-strewn balcony secured behind chicken wire and broken glass. She liked cartoons and knew how to use a sewing machine. She wore high-topped trainers with Velcro and her hands were always cold. She kept a handkerchief up her sleeve like old ladies do. She ate fruit like it was sweets and carried a miniature book of animal facts in the inside pocket of her coat. That was what got us talking. One of those *'who likes animals more?'* contests that I used to be so competitive about. Meda rose to the challenge. Took me on with some degree-level knowledge on meerkats and told me I was 'talking bullocks' with my assertion that hippos only had four teeth. I took the defeat uncommonly well. Made her laugh with an impression of a King Charles spaniel on a motorboat. We tossed some facts back and forth about Siberian huskies and Alaskan Malamutes. We got to know each other the way kids sometimes can. Best friends in the time it takes to drink a can of Fanta. She spoke with an accent. I thought she might be from Liverpool or Newcastle but she explained that home was a city called Visaginas, which looked like a butterfly if you saw it from above. She'd had a Pomeranian when she still lived there. Sasha, she said, though I thought that was more of a girl's name. Had to be brushed twice a day and he'd been stolen once by some men who were having some kind of dispute with her dad over money. He was on a farm now, out in the countryside, with grandparents who could give him room to run around. Sasha, that is. Not her dad. I told her about my cat, Ripper. Big fat face and fur the colour of turning leaves. Told her she could come meet him if it was all right with her mum. She looked like I'd told her it was going to be Christmas every day from now on.

I was breathless when I introduced her to Mum.

This is Meda, I said, pronouncing it properly. *She's Lithuanian. She's taught me to say hello and thank you and 'Welcome to the Jolly Bonnet'. She likes animals. Do you think we look alike? I do. She doesn't. We're going to open a sanctuary for mistreated dogs. But no Chihuahuas or yappy*

Yorkshire terriers. We don't like them. She knows her mum's number if you want to ring and arrange it. She doesn't live far from here. She walks herself home. You should let me do that. I know these streets. We could walk together . . .

I can see her now. Can picture her face. Two big teeth at the front and two little ones where her fangs would be if she were a vampire. Not the prettiest of girls, though her mum was a looker. She would have grown into her looks, I think. I don't know if she would ever have got any more elegant. She moved as though it was her first day in a new body. Bloody liability at showcase events. Sylvie had to stick her in the back row after the competition in Putney. With her big frame and long arms she'd seemed the best of all of us to be entrusted with the job of catching little Reena as she somersaulted down from the top of our three-tier human pyramid in a dazzling whirl of sequins and pigtails. Meda got into position a moment too late. Reena hit the wooden floor like she had fallen from a plane, arms and legs still fully extended. The imprint she left on the polished boards looked like a gingerbread man. We all heard the thud. All saw our parents and brothers and sisters wince in unison as the dark-haired little Bangladeshi girl hit the ground and stayed there, mumbling incomprehensibly into the shiny wooden boards. We kept dancing, like Sylvie had taught us. Kept high-kicking and back-flipping while Beyoncé bellowed from the speakers that girls run the world. Only stopped when the sound technician pulled the plug on our music and the St John Ambulance man shouted at Paulette for accidentally kicking over the oxygen cylinder. Meda felt awful about it all, though she still grumbled when Sylvie moved her into the back line at the next class. Reena was OK by then, although a rumour went around school that she could no longer count past the number six and would only answer to the name of Kevin. Even in the back line it was hard to disguise Meda's inadequacies. I can see her now, staring intently at the other girls and mimicking our actions an instant too late. Had she made it into the cast of Riverdance, the chorus line would have toppled like dominoes.

She was good at making me laugh. Everything sounded funny the way she said it. She didn't smile when she told jokes,

which somehow made them funnier. And she would get her
words wrong sometimes. She would try and use phrases that
somebody had told her we used in London but they always
sounded weird coming out of her mouth. She would tell me
that she had been 'bubble busy' instead of 'double' and it took
us ages to work out that she was trying to say 'stone the crows'
when she responded to some piece of gossip with the claim
she had been 'stoning her clothes'.

I don't spend a lot of time wondering what Meda would
have become. It's not that the thoughts make me sad or that I
get all maudlin about it. I just don't think there's any way
I could come up with an answer. We were only friends for a
few weeks. You could count the amount of time we spent
together in hours. One class a week, every Wednesday night,
from 6 p.m. until 8 p.m. Believerz street dance class. Two
hours of sweating and giggling and trying to keep up with the
black girls in the care of a passive-aggressive French lady who
lived on runner beans and water and had once appeared in a
video for a band I had never heard of and who Mum said
looked like she was made out of varnished baguettes.

Outside of the classes and competitions I only ever saw
Meda twice. She came with us to the Stepney Green city farm
one blustery Saturday. Fed the goats and did impressions of
the chickens and ate every scrap of the packed lunch that Mum
had made us. Spent her pocket money on a hot chocolate and
a little book about British birds. Picked up some leaflets from
the display stand and spent a few minutes watching a man in
a green jumper demonstrate traditional crafts and then chainsaw
some tree stumps into wooden toadstools. She came home
with us after that. Loved my room. Played with my stuffed
wolves and Polly Pockets and grinned like something from a
cartoon when she saw Mum getting ready for work and slipping into her Victorian wig and gown. She thought the whole
flat was 'exceptional'. She liked that word. Mum's artwork,
displayed corner to corner against bare brick walls, was 'exceptional'. The antique typewriters and microscopes and the
dozens of dead mice displayed in top hats and wedding dresses
on wall-mounted potato crates. The old doctor's bag and the
antique stethoscope and the dozens of fat old books stacked

like logs against the chimney breast. All were 'exceptional'. I could tell she was sad to leave.

Meda. My friend. Big and clumsy and happy to be in England. Loved having a friend who was a real Londoner. She was my friend and I was hers and if I think about anything other than what I know for sure, I might find myself conjuring up images of her worst moments, strapped to that stark white bed in that stark white room – watching her blood fall on to the starched sheets like rose petals on to snow. And I don't want to think about that. It brings back too many of my own memories. Memories of absolute darkness and brilliant, painful light. Memories of gleaming brass and shining glass and blood flowing into and out of my arm. Memories of a reflection – my face obscured behind a mask made of someone else's skin. And when I think of that, I feel myself growing bitter. Growing jealous of Meda. Of all the girls who didn't come back. They became one thing instead of another. They went from alive to dead. Their heart ceased to beat. Their blood ceased to flow.

I'm not so lucky.

I'm still somewhere in between.

MOLLY

Whitechapel. London.
Then . . .

This is the Polly Nicholls snug room; back bar of the Jolly Bonnet. It is a small, comfortable space that smells of meat pies and furniture polish. It is illuminated with oil lamps and candles. It contains a cosiness; an air of autumn. At the centre of the room is a table made from an old wine vat, its surface stained almost black by decades of spilled wine and beer. A trio of rickety leather chairs are positioned like points on a masonic star. In one sits a straight-backed, short-haired woman in her mid-thirties, dressed in a Victorian costume that speaks of steam engines, hair grips, gaslight and clockwork. She wears tight black trousers, knee-high boots and a lacy, high-throated white top with three-quarter sleeves, which she has pinned below her delicate jawline with a brooch embossed with a red skeleton. Her hair is a henna-brown that clashes with the ruby of her fingernails and the black of her fingerless gloves. A pair of wire-rimmed spectacles hangs on a chain around her neck. She is dressed to complement her surroundings, which give off an air of the sophisticatedly shabby; that luxuriously threadbare quality so beloved of glossy magazines.

The light flickers suddenly, as if a train has passed overhead. Black and gold, black and gold. A loose wire, perhaps.

'Cut it out, Polly,' says the woman under her breath. The instruction masks the sound of clumping footsteps. There is a fizzing sound and then the bulb flares bright white. The lamp pitches a golden blush on to the face of a young girl who is barging through from the main bar. She is a scowl of a thing; all wrinkled nose and bumpy brow. She's tall. A bit squishy in places. She looks like an overgrown cherub, with her big mop of honey-coloured hair, round eyes and apple-blossom cheeks.

She slumps down in one of the armchairs and throws her schoolbag on to the other.

Molly looks up from her book. She looks tired. She has had to apply extra make-up to cover an outbreak of tiny pimples that has emerged in her hairline and on her chin. She suffers with stress-related eczema. She is working long hours and her tongue is stippled with tiny ulcers that betray her current poor health. There never seems enough time to eat proper meals any more.

'Mum!' says Hilda, looking at her expectantly. 'You're just sitting there. You've gone dead-eyed again. You look like a corpse.'

They sit in silence for a moment. Molly's eyes return to her book. Hilda folds herself deeper into her chair and looks up at the ceiling, where steam from her wet coat and sodden hair is vanishing into the darkness.

'What's wrong with Polly?' asks Hilda at last.

'In a grump. Sick of it. Not happy in the slightest.'

Hilda nods, understanding. Neither of them has any real belief in ghosts or spirits but they have taken to referring to the Bonnet's idiosyncrasies as being the work of 'Polly' – the understandably restless spirit of Jack the Ripper's first victim. Molly has encouraged Hilda to remain silent about this fact during group discussions at school. She realizes that, out of context, it sounds a little odd. Much of Hilda's life sounds odd on paper.

'It's probably the weather,' says Hilda, wriggling herself upright. 'Cats and dogs out there. Worse. Cows and zebras.'

'Unicorns and porcupines,' says Molly, playing along. They could do this for a while.

Hilda gradually lets go of her bad mood. The apartment she and her mother share is two streets away, in an old pumping station transformed into stylishly shabby apartments. It is a nice place, and home to her fat-faced cat, Ripper, but it is this bar, where her mum is boss, that she thinks of as home. It is a gift for any child with a vivid imagination. Her mind has invented wonderful stories here. She keeps telling her English teacher that she should come in for a drink. Gushes with enthusiasm over the fixtures, fittings and finery. Gets her eras in a tangle from time to time. Mixes up the Tudor with the Victorian. Tells her teacher that the bar is the kind of place where Guy Fawkes might meet with his co-conspirators. The sort of place a working girl, a soiled dove, might down a final tot of rum before evaporating into the murk of Whitechapel for an assignation with a madman's blade. A lot of effort and money has gone into the creation of such an illusion. Though this building on the corner of Brushfield Street is several hundred years old, it has only been a hostelry for a few years. When the Ripper was doing his bloody business, the premises was a print works. Its only real connection to the world's most famous serial killer comes in the form of the posters that were printed on the presses during the panic which followed the third of the Ripper's murders, when rich and well-meaning women began a campaign to provide greater comfort and safety for the unfortunates of the hellish neighbourhood where the murderer seemed able to strike with impunity. One such poster hangs above the fireplace in the main bar. It is the first thing that tourists see when they push open the creaking double doors and gaze at the shabby elegance of the Jolly Bonnet – Whitechapel's premier Victorian gin bar.

'Homework?' asks Molly. 'Hot chocolate on the way?'

'Julien is doing it,' replies Hilda. 'He said he didn't mind.'

'He's sucking up,' scowls Molly. 'An hour late this morning. We were supposed to clean the lines and do a tasting for the new puddings. And he was still in the same shirt as yesterday.'

'I like Julien,' shrugs Hilda. 'He's funny.'

'He's not funny,' says Molly, then concedes that perhaps she is being harsh. She likes her junior barman. He's twenty-three, Croatian and is tattooed from his ankles to his neck. He has a moustache waxed into tips and looks splendid in his braces, bow tie and button-down shirt.

'You used to give me a kiss when you got in,' says Molly. 'It was the best bit of my day. Too cool now, are you?'

Hilda rolls her eyes but smiles as she rises from her chair. She rounds the table and gives her mum a cuddle, pressing their cheeks together. Molly smells of Cool Water perfume; of cake, tea and hairspray. Hilda is all wet clothing and outdoors.

'Extra marshmallows,' says Julien, arriving soundlessly from the main bar and placing a large, copper-coloured mug on the table. It contains steaming hot chocolate and seems to have been topped with most of the pick'n'mix in London.

'I haven't forgiven you,' says Molly, giving him a harsh look. Julien mimes slapping his wrist. Molly, despite herself, sticks out her tongue.

'Your friends are coming through,' says Julien. 'Lottie. Sheamus. The little fat one.'

'That's mean,' says Hilda.

'Christine's not fat,' says Molly, waving her hand. 'She's got a gland thing. It makes her puffy.'

Hilda is considering her response when the staff from the pathology lab at the hospital troop into the snug. Lottie is leading. She is a small, curvy woman with olive skin and bright purple hair. She is wearing a long black leather jacket over a tight black hoodie – unzipped to show off the cleavage that is responsible for many of her thousands of followers on social media. Her chest is tattooed with an anatomically perfect sketch of the human heart and lungs. She is a pathologist by day and YouTube darling by night. She is also thoroughly filthy, a part-time burlesque dancer, and Molly's best friend.

'Wetter than a herring's nostril out there,' says Lottie, shaking her hair, rubbing Hilda's head, pulling up a chair from the fireplace and taking a swig of her Gin Fizz in one fluid gesture. 'I've been gagging for this . . .'

Molly inclines her head to accept Lottie's kiss on her cheek. She looks up as the other morticians make themselves comfortable. She stands and directs the peculiar-looking gentleman into her vacant seat. His name is Sheamus. He is all skin, bones and ill-fitting clothes. Christine pulls up the other chair. She is drinking Baileys and eating crisps. Shorter than Hilda, she has large, slightly wonky eyes and doesn't say a lot.

'The Gargoyle is asking about the scarificator again,' says Lottie, sitting down and finishing her drink in one slug. She puts the empty glass on top of her head. 'You sell it to that abomination of a human being and I'll stab you through the eye.'

Molly sighs. The Jolly Bonnet has become a must-see destination for anybody with an interest in the murky world of morbid anatomy. Lottie has helped her friend source an enviable supply of specimen jars, death art and all manner of Victorian medical equipment. The bar is a paradise for women who wear black eye make-up and who used to draw skulls on their pencil cases at school. It is also popular with the die-hards, the fanatics who will travel thousands of miles to bid for eighteenth-century scalpels that were used to disembowel some notable asylum inmate in some experiment or another. Without really trying, Molly has amassed some decent exhibits and sometimes it is all she can do to stop some of the more rabid collectors from running off with her pickled spleens.

'I'll go be polite,' says Molly. She turns to Hilda. 'You've got an hour for homework and hot chocolate. If Auntie Lottie happens to do some of it for you then I'm not going to ask too many questions, okay? But there's no Believerz if it's not done and I know you want to see Meda. How's all that going anyway?'

Hilda coughs, theatrically. '*Sveiki. Esu Hilda, nors aš kartais norėčiau buvo vadinamas kažkas. Sveiki atvykę į Jolly Bonnet. Aš tikiuosi, kad jūs neprieštaraujate mano Muma yra taip keista.*'

'Impressive,' says Lottie. 'I can ask for a threesome in Danish if that's any help.'

Hilda joins in the laughter and Molly hopes to goodness that she is only pretending to understand. Leaving the cosiness of the Polly Nicholls behind her, Molly makes her way down the dark, lamp-lit corridor to the front bar. There's a decent crowd in tonight. Half a dozen men in nice shirts and loosened ties, drinking pints of real ale and playing with their mobile phones. A man and a woman, sitting in the window, arguing about something unfathomable as they share a triple burger, taking their bites in turn. A French girl, drinking white wine and typing ideas into her laptop. The old boy, hand over his face like he's got the worst migraine in the world. And *him*. The collector. The one Lottie calls the Gargoyle. Back for more.

'Your Grace,' says Brendan, effusively. He has thinning hair swept back into a nasty little rat tail and there is a mottling of grog-blossoms on his nose and jowls.

'Brendan,' says Molly. She allows him to bow and press his damp lips to the back of her hand. She manages a smile, which turns to horror as she sees what he has brought with him. 'Oh, you dickhead, there's eyeballs on the bar!'

A wooden case sits on the bar in front of Brendan in the sort of position most people would deposit a laptop. Inside are fifty glass eyes, carefully arranged into beautifully crafted wooden squares. They are a variety of different colours and are staring out in all directions.

'Are they not beautiful? They arrived today.' He looks at the eyeballs as if they are children and they stare back without expression. He preens a little. 'Nine hundred and eighty pounds at auction, but it was worth it to defeat Autolycus. Manufactured by the wonderful Lemoine Flizet Peigné in Paris a century ago. Only one tiny chip to one specimen. I find myself utterly transfixed. I have not yet utilized them for their original purpose as prostheses, but perhaps if my lady commands . . .'

Molly pulls a face, exasperated. Brendan is constantly bringing in his specimens and regaling the staff about his ongoing feud with a rival collector by the name of Autolycus. Molly has got very good at saying 'that's awful' while not really listening.

'You are so frigging weird, Brendan. What do you do with all this stuff? I mean, I used to collect teapots. I like oil lamps. All this medical stuff – it's a bit creepy.'

A whiff of strong perfume and damp clothes trickles into Molly's nostrils and a moment later she feels Lottie take her in a hug from behind. She peers over her shoulder and looks at the eyeballs. 'Nice,' she says, begrudgingly. 'Parisian?'

'Of course!' says Brendan, delighted.

'And they'll be going to a museum, will they?' she asks, sounding disapproving. 'You'll allow people to enjoy the craftsmanship . . .'

'I am a private collector. It is a long and noble calling. They will fit in at my private museum. My own Aladdin's cave. My palace of oddments and peculiarities . . .'

Molly rubs her forehead. She could do without this. 'You were trying to buy it,' she says, flatly. 'Again. You were offering money to Julien to turn a blind eye while you took it. And don't say you weren't. Or show me your blind eyes. Now, are we going to have to go through this again?'

Brendan has his heart set on a scarificator. It is a small device and currently shielded from dirty fingers within a tall glass case behind the bar. The Mallam scarificator allowed for vaccination against smallpox. All its user had to do was dip its four lethal-looking blades into the pustules of a person already infected, then flip the lever to stab the blades into their arm. It was one of the more brutally ingenious devices of the eighteenth century and looks to Molly about as appealing a concept as a French kiss with a shark.

'I am in funds, Duchess,' says Brendan. He is holding a brandy glass containing enough Courvoisier to house a gold-fish. 'I know you to be a fine specimen of womanhood. You are a collector, as am I. You strike a hard bargain and I applaud you for it. But if I do not have the item then I declare I shall be of miserable cheer for the rest of my days. I implore you, name your price.'

'Brendan, I'm tired, mate. I haven't got the energy tonight. Get your balls off the bar.'

'Wednesday, yes?' says Brendan, unexpectedly. 'Dance class. You and the *enfanta*. I would not dream of standing in your way. But please, I implore you – give me an indication that all is not lost.'

'Brendan, there are only so many ways I can say the same thing,' she says. 'The exhibits are on loan. If I sell one, or lose one, it will go to court. I only work here. I own nothing. And if you tell me I own your heart, I promise, I will glass you.'

Molly looks up as the man at the end of the bar gives a polite laugh. She hadn't noticed him before. He's not a big guy but he has broad shoulders and his big arms strain at the fabric of his brown leather coat. His hair has been trimmed down close to his skull and there is a map of scars upon his left temple. His stubble is a day away from becoming a dark beard and he is looking at Molly with eyes that suggest he is reading an invisible inscription on the inside of her skull.

'My dear, I would implore you to name your price,' says Brendan. 'I will make the cheque out to whomsoever you decree. Or perhaps I might pay cash . . .'

'Seriously, Brendan, have your drink and toddle off home. I'm not in the mood. Could I be clearer? Hilda gets this concept and she's only fucking ten!'

Brendan starts laughing, showing badly capped teeth. He seems about to return with a counter-offer when the mobile phone tucked into Molly's bra starts to vibrate. It's her alarm, telling her she needs to get her daughter home and changed for Believerz and try to feed her something halfway nutritious along the way.

'Mum, are we going? I really want to see Meda. And you know how Sylvie can be when we're late. Can we run?'

'We're going, we're going,' Molly mutters, looking through the darkened window at the diagonal rain beyond the glass. 'Can you keep up the pace?'

Hilda grins. 'Ready . . .'

'Steady . . .' says Molly.

They both cheat, and set off early.

Several pairs of eyes turn and watch them go.

An overview of Medical Cannibalism and the
Benefits of Vampirism
An article by Goldsmith's research fellow Eve Burrell
February 11, 2013

For many centuries, it was not uncommon for people in the western world to consume flesh and drink blood. These people were not vampires or cannibals in the sense that we would know them today. They were people seeking strength, sustenance and an extended life. Gruesome as it might seem today, the drinking of human blood, the smearing of human fat, and the distilling of human bones into a much-prized spirit, were done with the intention of healing.

Today, lifeless corpses are viewed as something unpleasant. They are something that inspires fear and revulsion. But for a long time the corpse was a veritable supermarket of ingredients for healing potions. The scientists of the time were somewhat literal in their prescriptions. Powdered blood was said to help bleeding; human fat helped bruising; ground-up skulls helped with migraines or dizziness. What's more, physicians and patients believed that ingredients obtained from corpses were most potent if they had died violently. The physician Paracelsus wrote that after a man was hanged, his 'vital spirits' would 'burst forth to the circumference of the bone'. It was thought that when death came suddenly, a person's spirit could stay trapped for at least enough time that the living might benefit from its power.

Epileptics of ancient Rome drank the blood of slain gladiators and the practice gained renewed favour as a health tonic during the Renaissance. The blood was typically harvested from the freshly dead, but could also be taken from the living. Marsilio Ficino, a highly respected fifteenth-century Italian scholar and priest, said that elderly people hoping to regain the spring in their step should 'suck the blood of an adolescent'. By the 1650s there was a general belief that drinking fresh, hot blood from the recently deceased would cure epilepsy, as well as help with consumption. Meanwhile, dried and powdered blood was recommended for nosebleeds or sprinkled on wounds to stop bleeding.

Skulls were another commodity prized for their healing powers. The seventeenth-century English physician John French offered at least two recipes for distilling skulls into spirits, one of which he said not only 'helps the falling sickness, gout, dropsy' and stomach troubles but also was 'a kind of panacea'. (The other recipe was better for 'epilepsy, convulsions, all fevers putrid or pestilential, passions of the heart'.) English King Charles II, an enthusiastic chemist with his own laboratory, is reported to have paid six thousand pounds to a professor at a local college for a recipe for distilled powdered skull, which thereafter became known as 'the King's drops'. The remedy was popular for a variety of complaints and seems to have often been mixed into wine or chocolate . . .

MR FARKAS

Mr Farkas lives in a big brown house at the end of Fournier Street in Spitalfields, London. Were he to open the shutters and lean out of the window in the attic room, he would be able to see the Ten Bells pub and the shadows cast by the great dirty iceberg of Christchurch. He would hear the carillon and call of the bells. Were he to strain his ears he would perhaps hear the occasional word drifting up from the street guides who lead tours around this historic neighbourhood. Some of the experts believe that Jack the Ripper lived here. Modern profiling techniques have been applied to the locations of his victims and this street, where working girls used to ply their trade and drink their gin, is at the very centre of the kill zone.

Mr Farkas does not care about the Ripper. He does not understand the fascination. He takes no notice of the crowds who gather near his front door and who wonder how a property on such a sought-after street could have been allowed to fall into such disrepair. There was a time when he would have been tempted to open the shutters and pour cold water on the guides in their frock coats and top hats and to listen to the squeals of the tourists who keep taking pictures of his front door. But Mr Farkas does not have the strength any more. He has not leaned out of the window of the attic room for a long time. He has dizzy spells and does not like the feeling of insubstantiality that overcomes him when he looks down from a height. He imagines himself torn away on the breeze like a shirt snatched from a washing line. Or worse – toppling forward and plummeting to the road beneath. He can see it perfectly. Can imagine himself coming apart like a bag of dropped offal and exploding all over the pavement. Mr Farkas does not like the idea of such destruction. His flesh matters little to him, but the thought of his blood being so ill-used is a horrifying one.

Mr Farkas is a thin, reedy sort of man. His greying hair is

thick and neatly parted and covers his ears on both sides, as was the style when he attended university. He has a large nose that does little to draw attention away from his bushy, impressive moustache. He is very pale. His fingers look like candles on a birthday cake and his lips are the sickly grey of soggy paper. There is a sheen of sweat upon his skin.

Mr Farkas is sitting in one of the rooms on the second floor of the house. He does not remember entering it. He is accustomed to these moments of returning to himself without recollection of where he has been. He is an educated man. A respected academic. It is true that these moments of disassociation, of disconnection, are becoming more frequent, but he tells himself he has been under a great deal of pressure recently. He does not sleep well. He eats infrequently. He is cold much of the time, despite the perspiration on his brow. Lately he has made the decision to stop taking his tablets.

Mr Farkas blinks, slowly. He takes stock of the environment in which he finds himself unexpectedly situated. He is in the room that his wife used to use when she dabbled in art. It faces out on to the street instead of into the enclosed back garden and the light from the streetlamp casts a lurid yellow glow through the open shutters. It mingles with the blue light that shines from the laptop computer by his feet. He is sitting down in a leather armchair. It is plum-coloured but appears a deep shade of ox blood in this light. The rest of the room is largely bare. A stack of books are piled in a ruined pyramid in the corner and an easel with a broken leg leans against the shutters. A paintbrush sticks through the canvas, skewering the eye of the vaguely female face that smiles dazedly out from the smears of paint.

Mr Farkas examines himself. He is dressed in his finery. Grey-black, high-waisted trousers in brushed cotton. High-collared white dress shirt and waistcoat in herringbone tweed. He wears a blood-red cravat at his collar. He is draped in a soft blue smoking jacket, embroidered with turquoise threads. There is a patch worn smooth on the velvet of the collar and he finds himself stroking it as he casts his eyes around him. He is dressed as she likes. He is her creation. Her anachronism. Her old-fashioned Daddy.

Mr Farkas thinks of Beatrix.

Of his *cica*.

His blood.

Mr Farkas rarely allows himself to speak in his native Hungarian. His English is almost without accent and the academic textbooks that he has written are regularly praised for their precision and mastery of language. Through training and willpower he has ensured that his thoughts invariably arrive in his head in his adopted language. He only allows himself this one indulgence – this one word from his childhood. He calls his child his *cica*. His kitten. It suits her. She is soft and languid and seems to purr when he strokes her hair. She is playful and inquisitive and has the same piercing eyes as her father. She is the blood of his blood. She is made of the same things as he is.

Mr Farkas stares at a patch of damp on the patterned wallpaper of the chimney breast. The paper was expensive. Game birds and exotic fruits upon a rich blue background. It seems to shimmer in the peculiar light. Mr Farkas stares. After a time it becomes a face, the way clouds become dragons and flames form into dancers. It is a round, well-fed face. Dark, deep-set eyes and a slack mouth, as if the jawbone has been dislocated and improperly set. The face has a dark widow's peak which disappears into some form of flamboyant periwig, and the throat is bisected by a disk with ruffled edges. It becomes clearer the more he looks. Becomes more precise. More real. Soon Mr Farkas is unsure whether he is looking at the pattern in the damp, or whether it is looking at him. It is no longer a part of the picture. The alchemist is standing in front of him. Heeled shoes and breeches. Stockings to the knee. A dark, formal coat over a blood-red waistcoat. He is considering Mr Farkas critically, as though mentally disassembling him into his component parts. He moves, and Mr Farkas thinks of magic lantern shows from his childhood. The alchemist moves fluidly; a gracefulness made up of flickering images, all minutely different from the last. It is as if the alchemist is disappearing and reforming too fast for the eye to process. Mr Farkas finds it unsettling. The alchemist's presence always precedes a terrible headache and nausea. The doctor has urged him to be alert for any such symptoms. He has allayed the doctor's fears. Told them that he is not experiencing any hallucinations, painful cranial pressure or hearing the soft, sibilant voices that have undone him at different times of his life. He is only half lying. Mr Farkas does not believe he sees hallucinations. He knows the alchemist is here. He is simply the only one who can see him.

A creeping feeling of disquiet inches over Mr Farkas. He is overcome by a sensation of having done something shameful. It is a feeling he can only liken to waking from a dream having committed adultery. He feels grubby, despite his fine clothes. He feels as though he has dressed in splendid garments while still unwashed and caked in filth. He does not like it. He feels himself shuddering and becomes aware of a chemical taste in his mouth. He does not remember taking any medication but he cannot say for certain that he has not. He knows himself to be an occasional slave to his pleasures. He has been known to sip from his cache of illicit prizes from time to time. One entire room of his house is given over to the oddities that he has collected over the past thirty years. He has a love for medical paraphernalia. Mr Farkas regrets that he did not train to become a doctor. Were he given his chance again, he would train as a surgeon. Instead, he has made a living as an expert in the history of medical advancement and is one of the world's leading authorities on antique medical equipment. His home contains artefacts worth almost as much as the property itself. He has been known to help himself to the occasional sample from his private museum of curiosities. He has routinely dropped laudanum on to his tongue from an original pipette manufactured in Belgium in the 1840s. The dealer from whom he purchased the item claimed that it had briefly been owned by Lewis Carroll, though he had been unable to verify the claim. The provenance does not matter to Mr Farkas. He cares little for Carroll. The laudanum helps Mr Farkas *see*. It helps him find the right mental frequency, tuning him in to the voice, the vision, that has provided him with such comfort these many months. Were it not for the chemicals, Mr Farkas is unsure whether he and the alchemist would have found each other. And without the alchemist, Mr Farkas would never have understood what was required of him. He would have continued to think of life and death as distinct states. He would have thought his bloodline dammed. Instead, something approximating his offspring continues to breathe. And that pleases Mr Farkas and the alchemist very much.

For a time, a young research fellow used to help Mr Farkas with his experiments. She compiled a thick folder of the documents and scribblings that they had pored over together. She had drawn exquisite anatomical specimens and her neat handwriting had turned Mr Farkas's scrawled notes into something close to art. Mr Farkas had been touched by the gesture and his rare, awkward smile had made the girl grin in a way that made him uncomfortable. It made him wonder if his wife had been right when she told him that it was folly to invite her into their home. Folly to encourage her burgeoning obsession with the professor who had been appointed to oversee her PhD. He had dismissed his wife's fears. Told her that he had tutored thousands of students and that it would take somebody extraordinary to turn his head. He did not want her for anything other than her willingness to do as he asked. It was her approval that he liked most – the way she condoned what must be done in the name of advancement.

The documents within the young student's scrapbook have long since been ripped into scraps. The home which used to mean so much to Mr Farkas and his family is now a broken-down mass of shadows, damp and fallen brick. The garden is overgrown and most of the rooms are empty. Mr Farkas will eventually make things right with the property but for now he has other concerns. He must make things right with his daughter. He must make things right with his blood.

Mr Farkas breathes in and catches the whiff of it. That tang of iron and vinegar.

A memory surfaces.

Beatrix.

Angry conversations about platelets and blood counts and urgings that he should prepare himself for the worst.

He screws up his face as if biting down on the memory. The picture bursts and his mind floods with the juice of other remembrances. Exertions. Recent undertakings that left his chest heaving and his skin coated in mud, sweat and blood. He cannot quite recall how Beatrix had evaded him when she sleepwalked away from her bed in the cellar but it had been a hard job to find her and bring her home. He seems to recall having to hurt somebody but he is not sure whether the memory is real or something he has read. He fancies that it is the work of imagination. He knows he is not a violent man.

Soon, Mr Farkas will walk downstairs and into the kitchen. He will pull up the heavy door in the floor and descend into the specially adapted cellar room beneath. He will sit by his daughter's bedside and he will read her one of her favourite stories. These moments are precious to him and he knows what they mean to her. They distract them both from feeling too negatively about the future. He cannot deny that she is getting sicker. Her face looks pale and ragged, no matter how hard he tries to apply lipstick and rouge to her greying features.

Mr Farkas would suffer far more in these moments of despondency were it not for the alchemist. He has reached out through the centuries and spoken to Mr Farkas. He has given him instruction on what can be done. What *must* be done.

Tomorrow he will give Beatrix her medicine. He will attach a rubber tube to the goose-feather quills that puncture her veins. He will bleed her into a gleaming silver cup. He will fill her full of the refrigerated blood that he guards as if it were treasure. And then he will lay his head upon her chest and listen to her heart beat, hard and true, with a blood that he will never allow to die.

Mr Farkas casts an eye on the computer screen. She will be talking to him soon. The girl with the blue hair and the large breasts and the understanding of what goes on beneath the skin. He enjoys her. She has spirit. Her understanding is rudimentary but he would like to talk with her some day. He believes that she may be crucial in raising awareness of the alchemist's work. He has sent her several messages on the discussion forum on her website, urging her to consider turning her attentions to the forgotten master. Perhaps she will do so tonight.

The thought causes a frisson of excitement to course through Mr Farkas's veins. He slides towards the computer. Opens up the document he is working on. It is a short article for an academic magazine detailing the life of a seventeenth-century anatomist and surgeon. He is satisfied with the article but is not yet ready to send it. His work requires a conclusion. He fancies that when Beatrix sits up and holds him and stares out through new eyes, he will glimpse at once an end, and a new beginning.

LOTTIE

'Do I have lipstick on my teeth?' asks Lottie, pulling a face at Christine. The gurn is extravagant and more than a little manic.

'No, you're fine. Pearly white.'

'My sort of fine or a general fine?' asks Lottie, concerned. 'The sort of "fine" I say when it's really not very fine at all, or a general kind of "hey, that's damn fine"?'

'Could you stop looking at me like that please? You look like a chimpanzee on a rollercoaster. I'm a bit out of my depth . . .'

Lottie looks as though she is going to push for more and then takes pity on her friend. Christine is socially awkward and always seems to be doing battle with a surfeit of saliva. She is at her happiest labelling exhibits at the pathology museum and writing long and impenetrable blogs with titles like *The Death of Death* and *Is Cremation a Feminist Issue?* She has a lot of followers on social media but has never used her own image to promote her output. She prefers to hang back in the shadows. Lottie presumes that she lives with her parents and that her bedroom is all black potion bottles, Edgar Allan Poe stories and Buffy the Vampire Slayer posters.

'Nothing up my nose?'

'Lottie, I don't want to look up your nose.'

'Why? Is there something up it?'

'This was never in the job description!'

Lottie laughs and starts blowing raspberries to make her lips look fuller for the camera. Christine mimics her, but while Lottie looks cheeky and sweet, Christine seems to be doing an impression of a motorboat. Lottie looks away. She sometimes wonders if she has befriended a version of herself from an alternate reality. Lottie was just as shy as Christine during her school days in Reading and if it were not for a conscious decision to embrace her own uniqueness, she could have easily become a timid and introverted adult. She knows what it is like to be the victim of endless dead arms and Chinese burns and has fished her exercise books out of so many toilets and rubbish bins that she has never got out of the habit of doing duplicate copies of her homework. But at 15 she decided that it was better to be different than to blend in, and spent her birthday money on the kind of black boots that figure in a certain kind of person's darkest fantasies. She started wearing white foundation and thick black eyelashes and eyebrows. Started dyeing her hair a deep purple-black. Started wearing chokers and little purple corsets over tight black skirts. Half a lifetime later she is Dr Lottie. She's the darling of the Death Salon, the Queen of the Coffin Club. She's a well-respected pathologist and an excellent curator of the necro-museum she personally established, and she is a recognizable figurehead for the whole sub-culture of morbid anatomy. Her regular webisodes on her own YouTube channel have got huge viewing figures and the work on mainstream TV is picking up. She could easily be dining at The Ivy or quaffing champagne at a gallery opening right now, but she feels more at home in the Jolly Bonnet. There is something comforting about the place. It feels a little like a wrinkle in time – as though she could constantly open the door to another era. She wouldn't be surprised to hear that a regular had been killed by Jack the Ripper or that the guy who drinks Guinness and wears Crocs has lost his house in a Luftwaffe raid.

'Could you hold it for me please?' asks Lottie, handing her phone to Sheamus. They are sitting at the circular table in the snug. Christine has eaten three packets of crisps and Sheamus has switched to water in case he is too sleepy to play on his Xbox when he gets back to his flat.

'Just a trailer, is it?' asks Christine, softly.

'Agent says that's what I should be doing more of,' says Lottie. 'Little bursts. Gifs. A few seconds of this or that. It's about staying in the consciousness of your followers, which is a sentence I never thought I would say.'

'But they must be people with an interest in anatomy and death,' says Sheamus, confused. 'And that's not something you can just whiz through . . .'

'A lot of the viewers just want to see an example of mad

stuff that's been removed from rectums,' shrugs Lottie. 'Others tune in for something a bit more in-depth, which sounds crude, though I don't know why. Some people really do want to know about the history of the profession and some of the stories from around the world. People waking up in body bags. Ninety-year-old smokers with magnificent lungs. Bullets found inside the bodies of people who have no idea when they got shot. The weird stuff. They love all that.'

'And you,' says Christine, almost too quietly to be heard. 'They like you.'

'Well, I suppose,' says Lottie, wishing she had a stock response to such praise. 'I'm cheaper than porn, I suppose. But this is just me. And if it helps get people interested in the craft then it's no bad thing.'

Christine pulls a face. For a moment she looks like a rabbit about to burst into tears. 'Do we want more people in the craft? I mean, my numbers of followers are going up. There are more and more people coming to the Death Salon meetings. I mean, it's meant to be an alternative lifestyle . . .' Christine trails off, seemingly appalled with herself for having spoken. Lottie pats her arm. She understands the feeling. She used to be part of an exclusive club. Now everybody seems to be worshipping Day of the Dead masks and doing interesting things with human remains.

'Guilty as charged,' smiles Lottie. 'That's what we're trying to do, isn't it? Get the conversation going again. Get people to recognize their own mortality and to embrace it.'

'Sounds like a suicide club,' says Sheamus, shoving his finger in his ear and twisting it, as if chalking a pool cue.

Lottie feels her enthusiasm waning. She decides to leave it until Molly returns before she films herself. She always feels more vibrant in Molly's company. She brings a sparkle to her eyes. Puts colour on her cheeks. Her last three casual boyfriends have all subtly implied that she sees Molly as more than a friend. She has not dignified the accusation with an explanation. She doubts they would understand. She does love Molly, but it is not in any way that her occasional bedroom partners could understand. She just wants to be near her. Wants to please her. Likes breathing in the same air she has breathed

out. She is her best friend and something more. Something
indefinable. Something that makes her a pathologist and
morbidity scholar who actually believes in souls. She has dug
around inside enough corpses to know that not everything can
be found with a scalpel.

'Not bothering?' asks Sheamus, as Lottie puts her phone
down on the barrel.

'Maybe in a bit. I need inspiration. Or another drink.'

'I'll get them,' says Sheamus, and takes her empty glass.
'Spare you having to talk to the sweaty chap again.'

Lottie smiles her thanks. She likes Sheamus. He's physically
on the repulsive side but she imagines she will probably allow
him to have sex with her some day. He is a good friend and
has helped her with lots of research projects and she fancies
it would be rude not to give him something that he would so
obviously enjoy. She has told Molly as such, only to be told
off for valuing herself too cheaply. Lottie spent a lot of time
thinking about the scolding and eventually realized what her
friend had been trying to tell her. On the back of the telling-
off, she has decided not to have sex with people until they
really deserve it. That way, the reward has more value.

'I'm sorry if I sounded like I was going on,' says Christine,
and Lottie is horrified to see tears in the young technician's
eyes. There is steam on her thick glasses.

'Oh goodness, don't be silly,' says Lottie, feeling awkward
and putting a hand on her well-upholstered arm. 'You're my
friend. I love to hear your opinions.'

'I always let myself down,' says Christine, looking at her
shoes. 'My dad always said so. So much potential and then I
spoil it with my big mouth.'

Lottie looks around, hoping for rescue. None is forthcoming.
She is stuck with this shy, sad little Goth girl and her rucksack
full of assorted woes.

'Hey, actually, I wanted your opinion on something,' says
Lottie, desperately trying to distract her companion.

'Oh yes?' asks Christine, looking up.

'Yes . . . erm, yes . . . that creepy chap in the front bar.'

'Brendan? He collects medical equipment. Specimens.
Victorian paraphernalia. He's quite interesting.'

Lottie cocks her head, surprised. 'Really? I didn't know you'd spoken.'

'Yes, I knew him before I started drinking here. He's a bit of a drinker but he has a good collection. He's the one I suggested you have on for an episode, remember?'

Lottie keeps her face impassive. She receives a lot of messages from Christine and tends to skim most of them or delete them undigested. 'Oh, right. Sorry, two and two didn't make four for a second. I'm such a ditz . . . How did you know him, then?'

Christine shrugs. 'We were at the same auction. He knows his stuff, like I said.'

Lottie has a hazy memory of Christine's original application for the intern position at the hospital. She had listed her interests as 'taxidermy, morbid anatomy and the study of surgical equipment'. It had accompanied a degree in histopathology and a philosophy diploma. She'd seemed absurdly overqualified on paper. Only when she interviewed the timid little thing did Lottie understand why she had struggled to find a better position.

'Do you have much of a collection then?' asks Lottie, hoping that Sheamus will hurry back with their drinks.

'I wasn't buying,' said Christine. 'This was for a research paper I was putting together. The history of transfusion and the symbolic role of blood. Some of Jean Denys's papers were available to be viewed. I couldn't resist. Neither could he. He's a big fan.'

Lottie screws up her face as she tries to place the name. 'Anatomist,' she says, wincing. 'Transfused calf's blood into a mad bloke in Paris to try and calm his troubled mind. Ended up charged with murder.'

Christine nods, appreciatively. The tears in her eyes are sparkling now as she warms to her theme.

'Did you know that in ancient Rome, people would pay to drink the blood of dying gladiators so that the strength of the fallen could pass on to the living? The blood contained the essence of a person, you see. Fifteen hundred years later, people still believed that. When Denys transferred the blood of the calf to the mental patient, it was in the certain belief that the calf's "mild soul" would quieten the heated, troubled blood in the recipient's body. Of course, that's the tip of the iceberg. You wouldn't believe the lengths that he and his rivals went to practise their techniques. There were anatomists transfusing milk and wine and vinegar into their pets to see what effect it would have on their disposition. I'll send you the link if you think there could be a webcast in it. For you, I mean. Not with me, or anything . . .'

Lottie nods. She has never seen her friend so energized. She has a sudden mental picture of Christine's home. Can imagine a lot of dead birds and stuffed rats in wedding dresses. She would put good money on candles in empty wine bottles, pictures of cemeteries taken through cobwebbed railings, and at least one top hat crowned with feathers. She feels a sudden surge of fondness for Christine and her ilk. She likes the idea that there are thousands of people out there, all fascinated by her work and her webcasts and the work she is doing to make death as sexy as it used to be.

'She can talk,' says Sheamus, returning from the bar.

'Molly? She's back?'

'No, old girl. Looks like something from a fairy tale.'

'Connie?'

'Apparently I'm a right *skinnymalink*, whatever that might be. Need a good sheep dip. Smarten myself up a bit and get the mice out of my beard and I might be a looker.'

Lottie laughs. 'She's got character. Molly says her nan gave evidence at the Mary Kelly inquest. Spotted Mary with a gent in a tall hat the day before she died.'

Christine looks startled. 'Is that true? Her own grandmother?'

'Well, if Connie was born about 1930 then of course it would be possible, but no doubt half the East End can lay claim to the Ripper story.'

'Doesn't she talk about it? That would be fascinating.' Christine looks as though she has just learned that she is in the presence of a megastar. 'Would she talk to you?'

'Don't even go there,' says Lottie, affecting an American accent. 'She hates all the Ripper stuff. Reckons we should all get over it.'

'But she drinks in a Ripper bar!'

'She likes the atmosphere, so she says. Likes the way Molly handles problems. Thinks I'm a right mess of a human being. Doesn't like the hair, although I bet you half her neighbours in sheltered housing have a blue rinse.'

They drink their drinks and Lottie feels herself becoming more enthusiastic about a broadcast. She checks her reflection and the phone's connection and a moment later is talking into her phone.

'Evening, Coffin Club. Bloody horrible night, isn't it? I'm not sure the rockabilly curl will last all the way home. I'll be looking like a drowned Fraggle by morning. Just wanted to drop you all a quick hello from yes, you guessed it, London's finest gin bar. It's been a fine night in the company of these fabulous people.' She spins the camera and Sheamus waves. Christine covers her face, as if the light of the phone will burn her. 'We've got a shy one! You'll have to excuse us. We've had a shock. A fellow enthusiast of all things curious has just proudly displayed his collection of optical prosthetics. That's glass eyes to you and me. All different shades, from iris to the whites. I'm not sure which shade I'll need come the morning. Old piano keys, I reckon. Smoker teeth. Anyways, if you're interested I'll ask him to have a root through his collection and unearth a few oddities for your pleasure. Any requests? Anyhow, go and play with your pickled livers. Dr Lottie, out.'

Lottie gives a sigh of relief. Got it first time. She can expect at least 50,000 views. Her agent will be happy.

'Don't do that to me please,' says Christine, quietly, in her ear. 'I don't want to be seen. I've told you that before. I'm not like you.'

There is an icy tone in Christine's voice. She has gone pale. Lottie feels instantly terrible. 'Oh, darling, I'm so sorry! I forget. It just comes naturally to me, I suppose. But I promise, I won't ever point the camera at you again.'

Christine seems mollified. She gives a little nod and starts to put on her coat which has been hanging on the back of the chair. Lottie waves a hand in front of her own face, wafting at her eyes. There had nearly been tears. She feels chastened and the sensation is an uncomfortable one. She finds herself feeling both guilty and ill-used at once. She hadn't meant any harm. And sure, shyness is a horrible thing, but you can overcome it. She's proof – you can become somebody new. The girl needs to go drink some gladiator blood.

'I could use you in early in the morning,' says Lottie, breezily. 'The syphilis specimens need to be moved to a new jar. Is that cool?'

Christine gives a nod. Her eyes are hard to read behind her glasses. Lottie realizes she is being a cow and tries to make amends. 'Thanks for all that info on the blood chap. I'll look into that, yeah. Could you send me the piece you wrote?'

A little grin splits Christine's face and Lottie feels relieved. She is not great at dealing with emotional people. Her expertise is the dead.

Lottie sits in silence with Sheamus for a time. She can think of little to say. She would like to be on camera all the time. She seems better able to communicate when she has an audience instead of a companion.

'Shall we go sit with Connie?' she asks, at length. 'We can hear what she thinks of my career choices and shoes.'

'If she calls me a lanky fucker one more time I may cry,' says Sheamus.

'Prepare yourself for tears,' says Lottie, and lifts herself from the chair. As she glances at her phone, she sees that Christine has already sent her half a dozen links to different articles on Jean Denys. She rolls her eyes and sends a smiley face of thanks. She'll read them later.

'Anything?' asks Sheamus.

'A sea of blood,' says Lottie, shrugging. 'Honestly, Christine needs another hobby. You can't live on taxidermy and specimen-labelling alone.'

'That's what my old Mum used to say,' mutters Sheamus, as they emerge into the front bar. Connie is sitting in her usual position and she covers her eyes with her gnarled hands as she looks at the duo in the doorway.

'Facking hell, it's the Munsters.'

'I love her,' says Sheamus, sitting down at the bar. 'Connie, I love you.'

'Fack off, Beanpole.'

'Now now, Connie, no need for that . . .'

'And you look like a . . . what are those things? Funny shoes? Out on the common. Pick things up . . .'

'A Womble?' asks Lottie, hopefully.

'No, a hooker, that's it.'

Lottie shakes her head, face all smiles. She loves this place. Loves it here. Loves London, with its rain and its noise and the feeling that every breath has been through a million other lungs before it reaches your own. No wonder it attracts people like Christine, she thinks. No wonder it's a Mecca for those with a hunger for bones and blood. The city is built upon so much of it that it's amazing the East End doesn't sink.

'Your health, Connie,' says Lottie, raising a glass.

'Fack off.'

HILDA

Late for everything, Mum and me. Never turned up anywhere without the need to spit out an apology while sucking in oxygen and looking around for a water fountain. We were the scatterbrains. The dizzy duo that the sensible parents would scowl at as we ran across the playground, eating a sausage roll from a plastic wrapper and gamely licking yesterday's graffiti off the back of my hand. Sometimes Mum got upset at the disapproving looks she received from the other parents who sat double-parked in their Land Rovers and Porsche Cayennes and spoke with their stylists and trainers and poodle orthodontists on hands-free mobile phones. I'd heard other people call them 'yummy-mummies'.

We were late on the night we learned about Meda. It was 6.14 p.m. by the time we made it through the blue door and up the stairs that led to Sylvie's studio. Wet hair and soaking shoulders and one leg of my jogging pants soaked to a darker blue than the other. We stood outside the door for a moment, catching our breath.

'Got your snack?' asked Mum, looking me up and down.

'Two mini cheeses and a Kit-Kat,' I said, patting the pockets of the soaked denim jacket.

'Eight, yeah? I was going to head back to the pub but by the time I get there I'll have to come back. You could go with Meda's mum but I've lost her number . . . Oh, yes, there's that chicken place up on the busy road. Or that nice old bar in Limehouse. Do you think I could get there in time? Why am I asking? Go on, get in, love you . . . be brilliant!'

I had a grin on my face as I opened the door. Mum always said that. Said it every morning when she dropped me off at school. It was as much a part of our life together as 'love you, daisy-brain' before she switched the light off and 'wake up, numpty-face' each morning.

Sylvie was demonstrating the new routine, all sinewy and

stretchy like she was made of knotted tights. The girls in the front row were focussing. Mimicking her moves, bright eyes and lineless faces. Nobody even looked as I scampered to my place in the back row, pulling off my jacket and shaking my hair. I chucked my stuff into the pile and did a quick couple of stretches then slotted myself in at my usual position. Greza, the Turkish girl with the huge brown eyes was smiling at me from my right. I gave her a grin back and looked past her for the familiar bulk of Meda. I couldn't see her. Next to Greza stood Priya, with her perfect black hair sleek and dark and silky, like fancy pyjamas. I looked around to see if Meda had been moved to a different line or whether she was sitting on one of the benches by the window nursing a sprain of some kind. She wasn't there. I glanced at the pile of coats and bags and could see nothing of hers. I scanned the room, hoping to see her big, daft shape. I can picture it perfectly. There were a few posters on the wall from performances that the class had taken part in and a big framed print of some pop star from Belgium and a woman who looked like a younger version of Sylvie. Kids in front and behind me and everything reflected back from the big mirror that covered the whole wall by the door. A black and silver stereo system hooked up to a triangular speaker, reverberating each time the bass line thumped. But no Meda.

'She's not here,' said Paulette, leaning in. She was a big girl herself, with a deep voice and breath of cheese and onion. 'She wasn't at school either. Maybe she's got that bug. My auntie had it and she was in bed for three days. Makes you sick so much that your eyes pop.'

I was disappointed. Dance class had been fun at first but I'd been bored for the few weeks before Meda and I became friends. I wasn't as good as I wanted to be but the amount of practice required to make me better seemed like an awful lot of effort. Wednesday nights had become more about catching up with my friend and the thought of waiting a week to show off my new language skills seemed unfair. There was a distinct listlessness to my dancing that night. I was the little black cloud at the rear of the studio, scowling every time I spun. The dance music seemed too powerful and enthusiastic. I wanted to pull the plug and listen to the sound of the rain on the glass and the swish of tyres on wet road.

Sylvie had no answers when I managed to grab a moment with her at break time.

'Did Meda's mum call? Did she say if she was coming? She might turn up after break . . .'

Sylvie gave me one of her shrugs. She was good at shrugs. She had the cheekbones and shoulder blades for it. 'I have heard nothing,' she said, sticking out her lower lip and opening her hands wide to emphasize her point. 'You are her friend. Call her. Do you have Facebook? Is she on that? Tell her mother we pay in twelve-week blocks so she must bring her money next week, yes?'

I sought out the other girls who attended the same school as Meda. Sian was one of the better dancers and normally looked at us back-rowers like something a tramp had just coughed up. But I must have caught her on a good day because she stopped dipping her banana into toffee yoghurt and gave me her attention.

'She normally walks past my bus stop but she didn't yesterday or today,' she said, tugging at the tail of one plait and cocking her head at the strip lights on the ceiling. 'And my friend Sofia sometimes walks with her to the chicken place on the way home and she told me on WhatsApp that she'd been on her own when that lad with the tram-lines in his eyebrow said those things about her sister being a slag and if Meda had have been with her she would have said I'm sure so maybe she's just off sick or something.'

I replayed what she had told me a few times and put in the things she had missed, like pauses and sense. I asked questions but she didn't have any answers and she got bored quite quickly. She started playing with her phone and I felt myself getting hot across my back as my temper prickled. I'd received a mobile phone for my birthday but had lost it within three weeks and would not be getting another one until I could prove I could look after something expensive. Mum said I certainly wasn't going to be allowed to set up any accounts on social media. She'd read about some girl of my age who had thought she was talking to a distant cousin on Facebook and was actually talking to a dirty teacher from her school who persuaded her to send him photos of herself without her knickers on. I promised I would never send anybody any pictures of anything but it would be a while before I changed her mind.

'Is she on there?' I asked, nodding at the phone. 'Could you see? She's got a big family and one of them might say if she is OK.'

Sian looked at me like I was simple. 'I haven't got her number.'

'No, Facebook. Are you friends?'

Sian pulled a face. 'I hardly use Facebook. It's for old people.'

'But Meda does. She said so. Said she uses it to talk to her grandparents back home. She likes putting on photographs of animals and did a video of herself talking about why you shouldn't wear fur.'

Sian blew out through her sticky lips and eyed her yoghurt. 'What's her proper name?' she asked at last, behaving as if she were doing me the biggest favour ever.

I shuffled about, looking at the clock on the wall, as Sian played with her phone like she were a hacker from a movie. We tried a few spellings of the family surname but everything we managed to find was in some language that looked like it should have been carved into the wall of a cave and the few pages that were in English were of super-pretty teenagers with big boobs and white teeth.

'She's not on it,' said Sian, shrugging.

'Try the Believerz page,' said Paulette, who had lumbered over and joined in the conversation. 'There were the pictures that Sylvie stuck on after the competition. Loads of families put on nice messages for Reena. Maybe somebody commented.'

Sian handed me the phone and picked up her banana. 'You do it,' she said, exhausted by it all. 'But don't look at my selfies. I haven't edited them.'

I found the page in moments. Most of it was devoted to pictures of Sylvie and her favourite three dancers, beaming for the camera and striking perfect poses. I opened different pages at random and eventually found an album titled 'Putney/

Reena'. I spotted a few pictures of myself in among the hundred or so snaps of our troupe giving our all. I looked like I knew what I was doing, though my face was all red and sweaty and if you looked closely you could see that the label of my leotard was sticking out. I lingered for a moment on the pictures of poor Reena, laying there like a starfish as we danced around her and the parents urged the paramedics to push their way through. Then I started flicking through. I've always been a fast reader and it didn't take me long to scroll through the dozens of comments from family, friends and witnesses who were all wishing Reena a speedy recovery. Among them was a comment from a Rita Cicenaite. It was in a reply to a suggestion from one of the other dance mums that the girl who had failed to catch Reena should feel ashamed of herself. Rita was defending Meda. Her observation was simple. 'If you have nothing helpful to say, keep quiet. She feels awful.' I touched the screen and brought up the girl's profile. She was in her late teens and much prettier than Meda. She had nice green eyes and pinkish lips and had taken her profile picture in front of a brick wall at a funny angle. She was being followed by 113 people and she had four friends in common with Sian. The top post on the page had been written just three hours before.

> *Feeling so helpless. Why can't the world be nice to the nice ones? I love you, cuz.*

The words captioned an image of a girl, aged around five or six. She was lying on the back of a huge, shaggy-maned white dog, grinning for the camera with a mixture of teeth and gums. There was no mistaking Meda. You could tell from the picture that she was already big for her age and the dog didn't look as though it was going to take her cuddles without complaint for very much longer.

Underneath the picture were a variety of other messages written in another language. A dozen different people had commented on her words. The screen filled with consonants and accents and a jumble of emojis. A teenage boy called Matas had left pictures of teardrops. A blonde called Renata had included a link to a song by Coldplay. Atia had left question marks and a picture of a little posy of daisies. I felt hot and cold all at once, as if I was running through melting snow. The buzz of a dozen different conversations seemed to turn into a drone of static and jet planes. All I could think of was some desperate need to grab somebody who spoke Lithuanian and demand they translate the mass of pointy gibberish into an explanation about my friend.

'Time,' shouted Sylvie, and she turned the music back on. My grunt of frustration was snatched away on a wave of techno and Sian took the phone from my hand.

I barely paid any attention to what came after. I sleepwalked through the choreography and barely even looked up when Honey slipped on some squashed banana, pulled a box split she wasn't expecting and needed to go and lie down on the bench and moan into the wood. I kept making fists with my feet inside my shoes. I got jittery every time I sat down. Something had happened. Somebody was worried for Meda and, as her friend, that meant I should be too. By the end of class I was convinced that Meda had changed schools or moved back to Lithuania or that she was dying of one of the illnesses that strike you like lightning and leave you lying out cold and bare beneath a white sheet with tubes coming in and out and flowers dropping their petals on your feet.

I needed answers. I needed to make sure everything was OK. I needed Mum to put things right.

And I'm still so bloody sorry for what I began.

MOLLY

Molly leans back against bricks the colour of rotten wood and luxuriates in the fantasy that she is a *soiled dove* – the gentle name for a Victorian whore. The rain is coming down hard and the sky has turned the same shade of bruising that she imagines her character would display upon her sore forearms and knees: all indelicate hand marks and imprinted cobbles mottling her grimy skin.

She can see her reflection in the dark glass of the blue van parked with one wheel half up on the kerb. She enjoys being able to look at herself. She is still wearing her Jolly Bonnet clothes and the cold night air has leeched the colour from her skin, accentuating her red lips and dark lashes. She experiments with her position. Places one boot upon the wall behind herself – forming a neat figure-four with her legs. She pulls down her blouse a little and pushes up her breasts, pouting at her reflection. She wrinkles her nose, dissatisfied with the presence of the van. It is an anachronism she cannot fantasize around. She would prefer to look upon the black lacquer of a coach and horses, embossed with a tasteful gold crest and plum-coloured plumes. She has passed a pleasant twenty minutes here, comfortably inconspicuous in the gap between the two circles of light that spill from the streetlamps overhead.

For a time, she imagines herself to be called Alice. She came to London with her father and four sisters. Perhaps Irish-born. Welsh, if not. Sought work in a city where there was no comfort or succour to be had. Married a gin-soaked brute who spent what little money she had saved from her work as a glover's assistant and who beat her mercilessly before, during and after their brutish couplings on their stinking straw mattress in their one-room Spitalfields hovel. She imagines that Alice would take comfort in gin, but not to the extent of the other girls who offered to spread their legs for the price of a quart of ale. She imagines a quiet defiance in her eyes – an intelligence and intensity that would continue to burn even as a procession of rough-handed men slipped coins into her hand. She enjoys being Alice. Decides that when she and Hilda get back to work she will start work on a new cocktail in honour of this new Victorian alter-ego. Starts thinking up possible names for the tipple and giggles to herself as she imagines writing the name 'The Whore's Drawers' on to the blackboard behind the bar.

Suddenly she hears feet slapping hurriedly along the wet pavement. Hears a name she has never really grown used to being called.

'Mum. Mum, it's Meda. She's not at dance. I've been on Facebook. I know you said I shouldn't but I was worried and I really think there's a problem. Can we go check? I know where she lives. And you've got her mum's number. Could you ring? Have you been out here all this time? Why didn't you go to the burger place? It's freezing. You're soaked through . . .'

Molly drags herself from her fantasy and looks at her daughter. Her sweat has frizzed her hair at the temples and her face is at once pale and flushed. Her coat and bag are both slung over one arm and she has a look of real concern in her eyes.

'Sorry, sweetheart, I was miles away. How was dance? Did you do OK? How's Meda?'

Hilda seems ready to stamp her foot with frustration. She locks her jaw and takes a breath. She stands still as Molly reaches out to take her hand.

'Mum, listen. I just said. Meda wasn't there. She hasn't been at school. And I went on a Facebook page and there were all of these people saying stuff in Lithuanian about something happening to her . . .'

'You went on Facebook? You're not allowed on there. You're too young. And you lost your phone . . .'

'Mum, you have to listen!'

Molly looks at her daughter and realizes she is being serious. She feels bad at once for being too lost in her own flight of fancy to give Hilda her full attention. She softens her expression and spreads her hands. For an instant she feels like a police officer again – using expansive and welcoming body language to persuade a child to divulge a secret about what they have just seen. Out of habit, she begins to reproach herself, then realizes that such an avenue of introspection will again cause her to stop giving the child her concentration. She forces herself to focus.

'Right, tell me the lot. I'm all ears.'

When Hilda has finished, Molly gives a nod. She isn't quite sure what to think but instinctively she feels an urge to minimize the situation. Often she feels like this is her main role in life; that it is her duty to modulate every new occurrence, whether it be a poor mark at school or the loss of a favourite toy, all the way up to the end of a relationship and complete financial collapse.

'I'm sure you've got the wrong end of the stick,' says Molly, and the face she pulls suggests the gentle scepticism favoured by doubtful parents the world over.

'Did you not hear me?' demands Hilda. 'And don't say I'm being dramatic. I'm worried. There were flowers, Mum. A little emoji, and all these words of sadness and all sorts.'

'She's probably got the flu,' says Molly, kindly.

'The flu?'

'Or maybe she's having to go away or something. Or her dog died.'

'Her dog died? The only dog she knows here is the homeless man's. Banky. Nice man, she says. I wonder if he has seen her. She buys treats for his dog sometimes. He lives in a sleeping bag in a park. He's nice. Scottish. Do you think we should find him?'

Molly rubs her thumb and forefinger over her eyebrows. She would like to be back in 1889, waiting for a date with Jack the Ripper.

'What is it you'd like me to do, Hilda?' she asks.

'Call her mum!' says Hilda, and Molly notices that she is opening and closing her hands as if squeezing a ball. 'You've got her number. Just check. Please, Mum.'

Molly is about to say no when she realizes that she has no good reason for doing so. Behind Hilda she can see the other girls trooping out of the blue door in the old brick building. Most are getting into waiting cars, huddling inside their hooded tops. A few other parents are waiting on the pavement, extending hands to take bags and coats and sweaty palms for brisk walks to Tube stations and taxi ranks. Meda's mum should be up ahead, all sharp cheeks and pinched features and too-blue knock-off jeans. She should have just finished her cleaning job near St Paul's and have the look of somebody desperate for a bag of chips and a sit-down. Molly has only spoken to her a handful of times but she knows Meda well enough that she does not think it so great an imposition to call and see whether the child is poorly. She realizes she is worrying about whether there is some cultural impediment to ringing. That she is worried, on some level, that in Lithuania it would be an act of gross insult to call an acquaintance and enquire about the wellbeing of an offspring.

'Text her if it's easier,' says Hilda. 'Or a direct message. I can show you how to use WhatsApp . . .'

Molly sighs. She knows she will give in to her daughter's demands. She pulls out her phone and scrolls through looking for the right number.

'You're making a mountain out of a molehill,' she grumbles. 'I'm going to look like a right bloody bell-end.'

'You always tell me it's better to be safe than sorry,' says Hilda, and while she falls short of putting her hands on her hips, she looks as though she is considering it.

'Right, got her,' says Molly, ignoring her daughter. 'I don't know what I'm going to say . . .'

She listens to the phone ringing and her mind is filled with imaginary pictures of Meda's life. She sees a brood of brothers and sisters; cigarette smoke and vodka; a flat-screen TV and furniture still packed in plastic. She feels bad at once and wonders whether Meda's mother would presume that her own house be all mock-Georgian sideboards, stuffed stag-heads and grandfather clocks.

'Nobody's answering,' says Molly, after a time. 'If it goes to voicemail, I'll just leave a message, and . . .'

'*Kas po velnių yra?*'

Molly almost swears, biting back the curse at the last moment as the gruff male voice startles her.

'Oh, I'm sorry,' she says, sounding suddenly a lot more English than she had when speaking to her daughter. 'Yes. Forgive me. This is Molly Shackleton. I'm Hilda's mother. From dance class. Erm, my daughter . . .'

'*Kai anglų kalė. Aš atsikratyti ja*,' says the man, and though she cannot understand the words, she fancies that he is talking to somebody else. She hears her name, rendered almost unrecognizable by the thickness of the accent.

'Look, if this is a bad time, it's not that important . . .'

'Molly?' asks a female voice, and the 'l' at the centre of her name sounds impossibly extravagant in the thick Slavic tongue. 'This is Meda's mother. Meda not able talk right now. I sorry. I can't . . .'

Molly listens as the woman dissolves into a slur of sniffs and strangled syllables. She hears the male voice, brusque and businesslike, before the phone goes dead. Molly looks at the phone for a long moment before turning to her daughter, who looks at her with wide eyes.

'Well?'

'She couldn't really talk,' says Molly, trying to make light of it. 'I think they had people there.'

'Who was it who answered? That didn't sound like her mum.'

'He didn't say. Maybe her husband or somebody. Honestly, you've got ears like a bat.'

'We have to go round there. Meda's mum sounded like she had been crying. I know something's wrong. Please, Mum . . .'

It takes them twenty minutes to reach the property, huddling into their clothes as the rain sluices down from a sky that seems to contain all the motion and shapes of an angry ocean. The Stauskas family live in an apartment on the first floor of a soulless block of maisonettes on Portelet Road. The ground-floor properties enjoy gardens front and back but the homes above are half the size and can be accessed only through a communal entrance block and an angular staircase that smells of damp dog and takeaways.

'It's that buzzer,' says Hilda, wrapping her arms around herself. She is soaked to the skin and her lips look swollen with the cold.

'I know,' says Molly, jabbing her finger on the intercom and suppressing a shiver. Her make-up has run and her hair is plastered to her face. She will not make it back to work without first going for a hot bath, a hot chocolate and a couple of tequila slammers.

'Do it again,' says Molly, over the sound of a lorry rumbling by on nearby Globe Road. She steps back from the panel of buzzers and looks up at the flats above. To her left and right, most of the front doors are encased behind metal shutters and even the bicycles left out on the second-floor balconies have been chained to the drainpipes. There are lights on in most of the windows. Many seem to be illuminated by a bright, unshaded bulb, spilling out a harsh light into the wet, dark air.

'Should I press again, Mum? Should I?'

The clouds alter their shape as Molly looks up through the rain in the direction of the maisonette. For a moment she sees a curve of moonlight before the ragged clumps of mist reassemble themselves into a collection of scallop shells and broken feathers.

'*Ar Jūs bandote man galvos skausmas?*'

'Mum, they've answered. They've answered.'

Molly hurries back to the intercom. She is too cold and damp and grumpy to care about propriety and her voice is flat as she speaks.

'Yes, sorry, I think we got cut off before. I'm Hilda's mum. Is Meda there, please? We'd like to take her out with us if she's well.'

The impromptu greeting is met with silence. Molly strains to hear but there is only the empty static of the line.

'Buzz again, Mum. Buzz again . . .'

'Stay there,' comes the male voice that Molly recognizes. 'I'm coming down.'

Molly turns to her daughter. The child looks thoroughly bedraggled and her skin has gone ghostly. Molly opens hers damp coat and wraps it around her daughter. She kisses the soaking crown of her head and smells the strawberry of her bubble bath and the sweat of her exertions at dance class. She hopes that in a moment they will be holding hands and running through the rain towards the Tube, laughing at what silly scatterbrains they were and joking about all the things they had been imagining before they received some reassurance that Meda was absolutely fine.

A light flicks on inside the hallway and Molly steps from the shelter of the door and back on to the pavement. A dark outline forms into the silhouette of a tall, broad-shouldered man. The door opens and the light reveals his face. Molly is overcome by a sudden sensation of familiarity but the feeling is quickly overcome by anxiety as she sees the cold intensity of his stare.

'Hello, hello,' babbles Molly, unconsciously slipping into the role of ditzy mum. 'Thanks so much for coming down and I'm so sorry to bother you, but like I said, we just wanted to take Meda out. This is her friend, Hilda. Has Meda mentioned her? They're in the back row at Believerz together, and . . .'

The man wrinkles his nose slightly as she talks. He seems to be sniffing the air around her. He's a little older than Molly. There is a dark stubble covering his cheeks and upper lip and his short black hair is speckled with grey in a way that makes it seem he has been haphazardly painting a ceiling. He has dark eyes that make Molly think of tadpoles. He is wearing a white T-shirt beneath a V-neck jumper and the hand with which he holds the door open is adorned with two heavy gold rings and a jumble of indecipherable tattoos.

'Meda's not here,' says the man. He speaks quietly, and takes time over his words. 'There is a family emergency. A sickness. It would be best to come back another time.'

'What's wrong?' asks Hilda. 'Is it Meda? Is she poorly?'

'Poorly?' asks the man. He's handsome, in a brutish, brooding sort of way.

'Ill. You know. Sick. Is she sick?'

The man turns his attention away from Hilda and back to Molly, who feels a sudden irritation at the way he dismisses her daughter without apology.

'It's not that weird, is it?' asks Molly, adjusting her pose to seem more confrontational. 'She's her friend. She wanted to know she was OK . . .'

'Why you think she not OK?' asks the man. He steps out of the doorway and into the shadow cast by the balcony over-head. His face takes on a haunted, cadaverous aspect.

'There was something on Facebook,' butts in Hilda, before Molly can lead. 'A family member. All sad. Flowers and a gun and stuff. I had a bad feeling.'

A look of irritation crosses the man's face and he wrinkles his nose afresh. He makes a clicking sound with his tongue. 'Facebook,' he mutters, contemptuously. 'A curse, no?'

Molly is surprised to see him twitch his features into the most feeling of rueful smiles.

'I just use it for work,' she says, and seems bemused that the thought has become a sound. 'Maybe some pictures. Or a nice memory.'

'You post all that motivational bullshit?' asks the man, reaching into a pocket and retrieving a cigarette case. He retrieves a fat white cigarette and lights it with a cheap lighter. He breathes deep and huffs out a slow lungful of smoke. 'I hate that. All that shit about the next step being the first on a road to somewhere wonderful. All that "love yourself or nobody else will". Is that right? Have I said that right? Makes me want to puke. You let your daughter use?'

Molly shakes her head. 'She hasn't got an account but she still knows how to use it. Hard to stop them, isn't it? Like banning telly when we were kids.'

'I had no television when I was child,' shrugs the man, watching Molly intently. 'We had radio. Two stations. Propaganda and techno. I not like either.'

Molly finds herself smiling. She wonders where she has seen him before. She bites her lip as she tries to remember. Was he a customer?

'I talk to Meda's family about what they put on these websites,' says the man, almost apologetically. 'I tell them no. But they do anyway.'

'You're not part of Meda's family?' asks Molly.

'You head home, yes? Meda be fine. All be fine. But stay away for now, yes? Difficult time for the family.'

Hilda shoots an anguished glance at her mother. 'We're not just leaving it at that, are we?' she asks, indignant. 'I want to see her. I need to see her.' She stomps away from the door and on to the path. 'Meda!' she shouts, upwards through the rain. 'Meda, it's Hilda. Are you there? Are you OK?'

Molly turns to shush her daughter. As she moves, she feels the man brush past her. Gets a whiff of leather, vinegar and a pungent tobacco.

'You wake the neighbours,' says the man, approaching Hilda. 'The neighbours here – they are not happy to be woken.'

'It's not even bedtime,' says Hilda, turning to look at him and fixing her mouth in a defiant line. 'You've got her in there, haven't you? You've done something to her. Who are you anyway? I know all about her family and I don't know about you. You're not Uncle Steppen.'

The man stops, his cigarette hanging from his lower lip. 'I am a friend of Steppen,' he says, thoughtfully. 'An old friend.'

Molly hurries to where the two are standing. Hilda looks ready for a fight. The man does not seem bothered by the rain that has already soaked through his clothes. His jumper clings to well-defined muscles.

'Sorry if this is all a bit odd,' says Molly, positioning herself between them. 'We didn't mean to cause a bother. Do you think you could maybe call us when she is feeling better? Or when there's a good time. I run a pub called the Jolly Bonnet . . .'

'I know,' says the man, flashing his half smile at her once more. 'Nice real ale. Good meat in pie.'

Molly suddenly has a flash of recollection. He had been drinking in her pub as she and Hilda left this evening.

'That's a coincidence,' she says, coldly.

'No,' says the man. 'It's not.'

Before Molly can reply, a shout from overhead causes all three to look up. A man with short blonde hair is leaning over the railing. His face is a yellow colour, like farmhouse butter, and despite the dark and the rain, he is wearing mirrored sunglasses.

'Karol,' he shouts again, and the warning tone in his voice becomes more pronounced as he lets rip with a stream of syllables in his native tongue.

Slowly, the man called Karol turns his attention to the two girls. He gives a nod that could almost be apology. 'The football match,' he says, by way of explanation. 'There has been a goal. I go join my friend, yes? You go home now. Not think any more about this. Not call house for a while. Leave family to fix things, yes? Then we all be happy.'

Molly finds herself scowling. She does not like the way he spoke to her, though he has been nothing but polite.

'He didn't say anything about football,' protests Hilda. 'Meda's been teaching me . . .'

'Nice to meet you,' says Karol, turning away and heading back towards the doors. 'You pretty with your make-up washed away.'

Molly raises her hand to her face. She has not thought of a reply by the time the door bangs closed. She and Hilda stand still, saying nothing, unsure what to do except stand and listen to the sound of a million drops of rain thudding into the soaking ground.

They walk away in silence.

HILDA

We were back in the Bonnet by half past nine. Lottie was sitting at the bar, resting the weight of her face on the heel of her hand. Her friends had long since headed off and she had been making do with the company of strangers and the bar staff for the last couple of hours. She gave a huge grin as she saw us appear in the mirror behind the gin bottles and she turned around with her arms wide open as we pushed through the double doors. She was drinking black coffee from a pewter cup and from behind the bar Julien raised his eyebrows at Mum and nodded at her friend, indicating that Lottie had been on particularly fine form this evening.

The only other customer in the front bar was Connie. Red coat, red nails and a great tangle of fox-fur hair atop a face that looked like it had been pulled three feet away from the skull and then twanged back into position. She must have been at least ninety years old but there was nothing grand-motherly about her. She drank halves of real ale and got through three pickled eggs per session. Whether she chose to eat them with her teeth in depended upon her mood. She swore like a docker and had never heard a racial slur that she didn't like. She called me 'ratbag' and was full of stories about men with names like 'Hatchet McGinty' and 'Slagshagger Brown', and she would forever say things like 'Gawd rest him' when telling stories about the time such capital gentlemen hacked up some interloper who had pushed in front of her in the queue for bagels.

'Darlings,' said Lottie, and she elongated the 'a' to make herself sound like a Russian princess. 'You came back. I knew you would. Loyal, that's what I like about the pair of you. Committed. Decent.' She looked at Mum as she shrugged out of her coat and clomped behind the bar to get herself a gin and tonic. 'That dress is a poem, my dear.'

I sat down on the bar stool next to Lottie and rested my
face on her bare arm. She smelled of gin and wet clothes.
Something else too. A chemical whiff, like an air freshener
dipped in bleach. I felt her stroking my hair and wondered,
as I always did, how many body parts her fingers had pickled
and prodded in the past few hours. Oddly enough, I didn't
mind that Mum's best buddy spent her days with her fingers
fiddling about in other people's entrails. If I was ever on a
slab with my chest pinned back like tent flaps, it's Lottie who
I would want to weigh my stomach and liver. She's good at
it and has very soft hands. She certainly gave good cuddles
and she was the only person I trusted to cut my toenails. As
far as I was concerned, she was the only person with sufficient
professional training to be trusted with the task. Mum said
she was a godsend and I couldn't disagree. Before she became
our friend it used to take half an hour of arguing just to get
me to take my socks off and I wouldn't have my big toenail
trimmed unless Mum was sitting on my bum and holding my
ankle like the neck of a cobra while I screamed the words
'child abuse, child abuse' into the carpet.

'So sad,' said Lottie, softly raising my face. She looked into
my eyes. Her make-up was a little smudged and there was a
hair stuck to her lip-gloss but she was still great fun to look
at. 'Was dancing bad, my darling? Did you slip? It's OK if
you slipped. When I was your age I was so uncoordinated that
I would have thought it was a victory just to get up the stairs.
How's your friend, anyway? The big daft one who looks like
she's about to burst into a chorus of "No Cats in America".
Did you tell her the new words you've learned?'

Mention of Meda was enough to set me off. Lottie saw my
lip wobble and pulled me into a hug and everything that had
happened came pouring out as I snivelled and whispered and
babbled into the warm safe cave of Lottie's chest. I don't think
she understood half of what I was talking about but that didn't
matter because soon Mum was filling her in on the evening's
events. Julien joined us too. For the next half hour it was all
'I'm sure that can't be right' and 'that seems weird' and 'he
said what?' and Mum and I were overlapping and interrupting
and butting in and racing to the end of our sentences. I drank

another hot chocolate and ate some crisps and by the time we got to the end of the story I was feeling better all the way to my bones. That's the bit that feels odd, now. Telling the story about Meda's disappearance actually made me stop feeling so worried about her. I've never made sense of that. The doctors have told me that the nature of what is wrong with me will always make it difficult for me to understand why people act the way they do and why feelings are able to do what they want without permission or control. I should have been jiggling up and down in my stool and demanding to know when Mum was going to call the police. But being in the Bonnet, in a place I knew, with people who loved me, somehow made a silliness out of all of my previous dark imaginings. The world was nice, wasn't it? Friendly? Comfortable? Bad things didn't happen to little girls. Not really . . .

'What are you going to do then?' asked Lottie, and I noticed she was holding Mum's hand in hers across the bar. She was stroking the back of her hand with her thumb. I wondered if she was picturing the layers of epidermis and assessing the elasticity of the tendons.

'I don't think there's anything *to* do,' said Mum, turning her empty glass around and around on the bar top.

'Would the police think you were just being dramatic?' asked Julien. He was pulling at the points of his moustache but hadn't smiled as much as he usually did while we were telling him our story. He seemed concerned.

'I'm sure there would be eye-rolls all round,' said Mum. 'They'd tell us there was nothing to worry about.'

'And do you think there is or there isn't?' asked Lottie.

Mum noticed Lottie was holding her hand and gently slipped it free. She busied herself making more drinks, talking over her shoulder as she did so.

'It was just the way they dismissed us,' said Mum, and I could see her scowling at the memory. 'There was something going on but who's to say it's anything that should trouble the police? I mean, I barely know the family. We don't know Meda is missing or in any kind of trouble. They said to leave it alone. There's only a problem if we make one.'

Lottie sucked her teeth and turned to me. 'You said that the man in the sunglasses never mentioned football. Do you know what he did say?'

I let out a little laugh. I'd been so lost in the swirl of my thoughts I'd all but forgotten that burst of low, looping syllables and clacking consonants from the upstairs balcony.

'Have you got your laptop, Lottie?' I asked.

'Bag,' she said. 'Second peg.'

I trotted to the coat hooks at the end of the bar and found the big rucksack with the Day of the Dead mask embossed on the front. Inside was the laptop, resting against an empty Tupperware box and a pair of battered white trainers. Lottie couldn't walk further than a few feet in the towering, crystal-studded heels that she liked to wear in the bar. The times she stayed over at our house it was strange to see her first thing in the morning. Without her make-up or false eyelashes and at five inches shorter than she had been the night before, it was like she was two different people.

'I don't bloody know what's best,' said Mum, annoyed at herself. Her shoulders slumped a little. She'd never pretended to be one of those parents with all the answers. She was happy to say 'I don't have a clue' and habitually started her apologies with the words 'You know how I'm a bit shit . . .'

'There's a website,' I said, opening the laptop and passing it to Lottie so she could type in her password. She was permitted to use all sorts of encrypted websites and had special Home Office clearance for the kind of databases where you could find out how many days it takes for a bluebottle to eat its way out of an eyeball. I know this because she once left it logged in while she took a shower and I couldn't help having a little look. That night I dreamt I was sneezing out great handfuls of live maggots. I had to tell Mum that the reason for my nightmares was a scary movie I had watched on YouTube.

'Facking incredible.'

We turned to see whether old Connie was going to follow this up. She had half turned from her position by the window. The traffic outside had momentarily let up and through the condensation on the hazy, darkened glass, I saw all of our reflections. The hunched, talon-fingered crone in the rickety wooden chair. The glamorous, big-chested vamp. The moustachioed dandy in braces and bow tie. The elegant, thin-framed beauty in the black dress. It was a scene from another time. A time of steam and clockwork, of lives that could be bought cheap and sold even cheaper. A time of oil lamps and pestilence, mud and blood. I was the anachronism. I was the little girl in the pink hooded top, tapping away at a laptop on the bar. I was the wrong note – the only thing stopping the image from being a perfect recreation of a time long since dead.

'Incredible, Connie?' asked Julien.

'People vanish. Disappear. Die. Some come back, some don't. Sometimes you get answers, sometimes you don't. All this hand-wringing. All this "should I put meself forward" . . . Christ. What is she, this Meda girl? Ukrainian? Latvian?'

'Lithuanian,' I said, typing the website address into the search engine.

'That's one of the Soviet Union ones, isn't it? Russian, near enough. Bad lot. All of 'em.'

'You can't say a whole people are bad,' Mum began automatically. She had been through similar conversations with Connie plenty of times before.

'Yes you can! You can say what you like. Doesn't mean you have to agree with me or like it but I can say it if I fancy. What's anyone gonna do about it, eh? Tell me off? Facking hell, I used to live in the same block as Maurice the Mentalist and I wasn't scared to tell him to keep the noise down when he used to be torturing his cats during *Last of the Summer Wine*. So if I want to say the Russians are a bad lot then I bloody will. And you want to know why I know that? 'Cause my Hilary runs a building company and they've half put him out of business. They either work for next to nothing and he can't compete, or he gets the heavies coming along and insisting he employ this person or that person and could he do this favour for their uncle . . . And the facking Albanians! Christ, the scam they were running a while back. Would have Ronnie and Reggie turning in their graves, if they ain't already spinning on a spit in Hell . . .'

I turned big eyes on Mum. Suddenly I was cold again.

'Mum, we're wasting time. There are messages on her Facebook page. Tears and roses. There are bad men at her house. They won't let us talk to her. What do you think is happening to her right now?'

A huge wave of images rose up inside me. Suddenly all I could see was my big, lanky friend, hugging her dirty knees and dressed in a dirty grey shift, huddling in the dank corner of some terrible underground cell; snot and blood and tears on her cheeks and a desperation in her closing eyes. I felt it. Felt every tremble of fear that the character in my imagination was enduring. I felt an urge to reach into myself, to take the ugly fantasy in my great fist and pluck it from the darkness of my mind.

'Sounds a right facking nasty bastard,' said Connie, and there was a clink as her false teeth hit the lip of her glass. 'Told you, can't trust 'em. Like the facking United Nations out there . . .'

'Go back on the Facebook page,' said Lottie.

I did as I was asked, following the links back to the site I had visited earlier. I raised my eyes in surprise. The thread of messages and emojis had vanished.

'It was there,' I protested. 'I'm not making it up, I promise . . .'

'I didn't think you were,' said Lottie. 'It's obviously been taken down after you went to the house.'

'What are you thinking?' asked Mum.

'Post-mortem I did last year on an eastern European. Body found on that little patch of mud and sand at Wapping. Never got an ID on him but his tattoos and blood sample suggested an Albanian background. No fingertips and no face. Oh, sorry Hilda . . .'

'What's that got to do with Meda?' I asked, and the blood was rushing in my ears as I imagined in perfect detail the scene she had just described.

'The officer from the NCA said the victim could have been linked to a gang that was targeting immigrants. Burglaries. Shakedowns. Targeting people unlikely to make a fuss.'

'And Meda?' asked Mum, trying to get Lottie to explain her thinking.

'I read an article about it, I think. It rang a bell for some reason. Maybe it's just the word "cutters". That's what was used on the fingers, you see. Little bolt cutters.'

I shivered, tearing up, and Mum put her hand on my forearm. 'That'll do, Lottie. Hilda, she didn't mean that something like that was happening to Meda! Lottie, tell her what you meant . . .'

'No, no, not that. It's just . . . look, I'll find it.'

I sat with my hands in the pockets of my hoodie, staring at the surface of the bar. All I could see now was some terrible blond-haired man in sunglasses snipping off my friend's fingers like they were the stems of beautiful roses. Each time the metal touched metal I imagined the soft, sad splat of a snipped finger hitting a stone floor.

'Here,' said Lottie, and she sounded rather rueful, as if she realized she had said far too many things in front of a child. 'I'll read it to you. Was in the *Independent* ages ago. Just a big feature about life in the cosmopolitan East End. Where is it? See! It's all up here, you know,' she said, tapping her temple. 'Listen . . . big increase in numbers of kidnappings in migrant communities . . . Eastern European gangs targeting people who won't call police . . . here, right . . . *Last year, a group of Lithuanian men seized a young Lithuanian after overhearing his accent in the pub. They beat him senseless and then scrolled down the numbers in his mobile phone, calling friends and relatives to demand £200. Police rescued the critically injured victim, who spent weeks on a life support machine but eventually recovered* . . . Molly, that's what the cop told me about the faceless body – that he might have been involved in this trade and been punished for it. This is how they process the bodies in the Russian Mafia. No face. No fingerprints. Said something about how they'd messed with the wrong people this time.'

I felt Mum's grip tighten on my forearm. She didn't seem to know what to do.

'Maybe we're getting carried away . . .'

We jumped as the phone behind the bar rang. A short jangling trill burst from the antique unit, a splendid assemblage of twisted copper pipes and a sepia-coloured typewriter case.

Mum loved talking on it. Made her feel like a duchess in a big house.

'Jolly Bonnet,' she said, and her voice sounded like it had been stretched too tight.

I can see the change in her face as I write this. I can recollect it perfectly. Mum, half-turned, looking pretty and pale and chewing on her lip the way she did when she was thinking. She sort of froze. Just stood there, totally motionless, with a twisted half grin upon her face.

She never told me precisely what was said to her. She just hung up and slowly turned to face me, pirouetting slowly like a music box.

'We have to go,' she said, quietly. 'Hilda, be a good girl and get your coat. Julien, I think we should close early . . .'

The door opened before she could say any more.

The warning had come too late.

The bad men were here.

MOLLY

Three men. Two young heavies and an older, plumper figure. Eastern European. The young men could be twins. Low-cut vests beneath tracksuit tops and leather jackets; colourful trainers and hair brushed forward into precise fringes. The older man has a haggard look, as if life has been unyielding in its assaults. There is a droopiness to his form, as if he is puddling into his belly. He looks like a teddy bear propped up on a child's bed, though nobody would want to cuddle him goodnight. He has a pestilence about him; a suggestion that beneath his loud woollen jumper and stone-washed jeans his skin may be flaking off like the scales of a rotting fish.

'Hello,' says Molly, a little shrill. 'Awful night, isn't it? Welcome to the Jolly Bonnet. Would you like to hang your coats up? Fire's on in the back room if you want to warm yourselves through . . .'

The trio are standing in the doorway, looking at their surroundings in some confusion. They look as though they have taken a wrong turn and opened a door into another world. Their eyes linger on the tasteful pen-and-ink nudes before resting on the medical paraphernalia in the display case. There is a burst of quiet conversation between the two men. One mimes the use of a syringe and the other nods.

Molly flicks a glance at her daughter. The child's eyes are wide. Wordlessly, Lottie moves closer towards her.

'Shithole,' says the first man. It is said like a pronouncement, as though an incontrovertible judgement has been passed.

'Look like fucking brothel,' says the other.

'So you must be hooker, yes?'

Molly has run plenty of rough pubs. She has never been afraid to tell a customer that they will not be getting any more drinks this evening or to boot out some drunken stockbroker for grabbing one of her girls and saying something offensive.

She is rarely afraid. But the voice had sounded so absolute. The warning on the phone had been clear. *'They mean to do you harm. I will be as quick as I can but get out. Now.'* She had recognized the voice. Had no reason to doubt the validity of his words. Just had no time to respond.

'Drink, is it?' asks Molly, loudly. 'We've got some nice guest ales . . .'

'You're the boss, yes?' asks one of the younger men. His face is expressionless, his voice neutral.

'I'm the manageress,' replies Molly. She moves forward, subtly putting herself in front of Julien. On the other side of the bar, Lottie puts a hand on Hilda's shoulder.

'Molly, yes?'

Molly mimes looking for a name badge. She shrugs. 'Who wants to know?'

The man stares at her, hard. Then he nods, making up his mind. 'I do, whore.'

Molly cannot avoid her reaction. She has an expressive face. Disgust and ecstasy habitually make her pretty countenance twist into comic overreactions. Shock manifests itself as a wide-mouthed, cartoonish mask of amazement. She pulls such a face now, as if truly aghast at the stranger's brazenness.

'I beg your pardon,' she says, and her accent is that of a duchess who has just been called a knobhead by a serving maid. 'Were you directing that comment at me?'

'And this must be the little girl,' says the man, turning his attention to Hilda. 'Hilda, is it? That's an old lady's name. You're not an old lady. Maybe you never will be.'

'Don't talk to my daughter,' says Molly, cold, and she makes for the hatch at the end of the bar. 'I've had a right pisser of a day and I haven't got time for a bunch of fannies coming in here and fart-arsing around like you own the place . . .'

'You like Facebook, yes?' asks the man, ignoring Molly. He has cocked his head and is staring hard at Hilda. 'You like to look at people's lives, yes? Poke around? What is the word I hear? Is it "snoop"? Yes, that is it. Snoop, yes. You like to snoop around and make trouble? Learn secrets? Take risks?'

'I never,' says Hilda, shaking her head. She suddenly looks very young. 'I haven't.'

'You cause trouble. Cause danger.'

Molly lifts the hatch and steps into the bar. She can smell the sweet reek of alcohol coming off all three.

'Oi. Knobhead. I don't know what you want but it's time to leave . . .'

'Leave?' Now it is the older man who speaks. He has teeth missing in his top row. 'You going to throw us out, bitch? You and this faggot in his braces? This little girl and her tattooed friend with her big tits? Or this old witch in her red coat?'

''Ere, you can fack off right now,' says Connie, her voice dropping by two octaves. 'Coming in 'ere like you own the facking place, saying things to a nice young girl. I'd fack off before you get yourself hurt, you cant.'

All three men laugh, but there is no joy in the sound.

'It's good advice,' says Lottie. 'And thanks for the compliment about the tits. I'll happily repay you with some kindly observations about your tiny but perfectly formed dick, if you like.'

'What you say, bitch?'

'You like that word, don't you. Do you know any more?'

'Fuck you.'

'You don't talk to her like that. Get out or I will throw you out.'

Julien has barely cleared the serving hatch when the leading man pushes past Molly and grabs him by his tattooed throat and braces. He head-butts him hard in the face. Julien staggers and the man kicks his legs out. He sprawls on to the floor, knocking over a table, and the other young man steps forward and kicks him so hard in the face that his head snaps back as if his neck were a knee.

'Stop it! Leave it!'

Molly reacts on instinct, launching herself at the man who is attacking her barman. She slams a hard punch into the cheekbone of the nearest man. He swears as he stumbles back, hand to his face, mouth opening in shock, and then Molly feels hands around her waist and she is being flung, hard, into the side of the bar. The wind goes out of her as a fist slams into her guts and she hears the screeching of a wounded animal as she thrashes back and forth, kicking out and punching as strong, stinking hands push her face into the spilled beer and stained grain of the bar top and she hears glass smash and stools topple and the desperate cries of her daughter . . .

The pressure on her neck relaxes and she pushes herself up from the bar, roaring, yelling, grabbing out for a weapon of any kind, ready to stab and punch and stamp . . .

She stops as she sees the man called Karol. Where the hell had he appeared from? He has one of the younger men against the wall. The other is slumped against the far partition, bleeding from the nose and blinking, over and over, as if sending a message in Morse. The older man, who had been holding Molly hard against the bar, is closing his hand around the back of a chair, raising it high, preparing to bring it down on Karol's back. Karol spots him at the last moment and kicks his attacker squarely between the legs. The chair falls from his hands and smacks the older man on the crown of his head before clattering on to the floor. Karol grabs him by the back of the head and slams him, face first, into the glass panel of the door. The old, frosted glass cracks straight down the middle and the old man topples backwards. Karol knees him in the side of the head then turns back to the man he had pinned to the wall. He picks him up again, hand around his throat. He puts one thumb on the edge of the man's left eye and whispers to him. Molly cannot hear what is said but the man squirms and squeals and nods, frantic with fear.

Karol pauses a moment and then drops the man. He pushes him towards the door and then barks an order in his own language. Meekly, the man hands over a roll of cash from his coat pocket. He drops it on one of the unbroken tables and then hauls up the older man. Across the room, the bleeding youngster manages to get to his feet. They stagger out, all mutterings and curses and the drip-drip-drip of blood. Karol continues to stare at the double doors for a full thirty seconds after they have gone. Then he turns to face Molly.

'A vodka, I think,' he says. 'Make it a double.'

An hour later, Molly, Hilda and Lottie are sat in the snug at the back of the bar. Julien had come to moments after his

attackers left and decided that, on balance, he would rather
go home than go to hospital. His left eye was horribly swollen
and his lip was split down the middle but he declared that
the bottle of absinthe he had been saving for a special occa-
sion would work fine as a painkiller. Molly had got Connie
a taxi and gave in to a smile when the old girl told her she
was a 'facking head case'. They had then tidied the bar in
silence. Save for a few smashed glasses and one stool with
a broken leg there was not much damage. Even so, Karol had
insisted that Molly take the roll of money he had demanded
from the young man, and she had surprised herself by doing
so without protest.

She pours herself a shot of Bathtub Gin from the bottle in
front of her. Her face is burning and there is a tenderness to
her lower ribs. Hilda has her own chair pulled up close. She
keeps touching her. Asking if she is OK. Asking whether her
hand hurt from punching the man. Lottie is staring at Karol,
chin in palm, eyes wide and admiring.

'Are we sitting comfortably?' asks Molly, and she sounds
as snappy as she feels. She feels agitated. Ill-used. She has
done nothing but take her daughter to dance class and follow
up on a worry about a child's welfare and for her troubles
she has been insulted, assaulted and embarrassed. She has
been glaring at Karol ever since his arrival. Wanted to smash
him in the face for his arrogance as he sat at the bar with his
legs apart, drinking her vodka and playing with his phone,
glancing up every now and again to watch the women clean
and tidy the bar around him; a little half-smile on his face
every time he caught her eye.

'You seem angry,' says Karol, mildly. 'You probably make
profit tonight.'

'Angry?' demands Molly, banging her glass down on the
table. 'Oh, I wonder why.'

'You being sarcastic, I think.'

'Yes, I'm being bloody sarcastic. My face is killing. My
stomach hurts. My daughter just watched a friend getting
kicked half to death . . .'

'He fine. Bruise look good on him. Same colour as tattoos.'

'You're not taking this seriously.'

'I called you. I warned you. Ran red lights to get here. Probably got ticket.'

'But we haven't done anything wrong!'

Karol rubs his forehead. He reaches into his pocket for cigarettes and then stops himself. 'It's banned, yes? No smoking in pubs. And soon, no drinking, talking or laughing.'

'Please,' says Hilda, quietly. 'Just tell me about Meda. Is she OK? Were those the men who have her?'

Karol considers Hilda. He looks at her for an uncomfortably long time. In the half light of the snug, with its flickering candles and honey-coloured lights, he looks to Molly like a man out of time. She suddenly sees a different man; an intense and brooding battlefield poet, warming his cold skin beside a flickering fire in a draughty tavern. Dressed as a Victorian brothel keeper in her sumptuous East End pub, she feels well placed to judge.

'Meda is not fine, no,' says Karol, at last. 'I tell you what I know because I think you understand that this is important, yes? And I appreciate that you haven't mentioned the police.'

'Just tell us about Meda,' says Molly, chewing her lip.

'She has been gone three days,' says Karol, sitting back in his chair. 'Her mother sent her out for milk and something to put in her sandwiches for school. It was dark but the shop was only three streets away and she had been many times before. She did not come home.'

Hilda looks up at her mother. Her eyes brim with tears.

'You've called the police,' asks Lottie.

Karol shakes his head. 'They called me.'

'And you are?' asks Molly, unimpressed.

'I fix problems.'

'Could you just be a bit less of a big fat cryptic dick-face and tell us who you are and what's going on?' snaps Molly. 'It's a bloody school night.'

'Mum!' says Hilda, shocked. 'He just saved you!'

'No he didn't,' says Molly, indignant. 'I don't need saving.'

'I do,' says Lottie, staring at the side of Karol's face. 'I need somebody to save my brains out.'

'My name is Karol,' he says, shrugging. 'That not important. I used to be a soldier and now I am a specialist.

I help people with problems. Problems they run into in other countries.'

'Like what?' asks Hilda.

'When you are a foreigner, when you are far from home, it can be hard to know who to trust. It is not always a good idea to go to the police when things go bad. Sometimes they like to forget about the crime you are reporting and instead start poking about in your own life. Your own background. Your own papers. People do not want that. They want to work and be happy and be left alone. But bad people take advantage of that.'

'We read about that,' says Lottie, excitedly. 'Your friend Feodor. The name rang a bell . . .'

Karol considers her for long enough to make her ask what he is looking at. Molly can see him piecing things together.

'People get taken,' he says, at length. 'Bad people take other people and ask for money from their families. If that money is paid, they are released unharmed. If it is not, they do not come home.'

'And somebody has Meda?' asks Hilda.

'We think so,' says Karol.

'Have they been in touch?' asks Molly, quietly.

'Not yet,' says Karol. 'But there have been things like this before. Children snatched and parents made to pay. They will get in touch. The family will pay.'

'But what if it's not?' asks Molly, sitting up and knocking the table so hard that the gin bottle teeters. 'It could be any random nutter! She's a little girl and she's not come home and the parents have called in some mercenary from home rather than call the police! This is mental! No, Karol, I'm sorry, you have to get the police involved. She's a missing child.'

Karol pats the air, urging her to calm down.

'We know what we are doing,' he says. 'Meda's uncle is a rich man. An important man. Somebody has either been very brave or very stupid but either way, they will want money. That money will be paid. And Meda will come home. The others have been well treated. She will be sitting in a bedroom playing a computer game and eating fried chicken right now, I promise.'

'So who were those men?' asks Hilda. 'Why did you let them go? Do they have Meda?'

'They are family. Cousins to Meda's mother. They were embarrassed when my partner told them their sister had put messages on that bastard Facebook about Meda. They were told to make sure the messages disappeared but then they drank and their shame became anger and their anger became directed at the nosy English bitch and her daughter who made them look like fools. And they decided to make themselves feel better. I'm sorry this happened. It will not happen again.'

Molly is shaking her head, glaring at the floor. 'I don't know how you can be so sure that she's been kidnapped for ransom. There are bad people everywhere. For different reasons. Where was she last seen? Did she get to the shop? Who saw her? And why haven't they called yet?'

'Relax,' smiles Karol.

'Don't patronize me. I'm concerned. You should be too.'

'I am. I want her home. She not come home and Steppen not pay me. My partner get upset and then I have problems to solve. We want to go home. It's miserable in London in December.'

'How many have you got back?' asks Lottie. 'Hostages, I mean.'

'We not call them hostages,' he says. 'They just people on little holiday that cost their family some savings. And we get plenty back.'

'Children,' she says. 'How many have been children?'

Karol frowns down one side of his face. 'Two boys taken from a rich Latvian builder last year. They came home fatter and healthier than they left.'

'Little girls? Meda's age?'

Karol twitches; the merest flash of discomfort showing at the corners of his mouth. 'I know of one. The family did not get in touch until too late.'

'They didn't pay?'

'Little girl didn't know her parents' number. No call came. She must have become too much trouble.'

'What happened to the girl?' asks Hilda, and Molly reaches out to put an arm around her.

'Dumped,' he says, without emotion. 'South-west London. Left in a tangle of trees by the motorway.'

'There would have been an investigation,' says Molly, incredulous. 'I'd have heard about that . . .'

'You probably did,' says Karol. 'Probably saw a paragraph in the *Metro* and thought it was very sad, then turned to the fashion pages and got on with your life.'

'Don't act like you know me,' snaps Molly.

'I'm sorry,' says Karol. 'I'm tired. Still got to sit up all night and stare at phone. They will call. You need to know so bad? Meda got to shop. Bought what she came for. Four pints of milk, tin of tuna, packet of ham. We see receipt at shop. She bought extra tin of tuna with change. She seen twice walking back, swinging bag. Happy. Then she gone.'

'I don't know that area,' says Lottie, rubbing a knuckle against her forehead. 'My brain's going. What are we going to do?'

Karol gives her his attention. 'You do nothing. You leave to me. Meda be home for next dance class. You forget this and not speak of it and everybody be happy. Steppen most of all.'

'I liked Uncle Steppen,' says Hilda.

'He liked you too. That's why he send me to help you tonight.'

'And if he hadn't?' asks Molly, wrinkling her nose.

'You'd have handled it, I'm sure,' says Karol, and he stands up, barely making a sound as he does so. 'Please, go home, go to bed, wake up and enjoy the new day. That is all any of us can do.'

Hilda and Lottie are both polite enough to say goodbye. Molly just sits and chews her cheek, staring so hard at the table top that she expects it to burst into flame.

'Do you think he's right?' asks Hilda at last. 'Meda will be OK? She's playing video games and eating and it's all fine?'

Molly glances at Lottie and something passes between them. Molly puts on her best mumsy smile and cuddles her daughter.

'I promise,' she says. And her bruised cheek burns.

HILDA

needed the lie. I was a kid, after all. Still full of fairy castles and princess parties and dreams of becoming a groom to a stable of unicorns. Mum was probably right to tell me what she did. But promises count, don't they? A lie isn't really that terrible of a thing, but a broken promise? That's what some people would refer to as a sin. I sometimes wonder whether all that happened next was a punishment for that one sin. I shake that thought away whenever it bubbles up. That kind of thinking can lead to madness. It can make you think there's a reason to it all; some kind of cause-and-effect to the whole thing. It means that terrible things could have been avoided if you had just been better, and I don't want to think that what happened to me only happened because I forgot to say a thank you for something or said a mean thing or didn't believe in God.

I took comfort in that promise. Mum made it clear. Meda would be OK and nothing bad would have happened to her. Her words gave me a better night's sleep than I expected. She repeated them as she cuddled me to sleep, spooned up behind me in her big four-poster bed with its lovely red and gold quilt pulled right up over our heads. She moaned a bit in her sleep, wincing every time she turned over, but every time a sound woke me I drifted back into our safe little burrow and comforted myself with the knowledge that Meda was probably having a brilliant time. I kept up that jollity all through breakfast. Even kept up the cheerfulness in spite of the bruising on Mum's cheek and the pain that wrinkled her face as she brushed my hair and made my sandwiches. She was quiet on the walk to school. Hadn't put her make-up on and was wearing nothing more remarkable than a pair of ripped jeans and a stripy jumper. Didn't tell me to put my coat on and didn't say 'I-told-you-so' when the sky tore open and great waves of rain came tumbling down from sky the colour of dead skin.

'Love you,' she said, at the school gates, but it was automatic and forced. I wanted her to say 'be brilliant' like usual, or try and embarrass me by doing a twirl or an elephant impression in front of the yummy mummies. She didn't even wave. Just turned around and started trudging back home. I watched her go. She had her phone in her hand by the time she had cleared the playground. She was calling Lottie, I know that now. Starting to dig. Poking her nose in somewhere it didn't belong. Taking a step down a road that would end in so much of our blood.

MOLLY

I t's a little after noon and Molly is grumbling her way down Fournier Street. Were there any sun she would barely recognize the question mark that her shadow makes upon the old stones. She is somebody who usually walks with her head up. Past lovers have remarked upon the swan-like elegance of her neck. Her adoption of such grace, of that certain poise, was a conscious decision. The people on the estate where she grew up had a tendency towards hunching their shoulders and disappearing, turtle-like, into the collars of their coats. As a teen she decided to accentuate her height and to walk with something approaching panache. Her new deportment led to accusations of her 'having airs'. She was accused of thinking herself 'better than she ought to be'. Dismissed by neighbours as a 'snooty cow' and 'too big for her boots'. Her accusers would be delighted to see her now. She has pulled up the hood of her black coat and is hunkered down within it, wincing into the gale and keeping her eyes fixed on the slippery damp stone beneath her black knee boots. She is muttering to herself that the weather is 'bloody ridiculous' and knows that, in this mood, if she were to step in a puddle or topple off the kerb, she would either burst into tears or throw her handbag through a window. She considers herself as she comes to a halt. Were she sitting down, Molly knows she would be jiggling her legs up and down or tapping her fingernails on the table top. Walking through a rain that has been chopped into haphazard shapes by the tall buildings to her left and right, she is incapable of the sort of fiddly jitteriness that has always marked her sedentary moments. She contents herself with grumbling to herself and squeezing her hands into fists inside her soft fur mittens.

She forces herself to look up. Up at the imposing bulk of Christchurch. The guidebooks refer to its gleaming white façade and elegant snow-coloured arches and columns, but the ceaseless traffic has stained the stone and to Molly's eye, the whole edifice is the colour of water chestnuts and mildewed lace. She pauses where she stands. Re-adjusts her dress and coat. Checks her reflection in the darkened glass of the expensive salon. Looks back up at the spire. She feels a touch of connection, of significance, as she gazes up at the distant point. The Ripper's victims would have looked up at the same spire every day of their lives. They would have quantified their journeys, their boundaries, their nearness to home, using this church as a marker. And each were murdered within the sound of its chimes.

Molly spots Lottie as she pushes open the door to the Ten Bells. She is sitting in a battered leather sofa behind a low, careworn table. She is wearing a tight tartan waistcoat over a tiny vest top and her tanned, tattooed arms somehow look more beguiling than her constricted breasts. Behind her is a large painting of the pub's front doors as they would have been in Victorian times. Molly experiences a dizzying rush of peculiar displacement as she looks at this older representation of the space which she is currently inhabiting. It feels as if she could simply blink and find herself transported; to be within the painting staring out at a different century and imprisoned forever within scabbed swirls of paint. It is all she can do not to reach out to steady herself like some pitiable romantic heroin overcome by a swoon.

'Got you a Bloody Mary,' Lottie says, smiling. She half stands to greet her friend but the sofa is low and she is holding an armful of papers and gives up on the operation before actually levering her buttocks off the cushion. She points at her mug of tea and grimaces. 'I opted for a Bloody Awful.'

'Being a good girl?' asks Molly, slipping out of her coat and pulling up a wooden stool from a nearby table. Her head is pounding and she wishes she had given in to the urge to buy something greasy and full of sugar.

'Post-mortem in an hour. They like me to be sober.'

'Killjoys,' says Molly, and gives the barman a smile as he brings her drink. He gives her a once-over and seems to like what he sees. In a gesture of emancipation, she feels obliged to conduct a half-hearted appraisal of her own. Decides that, despite the sumptuous beard and pleasantly floppy fringe, she could never be with a man who has tattoos of Sonic the Hedgehog on his forearms. She turns back to her friend.

'Surprised you want to give your support to the enemy,' says Lottie, gesturing expansively at the pub. There has been a bar on the corner of Fournier Street and Commercial Street for more than 250 years. This is where they drank. The fallen women. The victims. The slain. This is where they sipped their gin and dulled their wits before venturing out to sell their bodies for pennies in the hope of finding enough coin for an evening's lodgings. It features on every Ripper tour in the East End.

'This place isn't the enemy,' says Molly, sipping her drink and giving an appreciative nod. 'We're the enemy. This place was the one for the proper Ripperologists. They've got authenticity on their side. We're the interlopers cashing in.'

Lottie considers this and tries to find a counter-argument. She gives up. 'Room for one more, I guess. And it's not as though they did it on purpose, is it? Not as though the landlord killed the hookers so that a hundred years on his business would have a nice marketing gimmick.' She pauses. 'Did she sleep OK? The little one?'

'Seemed to,' says Molly, nodding. 'She's a funny one, isn't she? Couldn't sleep on her own for a month after watching the Muppets for the first time but got eight good hours after watching Julien get his head kicked in and finding out her friend's been bloody kidnapped.'

'How is Julien?'

'Still asleep, I'd imagine. I've taken him off the rota. He went down like a right sack of shit, didn't he? Took a punch like a right fanny.'

'I like it when you go all Northern. Don't be too harsh on him though. He was defending your honour.'

Molly pulls a face. 'He didn't need to get involved. He just escalated things. I'm sorry he got hurt but I'm not some princess who needs saving. I don't need a knight in shining armour, thank you very much.'

Lottie sips her tea and grins at her friend as she considers a memory. 'You went mental. Never seen you go off like that. It was like somebody had shaken up a bottle of ginger beer.'

Molly folds her lips in upon themselves and lowers her eyes, looking bashful. 'Instinct, I suppose.'

'I thought you got trained in conflict management,' laughs Lottie. 'Arm up the back, that kind of thing. You hit him in the mouth. Full-on punch. With your fist!'

'I don't like bullies.'

'I could tell.'

They sit quietly, listening to the rain hit the glass and the occasional shouts of delivery drivers, cabbies and cyclists conducting their daily three-way war of attrition. This is Molly's favourite part of London. She buys most of her vintage clothes from the boutiques and independent traders across the road at Spitalfields Market. She has imagined running a stall herself, selling the kind of curiosities and knick-knacks to which she has always been such a slave. Can see Hilda beside her, all fingerless gloves and a money belt around her waist, haggling with customers and learning that effortless confidence that some Londoners seem to be full of. She likes the idea. Holds on to it for a couple of seconds before bringing herself back to the present.

'I'm surprised,' says Lottie, cautiously. 'Or maybe I'm not. I don't know.'

'What are you talking about?'

'Surprised. That you wanted to know. That you're not going to leave well alone. Is it the cop in you, do you think?'

'I don't know about any of that,' says Molly, dismissively. She gives it a little thought. 'Maybe I became a cop because I felt this way already and it seemed a way to get paid for it. I never really know what my motivations are for anything. I'm not sure anybody does.'

Lottie huffs out a lungful of air. 'Somebody's feeling cheerful. How's your face?'

'Sore,' says Molly, flatly. She seems agitated. She wants to explain herself more thoroughly but simultaneously wonders if there is any merit in seeking a better collection of words to describe a mind-set which she does not really understand. 'There's a little girl in trouble. That's wrong. That's something which nobody can argue with. It's wrong. She should be at home and instead she's with somebody who is using her as a tool to make money. And instead of telling the police they've brought in this great bloody thug . . .'

'That's a bit strong,' says Lottie, displeased at the description.

'. . . and they're going to pay whatever this person asks for and then no doubt beat the crap out of him as a warning to others.'

'That's fair enough,' says Lottie.

'Well, yes, but is it? I mean, there are laws. Systems. Ways of doing things. I get so cross about stuff when I think about it properly. It's like, until you need to access certain services you presume that they work and that they're there as a safety net if you need them. But when you need them and try to access them you discover that they don't really exist and if they do, the waiting lists are over a year, and you find yourself suddenly feeling like you live in Albania or the Middle Ages and you can't work out why all the immigrants want to come to this shitty little island . . .'

Lottie reaches across and puts her hand on Molly's arm. 'It's OK,' she says, soothingly. 'You went through something horrible. It's OK to sometimes still feel helpless.'

Molly gives a growl of frustration. 'It's not that. It's not about before. About back then. This is about now. I don't know if it's being here, in this place, but sometimes I feel like we're no more advanced than they were.'

'Who?'

'The ladies. Annie Chapman. Polly. Mary Kelly. His victims. The ones who sat where we're sitting and talked about bad things happening to ordinary people and who ended up with their innards in the dirt. What's improved? What's better? We've got iPhones and microwave meals and we live longer but . . . oh, I don't know . . .'

'This isn't like you, Molly.'

'It used to be,' she sighs. 'Two gears, me. Manically happy and giggly and full of energy, or reflectively miserable and willing to stick my head in a blender.'

'That would be an interesting autopsy.'

Molly puts her head in her hands. She stretches her limbs while sitting still. Gives a little squeal of mock breakdown.

'I'm doing my own head in,' she says, pulling down the skin beneath her eyes and doing an impression of a chronically depressed bloodhound. 'I've been awake all night and I don't even know what I'm trying to work out.'

'Whether to call the police?' asks Lottie.

'I've already decided not to do that. I'm not arrogant enough to think I know best. Karol might be exactly the right bloke for the job and this time next week Meda could be back at school and none the worse for wear.'

'But . . .'

'I think there might be something else,' she says, turning her attention back to Lottie. She is struck for an instant by just how lovely her friend's eyes are. Struck by the Malamute blue and the intense black pupils that dilate like spilled ink whenever Molly looks into them for longer than a moment. She feels momentarily flustered and tries to gather her thoughts. 'If it's a ransom, they should have heard by now. Shouldn't they?'

'I don't know.'

'Well, I think they should. I know, I know, who am I, right? But I mean, what if she's gone missing and everybody presumes it's a ransom situation because there have been others a bit like it, but while everybody is waiting around for the call, somebody completely unconnected has got her. Some pervert. Some sex offender. There are girls being used as slaves in big posh houses all over London right now. We think we're so advanced and so far past all the ugliness but it's all around us if you just look.'

Lottie squeezes Molly's arm. 'I hate seeing you upset.'

'I don't feel upset. I'm irritable. I want it all to be clean and nice and sort of, well, advanced. But it's all such a mess . . .'

'What is?'

'Life. London. The way we all live. It's all so shapeless and tangled.'

Lottie looks unconvinced. 'Darling, I've seen your house. I've seen your accounts. You are not somebody who wants it to be neat and ordered. And you run a Victorian theme pub. When did you get so excited by the idea of gleaming metal worktops and fabulous efficiency?'

Molly has the grace to laugh.

Lottie looks at the papers in her lap. She straightens them and taps her nose, theatrically, with her finger. 'I feel like a spy, giving you all this. Like I'm being naughty.'

'You love feeling naughty,' says Molly, shaking her head and trying to focus on the here and now. She sits up a little straighter. There is a notepad in her pocket but she feels that to use it would be an act of make-believe, as though she were playing dress-up.

'It's a bit ugly,' says Lottie, apologetically. 'You don't want the photos, I'm sure. But I can tell you the basics.'

'Please.'

Lottie nods and consults the pages before her. She is holding the autopsy report into the death of an unidentified female found dead in a layby off the A3 in early January.

'I can't let you have it,' says Lottie, and she looks mortified by the admission. 'Printing it was bad enough and I couldn't email it without a great cage landing on me from the ceiling, but I can tell you what the pathologist found.'

'Whatever I need to know,' says Molly, and she cocks her head at her friend, aware she is deliberately taking her time.

Lottie stares past her at the scene beyond the window. The sky looks like it has been used to clean the paint from an artist's brush. The street is populated entirely by individuals; office workers on their phones, ricocheting off shop staff hurrying through the deluge to buy sandwiches and bottles of pop. The street is full of noise but nobody is talking to anybody nearby. Each interaction is conducted at volume, via satellite, over the sound of the ceaseless traffic.

'Body of an unidentified girl, aged eleven to twelve years old,' says Lottie, at last, in a flat and neutral tone she would never use on her social media platforms. 'Found in a copse of woods near Malden off the A3. Discovered by council workmen there for a refuse collection. Victim was clothed in a white, sleeveless, ankle-length gown. She had bare feet. She was laid on her back on a patch of grass at the foot of an alder tree. She showed signs of having been malnourished . . .'

Molly shifts in her seat. It feels as though her clothes are too tight across her back. She feels anxious. Her leg is moving up and down as if she is working a sewing machine.

'Height: 142.24cm. Weight: 32kg. Hair: brown, slightly curly. There is a small area of apparent alopecia measuring 3 by 2.5cm present on the posterior parietal-occipital area of the scalp. Eyes: conjunctivae: no jaundice; petechial haemorrhages not present. Sclerae: petechial haemorrhages not present. Iris colour: hazel/green. Pupils: equal diameter, each side 5mm. Ears: normally formed, without blood or other fluid in the external auditory canal. Mouth: lips are normally formed with no blood or other fluid or obstruction visible externally or in mouth cavity. Native dentition in good condition. Both upper and lower frenulum are intact. There is a recent injury to the buccal aspect of the upper right lip . . .'

'What did she die of?' asks Molly, quietly. 'You don't need to read it, you know it, I can tell.'

Lottie lowers the pages that she had been gripping in front of her as if they were a shield. 'Blood poisoning,' says Lottie, flatly. 'I was getting to the significant injuries. Puncture marks in the crooks of both elbows and ulcerations around the buttocks and calves. High volume of chlordiazepoxide hydro-chloride in blood stream . . .'

'That's like Prozac,' says Molly.

'A bit. Librium. Anti-anxiety medication. Used as a tranquilizer.'

'And the puncture marks – is that heroin?'

'None found in the bloodstream. No signs of diabetes. But signs of an irritation to the skin, as if from an allergic reaction.' Lottie pauses, unsure whether to go on. 'Skin sample demonstrated an intolerance to a form of prescription wormer used in the poultry industry. Panacur. It kills the gizzard worm in geese and ducks. Not easy to come by.'

'She was from an agricultural background, perhaps? Or she'd been on a farm . . .?'

'The sliver of a goose feather was found inside one of the puncture wounds,' says Lottie, looking down. 'It had broken off. There was blood inside it. Blood group O. No matches on the database.'

Molly sits still. Behind her, the door opens and a man in a

Homer Simpson T-shirt, jeans and woolly hat announces to the barman that he is wetter than a squid's pyjamas and demands an immediate pint of Brooklyn and a pickled egg to remedy the situation.

'The description,' says Molly, staring into her empty glass. 'Tallish. Brown hair. Hazel/green eyes.'

'I don't know,' says Lottie. 'I couldn't say.'

'Not dissimilar though. You could tick all of those boxes for Meda.'

'So? You could tick them for Hilda.'

'Goose quills, Lottie. Goose quills in her arms?'

'It's horrible,' says Lottie. 'But horrible things happen all the time. This is one of them but it's nothing to do with Meda, or you. It's nothing to do with me and I'm a pathologist. It's just more ugliness in an ugly world but if you start splashing about in it you will end up stained.'

Molly rubs her forehead. She looks tired. She lets herself think of Hilda for a moment, trying to comfort herself with visions of her daughter, but the first image that flashes across her mind is of she and Meda playing together, holding hands and feeding the animals at Stepney.

'What stage is the investigation?' she asks quickly. 'There must be an ID. Karol seemed to think he knew who it was, didn't he? Didn't you get that impression? Have you Googled it? Seen what the papers have said?'

'There's no interest,' says Lottie, soothingly. 'She may as well be one of the Ripper's victims, my darling. There's a different world just underneath us. Everything we think we know is a veneer. It's all gross and I'm saying that as some-body who is about to go and dissect a drowned tramp. But, sweetheart, you can't be thinking the worst or you will make yourself ill.'

Molly considers having another drink and then quickly talks herself out of it. She starts her shift in half an hour and won't rest until they have got rid of the last customer and cleaned down the bar. She can expect to see her bed around three a.m. None of it seems important. She feels irritated with herself. Sees a fool, playing dress-up and revelling in the gory happen-ings of a time that she always feels oddly at home inside.

'I've asked the copper in charge to give me a ring with an update,' says Lottie, and she seems unsure whether she has done right or wrong. 'I don't think there's any connection at all with what happened last night, but if it helps you sleep easier I'll be a good friend.'

Molly is scratching at the crook of her arm. For an instant she feels transplanted; removed; spliced into another existence. For a moment she is naked, save for a simple lace shift. The sharpened stem of a goose feather is sliding into her veins like a straw pushed into a carton of drink.

'Thanks for this,' says Molly, indicating the papers on the table. They have fallen open on a simple drawing of a human form and Molly's eyes are drawn to the sad little inscription handwritten by the pathologist. No breasts. No body hair. No evidence of sexual contact. A life still unlived, thinks Molly, as she slides her arms into her damp coat.

As she barges back out into the grey and sodden air, she feels the eyes of the woman in the Victorian painting upon her back. Wonders, if she turned around, whether it would feel like looking in a mirror.

HILDA

ottie was the coolest grown-up I knew. Everybody said Mum was awesomely stylish and funny but it's weird to think of your Mum as cool, isn't it? I mean, I've seen her sitting on the sofa watching *Emmerdale* in her onesie, eating Frosties from the box and trying to balance the remote control on her head, and none of that strikes me as being cool. Lottie was different. She was the rock star in our little world. When Mum wore her ace clothes and did her hair in wacky styles she always looked amazing, but Lottie had this look about her that suggested she would still be the most fabulous person in the room if she were wearing a traffic cone and a pair of waders. She cut up dead bodies. That was her job! She had her own YouTube channel. She ran a museum dedicated to the weird and wonderful things that had been fished out of the human body. She said 'fuck' a lot and had a habit of calling men 'total dick faces', though if I'm totally honest, I think she stole that from Mum.

I'm remembering, now. Getting my head into some sort of order. What came next? There was a day or two of not very much, when life was just life and the rain rained. If I had pens and paper I would draw a read-out from a heart monitor and in the space between hearing Karol tell us that Meda was missing, and then him telling us she was going to be OK, would just be a steady stream of *tick-tick-tick*. So I'll gloss over that. School. Lunch. More school. The bus . . . and then my memory kicks back in properly. Words. Full sentences. Facial expressions and clothes . . .

We were in the snug at the Bonnet and Lottie was showing me and two lucky spectators the new routine she intended to perform during the next event at her Pathology Museum. Lottie was the cat's pyjamas when it came to curating her specimens and slicing up bodies. She'd told me so, and I believed her. I'd seen loads of her videos online and even read some of her day-in-the-life pieces for the websites that thought she was awesome because she coloured her hair and painted her nails then shoved her hands into people's intestines.

'Did you know that the Grand Old Duke of York was so poorly embalmed that in 1997, he exploded during Evensong?'

I stopped what I was doing and looked at her sceptically. 'Like William the Conqueror?' I asked.

'Exactly,' said Lottie, looking pleased with me. 'You remember stuff, don't you? Forgot I told you that. They dropped the coffin and the great Conqueror pretty much popped into ten stone of flying mince and mulch in front of the congregation. Not a bad end, really.'

The husband and wife sitting in the arched area behind the metal barriers seemed incapable of leaving. They studied us with the sort of morbid curiosity that Lottie was capable of provoking in just about anybody. It helped that she was wearing her new costume – the one she would be wearing when she debuted her new character at the upcoming burlesque show in Clerkenwell.

'Do you mind me doing this again?' asked Lottie. She addressed her remarks to the husband. He was a middle-sized gent with unusually blond hair for a chap in his sixties. Grey eyes, big ears and a gut like a capital D. Surveying Lottie's form and timing the intervals between gyrations had kept him transfixed for the past hour. His face suggested that he didn't really think any of this was actually happening and that he was pretty sure this was the result of some coma which he was disinclined to leave. His wife, on the other hand, had the look of a frightened puppet. She had flat, lifeless hair that sat atop a wooden spoon of a face, spilling down into cardigan, floral print dress and sandals that revealed the kind of toes that looked as though there was a lot of formaldehyde in their future. Lottie could have studied them for days.

'You go for it, love,' said the man, adjusting his England shirt and seeming to mouth a silent prayer of thanks for the rain that forced he and the wife into this peculiar pub where they asked permission to eat their sandwiches in exchange for a pint of bitter and a port and lemon.

'What is this?' asks the wife, looking apologetic and confused.

'Burlesque,' I said, and tried not to give the impression I thought she was an idiot.

'We're only here on a coach trip,' said the woman, and her whole demeanour exuded remorse for her lack of knowledge. 'I think we've got a bit lost. What's burlesque?'

'It's like stylish striptease,' said Lottie, arching her back and pushing out her chest. She was wearing a white lab coat that she had adjusted to show off her chest, waist, stockings and suspenders. 'It's a parody show, really. Making fun of stuff. But tastefully sexy. Do you know what I mean?'

'Oh aye, love,' said the man.

'Not really,' said his wife. She groped for safer ground upon which to build an explanation. 'We're from Barnsley.'

I was laughing a lot that night. I had no reason to believe that everything was going to be OK but Lottie was a calming presence and there was something so comforting and homely about the Bonnet that it seemed kind of unthinkable that Meda was having a terrible time or something bad was happening to her. I was caught up in the moment. I was eating Scotch eggs and crisps and drinking hot chocolate. I was putting off doing my homework and had tied my school shirt in a knot across my tummy so I looked a bit older and fancier and a lot more like Lottie. I was happy, I suppose.

'It's this bit,' said Lottie, pouting. She rubbed a gloved hand across her crimson lips and snarled at her reflection as it flickered in the glass of the display cases. She looked cross with herself, even as she shone back from a newspaper clipping about the butchery performed on Long Liz by the Ripper in 1888.

'What bit?' I asked.

'Where I go into the crab,' she said, arching backwards and momentarily becoming a structurally unsound bridge. I heard the unmistakable sound of a rotund Yorkshireman saying the words 'bloody hell' and his wife hissing his name.

'I want to open my coat and have my breasts as perfect skulls but I worry about the light,' says Lottie, grumbling. 'They might just look like I'm wearing doilies. What do you think?'

She unfastened her coat and assumed the position.

I was laughing, I remember that. Big stupid grin on my face and some daft snorts erupting from my nose and mouth as the fat man started choking on his pint and his wife said the word 'blimey' over and over again. That's where I was. Where I was standing and what I was thinking as Karol came through from the main bar.

'We're popping out,' he said, more to Lottie than me. 'Molly is coming with me. She won't be told.' He turned to me and made his face unexpectedly soft. 'We've heard from the bad men. It will all be OK.'

He was gone before I could formulate a response. Gone before I could ask why he was here or what the hell it had to do with my Mum.

Out the door and into the night.

Out into a night that offered no promise of tomorrow.

MOLLY

The call came through as Molly was drawing her unexpected guest a pint of real ale. She has always enjoyed the act of pulling cask ale. She knows she has good arms and the light captures the definition in her biceps as she cranks the pump and spurts froth into the large tankard. She likes people to think of her as kooky and artistic but doesn't object to the occasional appreciative glance at her slim waist, round backside and graceful limbs. She has never been able to embrace the notion that being physically admired is an insulting gesture of patriarchal oppression. She has been to enough strip nights with her friends to be aware that women are happy to objectify men in the same way that blokes have been admiring the sorority for generations. The difference, as she sees it, is that women haven't spent thousands of years turning such appreciation into brutally invasive physical attacks. Sometimes she fancies that women will only have true equality when they work out a way to rape men. Then she tells herself off and decides to think about something easier on the brain, like how to solve the situation in Israel.

'I tried a pint of something calling Old Peculier,' said Karol, over the hubbub in the front bar. 'They spelled it wrong. Was that on purpose?'

'I've been to the brewery,' said Molly, brightly. Her hands were jittery and her voice was higher than she intended. 'Masham in North Yorkshire. Very pretty. They sponsor a crime writing festival every summer. I wanted to go when I thought about being a crime writer but never got around to it.'

Karol sipped his drink and nodded. He didn't seem bored by the burst of personal details that she found herself reeling off without quite understanding why.

'First time I try warm beer I think they taking the piss,' said Karol, twitching a cheek in a close approximation of a smile. 'Or that maybe they piss in it already. Now, every time I come to England I drink the stuff. Pork scratchings too.'

'I can only eat them when I'm drunk,' said Molly, busying herself with wiping down the bar top despite having just done it a moment before. 'I'm not sure that any snack should have toenails.'

'Toenails?' asked Karol, confused.

Molly thought about explaining herself then decided there were too many opportunities to show herself up. She poured herself a glass of water and decided to get a grip of herself. This was her place. Her environment. She shouldn't be feeling intimidated. She knew how to talk to people.

'Doesn't matter,' she said. 'You get over here a lot?'

Karol shrugged. 'Depends on the work. I go where people need me.'

'You sound like a superhero.'

'Superhero?'

Molly was about to explain when she caught the little glint in his eye that suggested he knew exactly what she was talking about. She grinned and pulled a face.

'You not like other women I meet here,' said Karol, thoughtfully. 'You dress different. Talk different. You pull faces and make fun of yourself.'

'You should come to Scunthorpe,' said Molly, rubbing her finger in slow circles on the tip of her nose and wondering why on earth her brain had sent such a message to her hands. 'There's loads of me.'

'Doubt that,' said Karol. 'You unique.'

Molly used every ounce of willpower not to preen. She had always been undone by compliments – especially when they were accompanied by the same intense gaze which Karol had suddenly fixed upon the place where her neck reached her breastbone. For an instant, she wondered whether there was something vampire-like about her guest; whether he was imagining the blood pulsing beneath the skin.

'I didn't do quite as you asked,' spurted Molly, putting her hands behind her back to stop them doing anything peculiar or unbidden. 'I asked some questions about that other missing girl. I think there's more to this.'

Karol sucked the inside of his cheek, his eyes upon hers. Molly forced herself to hold the stare. There had always been a defiance about her – an obstinacy that led to slaps and shakes as a child and the premature end of adult love affairs. She could never bring herself to follow instruction – even as each act of wilful disobedience created ripples of fevered anxiety within her.

'I figure,' said Karol, at last. 'You woman. You ex-cop. You friend of Meda. You not capable of leaving things alone.'

Molly searched his face for signs of rebuke but saw only a sly appreciation. She felt both relieved and disappointed. Some part of her had wanted his displeasure. Had wanted him to raise his voice in admonishment. She bit down hard on her lip, flicking her eyes towards Karol's mouth as she did so and breathing deep. She couldn't make sense of herself. Her thoughts were chaos and noise. There was sweat across her back and under her arms and her mouth tasted of pennies.

'I might not have to go home for a while,' said Karol, and as he leaned forward at the bar his shirt opened to reveal the complicated ink upon his lean, hairless chest. He caught the direction of Molly's gaze and moved back immediately.

'They're nice,' said Molly. 'I've got a couple, but . . .'

Karol held up a hand to stop her as he reached into the pocket of his dark trousers and retrieved his phone. He spoke only once, and his eyes seemed to become black as he listened to the voice. Then he nodded and terminated the call.

'Meda?' asked Molly.

Karol drained his pint and stood up. His leather jacket was hanging on a hook beneath the bar and he pulled it on as if slipping into armour. He did not seem to hear Molly's voice.

'Was it Meda, I said,' she asked again. 'Karol, was it to do with Meda?'

He turned to her, pulling his cigarettes from the pocket of his coat and placing one, unlit, between his lips. 'My partner get call. They want money. Meda is safe. Friends of ours trace IP address of the computer they use to make call. We go there now. Get her back. No worries. No problem. No payment.'

For a moment, Molly stood absolutely still. Just stared at him and breathed, slow and deep. Countless possibilities played out in her mind and she knew, with absolute certainty, that she could not do anything but follow her instincts.

'I'm coming too,' she said. 'I'm not a liability. You want to get revenge or whatever and that's all none of my business, but I care about Meda and I want to make sure nothing terrible happens and if you say no I'm going to have no choice but to call the police and neither of us want that. The girl who died, she had goose quills in her skin, and the kind of person who would do that is somebody who wouldn't think twice about hurting Meda if they heard a bang on the door, and I don't care what you say anyway because I will fucking follow you, and . . .'

She stopped in the face of Karol's bemused glare. 'I said OK,' he muttered, rolling his eyes. 'But change clothes. You bit fucking recognizable in your fancy dress. I tell your daughter.'

Molly pursed her lips into a line and declined to respond to the use of the phrase 'fancy dress'. 'Five minutes,' she said, and hurried over to the table in the window, where the other barmaid was collecting glasses.

Twenty minutes later, Molly is sitting in the passenger seat of Karol's car. It's a boxy, unremarkable family vehicle with plastic covers on the seats. It smells of pine air freshener and disinfectant. Karol wears gloves to drive.

'Horrible night,' says Molly, a little shrill. The rain is beating down hard on the windshield and the city lights are a dizzying spray of lurid yellows and blues. They are heading east, moving through heavy traffic, drifting away from the tourist spots and the architectural icons. Passing abandoned factories and shops that hide behind graffiti-daubed shutters. The names upon the supermarkets and clothes shops take on more accents and consonants. Larger satellite dishes bloom like mould upon the long, flat-roofed terraces. Cranes are black slashes upon the charcoal grey of the skyline, though whether they are erecting buildings or pulling them down is hard to say. She feels a sadness as they head further away from the areas she knows. Wonders how her own little network of familiar streets looks to outsiders.

'I haven't been out this far before,' says Molly, making conversation. She feels wired. Nervous. High.

'No reason to,' says Karol, moodily staring through the rain at the brake lights of the white van in front. 'This not London. This Lithuania.'

She gives him a curious look. 'Big community?'

'Big? Ha! This is biggest Lithuanian city anywhere. You live here, you shop in Lithuanian shops, talk to Lithuanian people, eat Lithuanian food. You just pay your taxes to Britain.'

Molly tries to work out her driver's opinion on the matter and realizes she cannot read him. 'You ever want to move here permanently?'

'I'd like to live anywhere permanently. But life's not that way for me.'

Molly takes a breath. Tells herself she is purely being chatty. 'You have a family?'

He shakes his head. 'Once. Something like a family, maybe. Girlfriend with a kid. It not work.'

'That's your type, is it?' she asks.

He ignores her, staring straight on. 'Was supposed to be big fucking deal this area. Thatcher loved it, you know that? This was where all the bankers were supposed to live. Pretty cottages with views of the river where the businessmen could commute to Canary Wharf. It look like that to you? Twenty minutes from the millionaires and you're in all this.'

Molly looks out of her window as they turn left on to a run-down street. The pavements at the foot of the lopsided trees are rising up where the roots are pushing through. There are battered England flags hanging from balconies of the three-storey apartment blocks above. The broken skeleton of a bicycle is chained to black railings around a parking area. There is a yellow clamp hanging half off the back wheel of the solitary vehicle parked on its pitted, rain-lashed tarmac. There are scorches on the paintwork where an axle-grinder has been taken to it.

'This is Beckton,' says Karol. 'You won't find many restaurants on TripAdvisor. It's OK though. Nice people. Even the Poles and Roms.'

'This is where she is?' asks Molly, as the car pulls to a halt

by the kerb. 'Meda? Are you meeting your partner? What do
they think is happening? Which house is it?'

Karol kills the engine and turns to his passenger. 'You ask
a lot of questions. Too many, sometimes, maybe.'

'I just want to know . . .'

'That flat,' says Karol, gesturing at a first-floor corner
premises indistinguishable from any of the others. 'IP address
is there. So I go upstairs and talk to the people inside. They
tell me where Meda is. If everything is good in our life then
Meda is up there eating ice cream and I bring her home with
me. That the end of it. If not, I persuade them to tell me where
she is. Then we go there. This my work. This what I do.'

Molly watches his mouth as he talks. His top lip does not
move much but his lower lip rolls up pleasingly around his
vowels. She wonders how she looks to him, sitting here on
his plastic-coated seats in her jeans and plain vest top, man's
shirt and borrowed denim jacket. She feels strangely naked
without her accessories. She finds herself wondering what it
says about her – that she could be sitting here, in this moment,
this now, with this man, and be regretting that she is not
dressed in high-throated corset and ruffled petticoats.

'You said you wanted to come,' says Karol, shaking his
head. 'Get that out of your head. You can be here to give Meda
a cuddle if she comes down with me. That's OK. But don't
come up.'

Molly is already shaking her head. 'No, that's not what we
agreed.'

'We didn't agree anything. I don't make deals. I say what
is what.'

Molly opens her mouth, showing her displeasure. 'You say
what's what? Not to me you don't. What do you think you'll
do if I just get out and follow you? I'm not some feeble little
thing. I want to help.'

Karol is shaking his head. The only light in the car comes
from the light of a street lamp a few car lengths away. Karol
is little more than an outline; a handsome, clearly defined
jaw, angled cheekbones and short hair. Molly suddenly realizes how little she knows about this man; how fleeting their
acquaintance. The absurdity of the situation strikes her. She

is miles from home, in an area of East London that she has never ventured into before. She is in a car with plastic sheets being driven by a stranger who wears gloves and talks of having no home and who makes his living recovering kidnapping victims and has criminal tattoos carved on to his chest. The sensation of disquiet in her chest begins to become a wave of something more akin to fear.

'I won't be long,' says Karol, and he pats the pocket of his jacket as if checking for the outline of his wallet. 'Don't touch the settings on the radio, the car belongs to a friend . . .'

Karol doesn't get to finish the sentence. His words are lost in an instant of sensory blackout; a moment in which her knowledge of herself, her physical being, her place within things, is entirely ripped away. She feels as though she has been consumed by blackness; swaddled in thick plastic and spun. She does not know which way is up or down, or which noises are in her head and which she can taste and smell. There is just the dizzying echo of the explosion and the certainty of pain as the windshield turns into so many shards of flying glass and the airbag flares in a sudden rush of colour and dust . . .

Karol is still bouncing back in his chair as the iron bar smashes into the window on the driver's side. Glass shatters and it feels to Molly as if she is on an aeroplane with a missing window. She watches as Karol is wrenched from his seat as if taken by a ravenous wind.

A sound pierces the fog. Angry shouts and curses that ring out like a shotgun blast. Molly shakes her head, trying to make sense of herself. There is wetness on her face and glass in her hair. She pulls at the door handle and stumbles out on to the damp stone of the footpath. She pulls herself up and slides over the rain-jewelled bonnet of the car.

Karol is on his knees. A man in a colourful tracksuit top is standing over him, raising something long and unyielding above his head. Molly's eyes fill with images from movies. She sees Samurai and Templars; arcing blades and the thud of decapitated skulls upon bloodied ground . . .

'Stop! Please, there's no need . . . no!'

Molly's voice sounds ridiculous to her own ears; a sudden

burst of English privilege piercing the rain-lashed air on this dark, derelict street. The man with the crowbar pauses an instant too long. The two men behind him, both barely distinguishable from the darkness that surrounds them, give a yell of warning, but the instant of hesitation is enough. Karol hits his attacker in the balls with his bunched right hand, an uppercut thrown from the floor. The man grunts and drops the crowbar, which thuds off his head and then tinkles down on to the road as Karol's attacker falls to his knees. Karol puts one hand on the man's face and slams his head into the pavement with the sound of splitting wood. He hauls himself up as the other two men rush forward from the shadows. Molly had expected broad-shouldered, dead-eyed criminals but these two men are young. Teens perhaps. One of them is shouting something in Lithuanian, raising his hands as Karol advances. If he is pleading it does him no good. Karol grabs him by the front of his hooded jacket and throws him at the side of the car. He bounces off as if he has been run over and Karol kicks him in the face as he tries to rise. The third man tries to grab Karol as he turns but Karol slides expertly out of the inexpert grip and thumps his fist into the younger man's back and neck, chopping him down as if felling a tree.

'Karol, stop . . .'

He turns at the sound of Molly's voice. There is blood all over one side of his face, and Molly finds herself thinking of Japanese symbols, as if his whole countenance had become an icon of Yin and Yang. The light catches the chunks and slivers of glass that cling to his hair and protrude from his neck. She opens her mouth in shock but Karol turns away before she can speak. He cradles his left arm in the hand of his right and Molly realizes he has been struck hard with the tyre iron. He hauls the man who did it into a seating position. Kicks open his legs and drops forward, kneeling on his bruised balls with all of his weight.

'Ooh, Jesus fucking Christ,' hisses Molly, wincing and looking away. She takes deep breaths, resting her hands on the warm metal of the car. She feels the rain upon the back of her neck. Sees lights flick on and then off again in the apartment blocks overhead.

'Meda,' she says, half to herself. The word gives her a sense of purpose and she moves to where Karol is crouching, his face millimetres from the anguish-filled features of the man who sits on the floor and tries not to puke as his testicles are ground into the road.

'What's happening?' asks Molly. 'Are they the ones? They have Meda . . .?'

One of the other boys looks up as he hears the name. Up close, Molly sees the boy is no more than sixteen. There are tears in his eyes and blood on his chin.

'We need the money. It wasn't our idea. It was wrong . . . I'm sorry . . .'

Molly looks at Karol, who releases his grip on his captive and crosses over to the boy who had spoken. He hauls him upright and hisses a stream of angry Lithuanian into his face. The reply is garbled and frantic and Karol spits blood on the floor when he is done. He grinds his foot into the frothy red sputum as if he is extinguishing a cigarette.

'Karol? Is she here?'

Karol pushes the youngster away and he sprawls on to the floor at his feet. He leans down and puts his thumb into the left eye and is rewarded with an instant scream of agony. Molly moves forward on instinct and Karol gives a shout of frustration and straightens back up. He swears to himself then drags the biggest of his attackers from his prone position beside the vehicle.

'You're saving these fuckers' lives,' rumbles Karol, and he fumbles in his pocket for his cigarettes. He wipes a hand on his face and seems to pay no heed to the blood that soaks his palm. He lights his cigarette and in the sudden flame of the lighter, Molly sees the streak of red on the white stem of the cigarette.

'What about Meda?' Molly asks again. She becomes aware of a pain above her right eye and raises a hand. She feels a sliver of glass poking into her eyebrow and she floods with a great wave of nausea and dizziness at the touch. She feels herself tottering and then Karol's hand is at her elbow and he is steering her to the vehicle and laying her, gently, in the back seat. She looks up, a high whine in her ears. Lead weights pull at her consciousness and she feels the dim sensation of Karol's blood dripping from his cheek to land on her upturned face, and then all she can hear is the purr of the tyres on the road and Karol's quiet voice, muttering into his mobile phone, as he tells his employers that they have been scammed. That his attackers never had Meda in the first place. That she is still missing and that nobody is claiming responsibility for her kidnap. He tells them that the girl is almost certainly dead.

Molly cannot hear the response of the man to whom Karol speaks. But somewhere inside herself, in a place that has witnessed violence and blood, she fancies that she can make out the white hot shriek of a soul in pain.

From: Harriet Johnson (deathbecomezher@hotmail.com)
To: Eve Burrell
Subject: Enquiry about death masks for doctoral paper
08/08/2013 8.48 p.m.

Hi Eve!

Sorry for the delayed response. The life of a mortician is just so rock'n'roll! I wanted to give a proper answer to your rather intriguing query. Do I make death masks? No, unfortunately that is not a request I have received, nor training I have. I am sure it would be possible, but I'm not sure how – would the casting material damage the skin? You see, some problems we have after embalming (and sometimes without embalming) include the skin on the face 'burning'. This is a drying out of the skin, causing areas to become a dark yellow/brownish color. Skin loses its moisture, and I wonder if doing a mask would work against me. BUT I would love to learn how . . . maybe that is something I could look into . . . also, desquamation would be of high concern . . . and the time it would take could be concerning . . . There are several guides on how to perform the process available online but I can't vouch for their usefulness. I understand William Blake underwent the process of having a replica made of his face while still alive and it showed him with a pained expression because the clay kept pulling his hair!

I DO get many requests for hair clippings, clothing to be returned, etc. We also fingerprint everyone and can send it to a company who uses the fingerprint to create jewelry and the like. One gal requested her husband's toe print . . . We didn't ask why . . .

A modern memento mori that I do on a regular basis would be separating cremated remains for the decedent's kids/family to have in a keepsake urn, necklace charm, blown glass item, etc. Each family member could have a separate part of the ashes of their loved one to memorialize.

Many families take pictures of their deceased loved one at the funeral. Even if I have someone prepared for closed casket, no viewing, I ALWAYS prepare them as if a million people will see them. This is one reason why.

I have been asked to return the clothing of the deceased before – depending on its condition, I have responded no. Also to take pictures of tattoos (I have heard of the company who preserves tattoos, but have not had a request to do so). I have seen hospitals do a plaster cast of children's hands and feet that families appreciated. Stones can be made out of these casts too. Hospitals and hospices can do hand prints too (this is easier when the person is alive).

You might have heard of people who request gold teeth/fillings to be returned. If they're in dentures, SURE! If they're attached to a tooth/mandible, NO WAY JOSÉ. The family can hire a dentist to come in and take it out. The fillings are worth a solid twenty-five cents. Maybe. (I may be exaggerating here, but it really isn't worth the trouble.)

One kind of 'reverse memento' I came across, this gentleman had kept a 'mumu' (an oversized, long, long-sleeved, busy patterned dress/nightgown) of his mother's. When he died, his wife brought it in to us and said, 'If he wanted to keep it so bad, he can be buried with it.' So I put it in the foot end of the casket.

Other than that, I can't think of any odd memento mori I have encountered . . . Then again, what's considered odd in this business?

I can't wait to hear about the paper you're writing. Do please stay in touch.

Harriet.

x

HILDA

I was asking questions the way I always did when I was getting over-excited. If I was a dog my tail would have been going like windscreen wipers in a storm. There was never any opportunity for the poor victim of my interrogations to reply to one question before I hit them with the next. I had the word 'chatterbox' as the password on my phone before I lost it and didn't object when Mum occasionally put her hands over her ears and warned me that if I didn't give her five minutes of peace, there was a good chance she was going to nail a brick to my tongue.

'Have you been to Lithuania? It's nice, apparently. Meda's city looks like a butterfly. People don't go there for honeymoons, do they? Did you know Verona and Paris both call themselves the city of love? Has anybody taken you to Paris? How about Verona? I'd love to go and see an opera there but Mum says the flights cost a month's wages. Is that true? Why haven't you got married? Are you and the skinny man seeing each other . . .?'

Lottie was starting to wince on the side of her face nearest to me. It was raining hard and the spray was hitting her liberally about the cheeks but I am pretty sure her expression was more to do with me than the weather.

'Which one do you want first?' she asked, raising her voice over the sound of the traffic that creaked past in a cacophony of horns and muffled music, hissing breaks and creaking tyres.

I thought about it. 'Why aren't you married?'

'I like to sleep diagonally,' she said, and there was a look on her face that, as an adult, I have come to think of as regret.

'You could still do that and get married,' I said. 'Just sleep in different beds. That's what Mum and Mike did and they seemed happy right up until they weren't.'

Looking back, I wonder why I said it. More than that, I wonder how that line affected Lottie. I wonder if I said it for effect. The truth is, I never had much interest in where Mike was sleeping. He was a phantom in our lives. It was like living in a haunted house. He was my dad but I wasn't allowed to call him that. He was Mum's boyfriend but nobody was allowed to know. He paid for things but it had to be in cash and there couldn't be any trace. He lived most of the time in a different house, with a lady called Ashley and two daughters who didn't know they had a half-sister and who had only heard Mum's name in the context of a colleague with a crush. As an adult, or the nearest thing to it, I can't think of those years without wrinkling my nose on Mum's behalf. She took so much shit. Thought she was doing right in insisting I have a relationship with the man she told me was my father. I engaged with him to please her but in truth, neither he nor I gave a damn about one another. It was all duty. If I had the choice of an afternoon in McDonald's and a shopping trip with Mike, or snuggles on the sofa with Mum, I knew what my heart wanted most. But it seemed important I embrace the idea of a dad, and so I kept telling her that I missed him when he wasn't there and that I'd be sad if we never saw him again. I still don't know why. I haven't seen him since she told him to go fuck himself and I don't feel any poorer for it.

'It's a good job I'm not married,' said Lottie, scowling at the blue-black air. 'Your mum would make him a widow this evening.'

'Stop worrying. Mum loves you.'

'I wish.'

We were on Globe Road, retracing Meda's last known steps. It was a little before nine p.m. We were soaked through. Lottie had abandoned her see-through umbrella with the curved handle and beaded trim – giving it to a homeless girl who sat in the doorway of Tesco and asked for a few pence with which to buy hummus. Lottie had been so taken with the specificity of the request that she had given her a £5 note and her umbrella and told the girl to treat herself to some sundried tomatoes too.

The owners of the corner supermarket had been reluctant to offer any help. I know now that Karol had already been in, asking the same questions that I had put to them in my rather less intimidating fashion. The lady behind the counter was Bangladeshi and there was a gap between her two front teeth that made me thankful for the fact I had never seen her eating spare ribs. She wore a gaudy sari and oval spectacles and she ate After Eights from the box as she told me she was sorry that Meda was missing but, like she had told the rude man two days before, they had many customers and could not remember them all.

'She was big,' I told her, and I tried to ignore the grumbles from the half-dozen people in the queue behind us. 'Big for her age. She bought bread and milk and tuna. Two tins . . .'

'She seemed pleased with herself when she worked out the change,' said the shopkeeper, flicking apologetic glances at the others in the line for service. 'She ran back and got a second tin. I do hope she is OK. Is she a friend of yours? I thought she was Lithuanian . . .'

I didn't understand what difference any of that stuff made. I didn't care that the lady shopkeeper helped me because I was English and pale-skinned. I just knew she was being kind to me, and that she saw me as more than a little girl with a rain-soaked jacket and a face laced with sodden hair.

'Had she been in before?' I asked, hoping to stumble on to something useful. 'You must have known her. She was big, like an ostrich. Clumsy . . .'

'I knew her face,' said the shopkeeper, closing her eyes as she said it, as though the memory made her sad. 'She was always full of smiles. She liked to dance, yes?'

That was when she told us the thing she hadn't told Karol. Chatting with a ten-year-old girl and her purple-haired friend, she told us something that a bruiser from the Lithuanian mob had never managed to squeeze out of her.

'It was for her friend, the extra tuna,' said the shopkeeper, under her breath. 'Most girls, when they get spare change, they buy a chocolate bar or a can of drink and they walk slowly home enjoying their little treat. She did something for the poor man. She bought a prize for Banky.'

The tumblers fell. I remembered a conversation, weeks before. She spoke of the man who lived in the doorway of the abandoned bank. He had a springer spaniel called Ray. He was Scottish and polite and shy and he cried the time she gave him her packed lunch and went to the Co-op and bought a packet of ham for his dog. He lived in a sleeping bag and he ate food from the tin. His teeth were rotten and his skin looked sore but he always had a smile for her and kept telling her how he liked her accent and that he had been to Russia for a football match and had a picture of himself somewhere outside the Kremlin. She had never corrected him about her origins. She just stroked his dog and told him that it would all be better in summer and promised to buy him something nice next time she got her pocket money.

We have to talk to him. That was the thought that pounded at my skull. I no longer truly knew what I felt about Meda's whereabouts or the circumstances of her disappearance, but I felt that if we had been given a clue of such obvious importance, we were duty bound to follow it up.

'You are so soaked,' said Lottie, looking me up and down. 'And oh my goodness that tastes amazing. That is literally a party in my mouth. I am biting the air. Hilda, please, tell me if anybody's looking – I'm about to start licking the window of this place . . .'

Lottie hadn't taken much persuading to take me out. With Mum gone and Lottie nominally in charge of my welfare, I'd been able to convince her without any real effort that I would sleep better and feel more settled if I had been allowed a stroll before bed. If that stroll happened to take us past the shop where Meda bought her supplies on the night she disappeared, surely that was a good thing all round. Lottie had agreed for primarily selfish reasons. Brendan was in, offering her his theories on the identity of the person who had outbid him on some weird object he was determined to own. Lottie couldn't face it that night. He was just too absurd a creature for her to keep indulging. I got a sense that if Mum didn't have a word with him, he was going to start costing us customers.

'She did take her mobile, yes?' asked Lottie. 'Your mum. She's OK, yes? Of course she is. She's tough. She's from Scunthorpe. What am I saying? I don't even know Scunthorpe. I just know my spell-checker thinks I'm being rude whenever I put it in an email . . .'

We were standing outside a chicken shop and I could tell that Lottie was feeling uncomfortably sober and very hungry. She had quite the appetite, did Lottie. I could always imagine her at work, tucking into a hamper of sandwiches with one hand and weighing heart and lungs and spleen of a flabby cadaver with the other.

'You know what she's like,' I said, and that covered most of what I felt at that moment. 'She's probably out of data or something.'

'Are you not worried?' she asked, and her eyes were big and wide and pale, like she was a drawing of a pixie.

'Worried about what? Did you not see her last night? She's tough, like you said. And Karol's with her.'

'You don't really know him either . . .'

'I know he fancies Mum. And he's well hard.'

'You think he fancies your mum? Why?'

'I know how people look at people when they fancy them.'

I've replayed that sentence a thousand times in the years since. I don't think I was being cruel. I don't think I was trying to tell Lottie that I knew her secret or that she had made a fool of herself in front of a child. But I know that it must have hurt her and I've always been sorry for that.

'She said she wasn't ready for another boyfriend,' said Lottie, and I seem to recall she was combing her hair with her fingers as she said it and her hand seemed a little firmer around my own.

'She's not. She thinks men are a bit embarrassing really. I asked her about it. She said she likes men but can't be bothered to get to know another one. All that stuff about who sleeps on which side and who gets to hold the remote controls and when it's OK to fart in front of them . . .'

We walked along in silence for a spell after that. I was a bit frazzled with nervous energy. And a bit burpy, truth be told. It's nice when the chap responsible for your evening meal has worked in Michelin-starred restaurants and thinks you're awesome. I'd eaten a tea of chicken and leek pudding in a rosemary and tarragon jus, and it had taken half an hour of thinly concealed belches before I felt able to refasten my trousers. It had helped to persuade Lottie of the need for an evening walk in the rain. I'd also promised her there was an awesome Lebanese takeaway near Meda's house and was beginning to wonder how she would react when she learned it wasn't true.

'Do you really think she likes him?' asked Lottie.

'I don't think it matters,' I said, dismissively, and I think I went out of my way to step in a puddle. 'She's sort of given up on all that, and . . .'

That was when we saw it. The blue lights and the yellow tape and the men and women in luminous jackets. That's when we saw what had happened to the man I had forgotten and who meant the world to Meda.

That's when it all made sense.

That's when I knew that if she ever came home, she would never be the same again.

That's when I saw them lifting Banky's body from the canal.

Red Gold – a precis of the work of visionary and pioneer Jean-Baptiste Denys

An extract from student magazine interview with Goldsmith's research fellow Eve Burrell about her chosen doctoral thesis

April 9, 2013

AG: Have I got this right? People have had blood transfused into their veins from different animals? Why haven't I heard about this before?

EB: Good question! But I frequently meet people who haven't heard about man walking on the moon so don't be ashamed to have a gap in your knowledge. Science is essentially a little bit ashamed of itself over the work of the early transfusionists but I'm optimistic that viewpoint will change. I personally admire the grandeur of the original vision and the desire to better understand and better use the human body. For me, and thankfully for my supervising tutor, Jean-Baptiste Denys was a genius.

AG: That's not a name I'm familiar with. Tell us more.

EB: In the seventeenth century, not long after blood circulation was theorized and proven, the scientists of the day began to think about the nature of blood. There were those who believed it somehow contained the soul. Think about it – we know that our loved ones are made of our flesh and blood. We talk about the nature of our blood and the calling of our blood. It's almost as if it contains who we really are. Would the blood carry personality traits? That was the question people found fascinating. And how could one's nature be changed by the injection of other substances? Scientists moved to animal models in which they were taking anything from water, beer, wine, opium, and injecting it into dogs to see what would happen. These experiments were being conducted in Britain by some great men

who next began to wonder whether animal blood could
have an effect on a human. Would the blood of a gentle
lamb or calf somehow cool the heated blood of a
maniac?

AG: Really?

EB: It was visionary stuff. But while the Brits were
dilly-dallying over the ethics of it all, a young French
doctor beat them to it. He performed the first transfusion on a young boy with sheep blood. It was a
success. The boy didn't die. What's more, the ailments
that had afflicted his mind were no longer present.
Soon he was the talk of the scientific community. For
the next transfusion, he used a butcher who was healthy
and who had likely provided the sheep for the first
transfusion. It was another success, though Denys was
curious to find the butcher getting drunk in a tavern
shortly after the procedure.

AG: But how was the procedure carried out?

EB: It probably sounds a little barbaric to modern ears
but essentially, the recipient of the blood had a vein
opened and emptied of a good quantity. The donor
blood was then poured in through a tube and a
syringe. The very earliest syringes were made of
goose feathers. There was obviously a good deal
of spillage and mess and the patients reported strange
sensations within themselves as the blood entered
their system, but there was no doubting the results.

AG: Tell me more! Are you saying they just stuck goose
feathers in people's veins?

EB: Well, they would puncture them with a lancet.
They would do a cut, and then they would slide a
goose quill inside and drain the blood out. Later on,
they had a more elaborate system using silver pipes.
At the Paris Academy of Sciences they used a scale.
One dog was on one scale. One dog was in the other.
They transfused blood and they were watching this
delicate dance between the scales to get an idea of
how much they put in.

AG: It sounds almost laughable.

EB: Not at all. It was primitive, of course, but that's where the purity of the vision has to be admired. This was uncharted territory. And yes, mistakes were made and yes, perhaps there were ethical concerns, but no great accomplishment has ever been achieved without some suffering.

AG: You sound like you're a big fan.

EB: My supervising tutor said that my zeal for the subject was what had persuaded him to oversee my work, so I suppose being a fan has served me well. I just think Denys needs to be better recognized. The public at large know nothing of what he achieved. He altered what we know about ourselves. There are those who believe he was close to finding the very nature of a human soul. I've put in request after request to study his actual notebooks and the original letters he sent to the British scientists after pipping them to the post, but they are in private collections that guard them very jealously. But fingers crossed!

AG: I understand Denys was eventually accused of murder after the deaths of one of his subjects.

EB: That was the result of a conspiracy. He disproved that charge in his own lifetime. The blood recipient was poisoned by those who wanted to stop Denys's work. These are the lies that myself and Mr Farkas will put right with my publication . . .

MR FARKAS

The bookseller is thin and limp and wrapped in a greyness that seems to go straight through to the bone. He seems to have too little blood in his body. Too little light in his eyes. His hands are forever fretting with the clutter upon his desk or patting at the air, like a blind man trying to find their way out of a phone box. His shirt is crumpled and though he is seated, his corduroy trousers look as though they will be too short to cover his stripy socks when he stands. He looks at home here, among the racks of paper and leather; the unwashed tea cups, the unwatered potted plants; the mingled scents of paper, polish and cat. He looks as though it would take little effort to fold him into a binding and store him next to the illustrated botany textbooks on the top shelf.

'It's a beauty. Exceptional, in fact. Going to hurt me to part with it.'

'It will go to a good home,' says the customer, his voice gentle as leaves upon water. 'It will be cherished.'

The bookseller nods appreciatively. He does not have any doubts that the volume will be cared for. The man before him has the look of a true bibliophile. He looks at the book the same way that the bookseller does – with a reverence verging on the obsessive. Within the bookshops on Cecil Court, just off Charing Cross Road, such a look is prized. This is where the serious booklovers come to buy their signed first editions; their rare hardbacks and limited prints. This is a paradise for the men and women who wear white gloves when they read and who would die in a house fire rather than leave their collections to burn. The purchaser standing beside the till in Wilkin's Antiquarian Bookshop looks the sort that can turn a bad week into a spectacular one and principal bookseller Vernon Halliday is having to keep his hands busy just so he doesn't start rubbing them together and mentally spending his commission.

'I know some of the stories,' says Vernon, holding the book upon his palm as if weighing it. 'Quite creepy, or so I remember. Beautiful illustrations. Worth every penny. You're sure, yes?'

The customer looks at the book and gives the slightest smile. He nods, once. He has dealt with Mr Farkas before. The man does not give in to displays of exuberance. He is soft-spoken and reserved. Vernon understands that in this moment, his customer is lost in something close to fantasy, completing a purchase perhaps decades in the dreaming. Vernon's own love of books is healthily zealous. He would not bankrupt himself or go hungry in pursuit of a rare first edition, but he would gladly walk to work for a month and forego the purchase of luxuries if it allowed him to buy a limited edition hardback signed and dated by one of his literary heroes. He has a withering contempt for the fly-by-night accumulators; those with a scattergun approach to amassing a collection of note. Nor does he admire the super-rich, who will buy limited edition Harry Potter prints and stick them on a shelf next to an original King James Bible so they have something to show off about over the sound of Emeli Sandé at dinner parties. He dislikes the majority of his customers, truth be told. He is not sure how he feels about Mr Farkas, other than quietly grateful that he chose today to wander in off the street and enquire about the artefact in the window. That's what he had called it – an artefact. Not a book.

'Do you think she will be afraid of it?'

It takes Vernon a moment to realize that Mr Farkas is asking him a question. He tries not to appear startled. He looks up and sees that Mr Farkas is staring at him, seemingly awaiting an answer. He feels unnerved by the gaze. He twitches his eyes towards the front window. Looks out through the golden lettering and rain-jewelled glass and into the little courtyard that has been home to booksellers for 300 years. Vernon has often fantasized that the shop is a portal; that if he just lets go of the present for long enough he could change the view beyond the glass and see men in top hats, pocket watches and splendid whiskers stalking by carrying the new Wordsworth for their betrothed. Mr Farkas, with his cape and hat and air of sculpted gloom, fits perfectly into the bleak picture.

'Pouring down,' says Vernon, feeling oddly uncomfortable. 'I'll double wrap it. Keep it safe. Is it cash or card?'

Mr Farkas hesitates and Vernon is struck by his stillness. He makes Vernon think of undisturbed water; a shimmering mirror reflecting back a thousand miles of sky.

'I asked if she will be afraid,' says Mr Farkas, again. 'I do not wish her to be scared. As a child I loved these stories but I have learned as an adult that often my preferences were unusual.'

Vernon breathes out, face splitting in a relieved grin. He feels on safe ground with such queries. He has no children of his own, but he knows books.

'Kids love the gruesome and the gory, don't they?' he says, nodding. 'Disney is far too clean. I watched *Anastasia* with my niece and it had a happy ending for the Tsar's family! I swear, if they ever make a Disney version of The Bible, Jesus will survive.'

Mr Farkas says nothing. Awaits a better answer.

'How old is she?'

'Eleven,' says Mr Farkas, without pause.

Vernon considers the customer. He is in his early fifties. Slim and loose-limbed. Large nose, dark eyes and a thatch of greying black hair. He wears a burgundy jumper beneath a suit jacket and holds a canvas rucksack in a hand all but carpeted in thick, dark hair. He looks to Vernon like an author photograph taken in the 70s.

Vernon busies himself with the folds of paper, creasing the soft tissue with his thin fingers. He likes this part of his job. Takes comfort in it as he prattles his platitudes. 'By eleven they're all playing video games where you can shoot nuns and blow up orphanages. I'm sure she will love it. It's a very generous gift.'

Mr Farkas blinks. He holds his eyes closed for a moment longer than Vernon would have expected, as if his eyelids are a mouth and he is swallowing what he sees.

'Bluebeard is the one I remember,' says Vernon, continuing to wrap the hefty pink volume in tissue paper. He remembers feeling similarly unsettled the last time Mr Farkas purchased something from him. There is an intensity to him, a lack of superficiality. He seems unnaturally desolate, even as he spends close to £900 on a book of fairy tales.

Mr Farkas subtly alters his position and stares past Vernon at the poster on the wall behind him. A children's author is giving a talk in a week's time to publicize the launch of their new guaranteed bestseller.

'Does she like them, your daughter?' asks Vernon, noticing the direction of his customer's stare. 'The series?'

'She has not tried them,' says Mr Farkas, and the 'r' in 'tried' sounds slightly accented.

'Not my cup of tea but the kids love them. I guess if your daughter prefers the classics . . .'

'Perhaps I will try them for her.'

'Read them first, you mean? Maybe wise. Sometimes you just don't know what they're going to stumble upon, though with the internet it's almost impossible to keep them innocent, isn't it?'

Vernon becomes aware of the silence in the shop. The courtyard beyond the window is deserted. The rain has stopped its drumming upon the glass. The crepe paper beneath his fingers has settled into place and hushed its soft scrunching. He looks up to see Mr Farkas staring into him as if trying to calculate the weight of his organs.

'Innocence?' he asks, unblinking.

'Pure,' says Vernon, making light. 'Hard to make sure they don't know about the nasty stuff.'

Mr Farkas continues to examine him. There is a scent coming off him. Something like still water. It is not a freshness. Though it makes Vernon think of new sap and cut wood. If dead trees could bleed they would smell like this.

'My daughter is pure,' he says, quietly. 'Truly innocent. She will always be so.'

Vernon nods, nervously. He wonders what it is about this man that so unnerves him. He flicks a glance at his eyes and has to suppress a shudder. They are black as Bible leather and they are boring into him.

'Cash, was it?' asks Vernon, smiling brightly. He feels oddly dizzy, as if he has stood up too quickly. The floor seems to be turning to sponge beneath his feet. 'Sorry, did you already say? I feel a little odd today. Maybe I should have eaten.'

Mr Farkas hands over an inch of notes. None are machine-fresh.

'Nineteen twenty-two,' says Vernon, with a last look at the book before he seals it inside the plastic wallet and slides it into a dark green paper bag. 'A different time. Different world. Lovely to think of your girl enjoying the same stories that kids did a century ago.'

Mr Farkas gives a swift, unexpected smile, like the slash of a blade in a darkened room.

'I enjoy this thought also. The continuity. The sameness of things. It was my own grandmother who taught me the fairy tales. She told them in her own way, with different voices and perfect actions. She could have been an actress, my grand-mother. I still hear her when I read these pages. I believed they were her stories. Hers and mine. It caused me pain to learn that the bedtime stories of my childhood were those of a Frenchman long dead. Charles Perrault. Creator of Red Riding Hood. Sleeping Beauty. Cinderella. They were stories that belonged to children the world over and eventually I learned to enjoy the fact that we were all connected by these stories. Perhaps things can be eternal if they are sufficiently beautiful. My daughter is connected by stories like these. She is linked to children four centuries dead. They laughed and squirmed and pulled up the covers upon hearing of Bluebeard's hands upon the throats of his wives. The blood that pumped in them pumps in her. Do you understand? So many do not.'

Vernon's eyes are wide. He has never heard Mr Farkas talk for so long. Their exchanges have always been brief. Within the ledger beneath the till are the names of the hundred or so customers that the shop staff contact when they are offered a particular rarity. Mr Farkas's telephone number is inside. It is a landline. There is no mobile or email address. No street name. He knows little about the man who is purchasing the illustrated first UK edition of this collection of grisly, fantastical yarns.

'I'm sure she will enjoy it,' says Vernon, ringing up the sale and putting the cash in the register. He writes out a receipt with his biro and imagines that Mr Farkas, if performing the same task, would use a fountain pen.

'I read to her,' says Mr Farkas, and his manner is warmer. 'She is sick, you see. She is too tired to read. But I treasure the moments when we are together and I am able to fill her head with pictures of strange and wonderful and fabulous things. It puts light in her eyes.'

Vernon seems unsure what to say. He looks back into the street. A small woman in spectacles is looking at the display of Raymond Chandler books in the window. He doubts she will buy.

'Do you do accents too?' asks Vernon, grasping for something worth responding with.

'I am shy,' says Mr Farkas, self-effacingly. 'My wife, God rest her – she say I would be good teacher if I had the courage. At first, my English wasn't good enough. Later, it was too late.'

'Your English is excellent . . .'

'Better than your Hungarian,' says Mr Farkas, and seems to find his joke tremendously funny. He gives a strange, close-mouthed titter of laughter – high and birdlike. Then it is gone. He reaches out and takes the parcel. 'You are still looking, yes? For my other request?'

Vernon nods, breathing out through his nose and trying not to look too relieved that the exchange is at an end.

'I have some good leads. I told you, it won't be cheap. There might only be a few copies left and it's not as if it's a storybook. I can't imagine this one's for your daughter.' Vernon glances at the pad in front of him, where he again scribbled down the name of the Victorian medical pamphlet for which Mr Farkas is willing to pay so handsomely.

'All is for my daughter,' says Mr Farkas, and he gives a tiny nod of dismissal. He turns away and crosses the wooden floor with barely a sound. Vernon watches as he opens his rucksack and pulls out the sodden tweed cloak that he had been wearing as he entered the shop. He shakes it out as if folding laundry and fastens it about his neck. It is an expensive-looking garment, with a crimson lining and fur collar. As he stalks away past the window in the direction of Covent Garden, Vernon is struck by the sensation he is again witnessing a person from a different time. He feels an overwhelming urge to bolt the door.

Ten minutes into Evensong and Mr Farkas is sitting on hard wood in damp clothes in this cathedral built of sugar and salt. The columns thrum like tuning forks, resonating with the high, bright voices of the children in their pure white cassocks and red cloaks. The harmonies are impossibly perfect. He sees the music rather than hears it. The treble clefs and semibreves, time signatures and codettas, forming into endless black strings in his vision, looping about the pews and columns, the other parishioners, the priest and acolytes; great black loops of inky hair twisting, binding, restraining. Mr Farkas thinks of rope-making. He sees cord being perfectly plaited. Interwoven. Pulled tight. Screws up his eyes and rubs at his forehead with his cold fingers. There is a pain in his chest, as though some-body is sitting upon him. The irony of the discomfort is not lost upon him. Before he stopped smoking he never had so much as a cold. Now he aches. The cold grey air of London seems to suffuse his bones. He feels as though his bones have become loose. Crumbly. He imagines his leg bones splintering like egg shells. Can see himself falling on to grotesque swan legs; bent at the shin; flapping as an injured bird upon the wet pavement as the pedestrians flow around this new obstruction as if he were a stone in a stream.

He swallows and it hurts him. He wonders whether he has eaten something he should not have. It feels as though he has vomited recently though he has no memory of it. He licks his teeth and tastes nothing. He checks again. The faintest trace of sugary cereal upon a back tooth. He must have had breakfast with Beatrix. Finished off whatever she did not eat. Her appetite has not been good in past days, despite his exhor-tations that she keep her strength up. Perhaps he will make something frivolous for tonight's meal. It will be their secret. He has always insisted that she eat wholesome, real foods. Meats, pulses, vegetables. Fruit for afters. Hot water with lemon. But he has found wrappers from chocolate bars in her room. He has seen the cream of sticky cakes upon her lips. It has been hard to admonish her for such betrayals. She has always been able to undo his resolve. She is his everything. His whole heart; his reason and purpose. It has always been an act of masochism to beat her.

The choir has fallen silent. The priest is talking. It's a bolstering drone, low lullaby of obscure promises and unquantifiable oaths. Mr Farkas is Catholic but does not believe in a creator. He does not have any sense of a heaven or hell. He believes the soul travels to the same place after death as it was before birth. He believes in the blackness. The nothing. The oblivion. That is why he has fought so hard to keep his daughter here. Sentient. Present. Within and beside him.

Beatrix would like it here. This church strikes him as motherly. The great façade of voluminous white stone is the skirt of a welcoming mother, held open to envelop all those willing to enter. Mr Farkas feels calmness descend upon him. This is a cool and peaceful place. The whiteness of it seems to have a cleansing quality. The dark wood of the stalls on the first floor is pleasingly black. The gold upon the high chandeliers is understatedly attractive. The bibles are neatly laid out. It is a gratifyingly exact space in which to spend a little time. Perhaps he should bring Beatrix. Would it be so impossible? There must be access for the crippled, must there not? He looks about and sees an elderly man in a blue raincoat with his legs in the aisle. He wears grey polyester slacks and has two sticks across his lap. He could not have managed the stairs. Would Beatrix feel comfortable using an entrance for the disabled? She is of that age. Easily embarrassed. Self-conscious. Before she got ill she was beginning to read magazines about make-up and fashion. She told him that the shoes he selected for her were 'old-fashioned'. She laughed at things that he did not understand and rolled her eyes when he tried to laugh along. Such gestures irritated him. Pushed his buttons? Was that the phrase? Yes, she pushed his buttons with such actions. It took an effort to keep his temper. He had made mistakes with her older sister and paid heavily for them. His wife also. He wishes to be all things for Beatrix and yet there are times when he feels as though she is not even listening as he reads her bedtime stories and outlines his beautiful plans for the life they will lead when she is well. He would give anything for that. Give every drop of his blood to see her sit up and ask to be held. Such images sustain him. Have sustained him long past the point of hopelessness.

'Will they sing again?' comes a voice, nearby.

Mr Farkas looks into the face of a large brown man in a colourful coat. His face has the look of a plump cat and he is smiling as if they are two naughty boys sharing a secret. 'I don't want to hear much more of the talking but the singing was good.'

Mr Farkas swallows. It hurts afresh. Was he sick? Did he eat something sharp and scratchy? He cannot remember. His memory is a picture sewn in lace. More and more of his sense of reality is disappearing into such spaces and holes. His sense of self and place seems to be unravelling.

'Sorry. You speak English?'

The man is American. Even whispering, his voice is gratingly loud. Mr Farkas is not given to displays of feeling but he allows his displeasure to show in his face.

'It is a church,' he says, primly. 'The prayers are why we are here.' He does not know why he adopts the character of a religious zealot. It is what his wife would have called 'sheer contrariness'. It took him a long time to understand the exact translation of the phrase. There was little in Hungarian that covered such a characteristic. Such moments of cultural divide have been rare in their lives together but they have always wounded him deeply. At times he has felt like an outsider in his own home; one man among three women. Him, the silly foreigner with his old-fashioned tastes and his peculiar ways and his sad little collections. Them, so sophisticated, stylish. So very much at home.

'Hey, sorry man, I like prayers too. Just got a train to catch. My bad. Y'all have a good one, y'hear?'

Mr Farkas retches; a cat with a fur ball; a child with too much gristle in their gullet. His throat fills with acid and mucus. He coughs and pinkish sputum flecks his chin. The American recoils, appalled, and Mr Farkas drags himself upright. There is a pain in his chest and he is swallowing down acid and blood and he can sense people turning to look at him. Beatrix's book feels heavy in the bag beneath his arm and his rucksack falls from his back on to the black-and-white tiles. It spills its contents: bottles of pills; vials of glass; great jars carrying ghoulish, lumped shapes . . .

'Sir? Sir, are you ill?'

Mr Farkas is on his knees, pushing his possessions back into his bag. He remembers suddenly that he is ill. He must take his medicine or he will get worse and then Beatrix will be alone and scared and helpless in the dark. He grabs his possessions and pushes past the outstretched hand of the old man who has come to try and help him. He emerges into the blue-black cold; the roar and dazzling lights of Trafalgar Square. He half slips as he moves down the slick steps, clutching Beatrix's gift as if it were a lifejacket. He needs to get home. Needs to take his medicine. The black cabs become killer whales as they surge forward on the dark road. He sees the great amber eyes and the glint of teeth and his blood seems to cry out within his veins as he staggers to the kerb and lurches into the back of the nearest vehicle. He can barely hear his own voice as he burbles out the address and he gulps and gasps as if drowning as more gorge rushes up his throat.

For a time there is nothing. Just the rhythm of the tyres and the squeal of the steering wheel and the distant banality of the cabbie's voice.

'Here you go, matey. Nice chatting to you.'

Mr Farkas climbs out of the cab and on to the quiet street. He stuffs two notes through the open window and turns away without change. Breathes deep. Holds it. Spray on the back of his legs as the cab splashes away through a puddle.

He pulls out his keys from the pocket of his trousers. Feels the great blanket of familiarity and comfort envelop him. Home. Here on this quiet street with its tall old buildings and its hidden little gardens; its neat symmetry and faded grace. Here, within the echo of Christchurch and the shadow of the Ten Bells.

Mr Farkas makes himself presentable. He cannot allow Beatrix to see him this way. He wants her passage into wakefulness to be a lovely thing and knows he must make his face

kindly before he puts his hand upon her wrist and urges her
awake.

The house where he has lived these past years is a converted
apothecary. The door used to be canary yellow but has faded
to its current lurid, mustard hue. In absolute darkness, Mr
Farkas keys in the code to the burglar alarm. He takes off his
wet shoes and hangs his cape upon the hook in the long, thin
hallway. He takes the long-nosed matches from their place on
the telephone table and lifts the oil lamp from the high shelf.
The match rasps as he creates a flame. His face becomes a
scrawl of charcoal lines. It takes the softer glow of the oil
lamp to make his features less ghoulish. He closes his eyes
until he can better deal with the new illumination, then walks
down the hall to the kitchen. The wallpaper in the hallway is
mildewed and hangs from the walls in ragged strips that always
make him think of tattered flesh. Lumps of plaster and brick
skitter away as he catches them with his feet. In the kitchen
is a long wooden table covered in papers, abandoned crockery
and books. A sheet has been pinned up in front of the windows.
There are photocopies of old newspaper articles on the wall
and a model of an unravelled human being has been drawn
on to a bamboo roll which hangs from a hook in the ceiling.
The room contains a smell that no longer troubles Mr Farkas.
It is the odour of festering meat, as if the walls have been
scrubbed with a dead cat.

Mr Farkas reaches down beside the table and fastens his
fingers around an iron hook in the floor. He pulls it, hard, and
feels the pain in his chest bite afresh. He props the hatch open
and closes his eyes. Lets himself enjoy it. Enjoy her. The
nearness of true love.

The room below the kitchen contains a Victorian bed with
a polished brass headboard. The sheets are stretched tight over
the form of the girl he calls his daughter. She does not move.
Only the slightest rising and falling of her chest gives away
the fact she is alive.

Mr Farkas inspects the girl by the light of the lamp. He
knows her face so well he could draw it from memory. Knows
her shape and scent.

He inspects the rest of her fairy-tale bedroom. Notes that

the flowers in the vase by the bed are turning brown. Decides to buy her some more tomorrow. Chocolate, too. A special treat. Perhaps some music. A CD of the choir from the church. He has a memory of being at church. A memory of a brown man asking him questions. Was that long ago? How many weeks was it since he last left the house? He should not leave her. Not his Beatrix. Not his beloved *cica*.

'Wake up, my love,' he says, rubbing her arm as gently as he can. 'It is story time. We will take a journey, yes? To an enchanted land. A story of villains and heroines and sword-fights on the steps of a mighty castle. See,' he says, pulling the book from the bag and unwrapping the tissue paper. 'See what I got for you!'

The girl in the bed does not speak. The eyelids that flicker do so beneath a mask of heavy synthetic flesh.

'You could say something,' says Mr Farkas, and his shoulders sag with disappointment. 'It wasn't cheap. Perhaps when we have read it you will like it . . .'

He pulls the wooden chair up next to the bed and sits down. He clears his throat. Begins to read.

In the bed, Meda gulps and swallows and fights for breath. A fever is eating her from within. The mask made from a dead girl's face is pushing down upon her features and she cannot breathe. There is a goose quill in the crook of her elbow and the blood with which she has been repeatedly filled is rotting within her veins.

'Once upon a time . . .'

LOTTIE

Lottie is blowing raspberries, quietly, behind her cupped palm. She likes her lips to look full for the camera. She wears a cherry-red lipstick that clashes extravagantly with her blue hair, which she has twisted into a 1950s curl. She is wearing clear-glass spectacles that curve upwards at the edges like cats' eyes and is dressed in a tight pinafore dress beneath a baggy red lumberjack shirt.

'Nearly there,' says Jay. He's an intern at the hospital and endlessly enthusiastic. He's a year out of university and is managing to support himself during his unpaid tenure at the hospital by doing some technical wizardry for the various professors and doctors who enjoy high-profile social media work. He has been Lottie's cameraman since the summer. It isn't a difficult job. All he has to do is point the camera and Lottie does the rest. She is a natural. Sometimes Jay is literally open-mouthed in his admiration. One day, she might let him sleep with her, but it will have to be as a going-away present. She finds him far too earnest and excitable to consider him for anything more than a one-nighter. She gets the impression he would do irritating things, like get up early to make her breakfast, or do all her laundry as a nice surprise. She has no time for such largesse. It makes her shudder.

'I think we're good,' says Jay, looking through the scope of the large black camera and double-checking the screen on the laptop at his side. The camera is trained upon a brown leather chair in which Lottie sits like a founder member of a gentleman's club. She has her legs crossed at the ankle and her hands upon her knees. Behind her is the pathology museum that she helped to establish during her own internship; row upon row of clear glass jars containing perfectly preserved samples of human anatomy and labelled in her own neat hand. This place has become one of the standard bearers for the burgeoning world of morbid anatomy – a subculture filled with people fascinated by the art of death. Her YouTube videos detailing some of her favourite specimens regularly get more than a million viewers, though she suspects that many of those tuning in do so to get a glimpse of the crazy blue-haired lady in the mini skirt. She curates endless exhibitions and organizes guest lectures and theme nights. She writes a popular blog about her daily work and is the go-to girl when radio stations and TV shows are seeking somebody photogenic to give a layman's terms description of something scientific.

'You're blocking the spleen,' says Jay. 'Just a touch to the left.'

Lottie shifts her position and gets a thumbs-up. She blows a final raspberry.

'Just lost the Facebook Live feed,' mutters Jay, holding up a hand and checking the laptop. 'Plenty people logged in. Your pal is back. Eyeballz12. Wants to know if you'll rub the liver like it's a sea cucumber. Do you think he's being rude? And some woman called Nessa wants to know where you got your shoes . . .'

Lottie sighs, disappointed at the interruption. She wants to get this over and done with. Normally she adores these sessions but today her mind feels like an open bin liner, her thoughts billowing like raked leaves. She's worried, for the first time, that she might make a mess of her live show. She has no pre-prepared script. She usually finds talking to the camera effortless. But today her mind is full of Molly and Hilda and the injuries to her friend and the dead tramp in the canal. She spends her days among the dead and has never felt any unease about touching innards or slicing through great ripples of flesh and fat and muscle, but it was all she could do not to cry out when Karol brought Molly back to the Bonnet. There was blood over half her face and her eye was bulging and swollen. Karol's arm was hanging limp and there was more blood on his skull. Lottie had presumed that professional instinct would take over, but her hands shook as she gripped Karol's bruised hand and yanked it and heard the ugly crunch of the elbow slipping back into the joint. She had been more at ease sliding the shard of glass out of Molly's eyebrow. She had been gentle with her. She was more used to working with the blissfully

dead and she was grateful when Molly told her that she had
lovely soft hands and had made it as painless as could be.
Truth be told, Lottie had enjoyed the intimacy of the moment.
They'd closed the doors of the Bonnet and sent the bar staff
home and Lottie had performed her little surgeries by lamplight
in the snug. It had felt perversely pleasurable, bending over
her friend as she lay back on the wooden bench and tried to
be brave and not to shudder as the large chunk of glass slid
free from her skin. Lottie had stroked her hairline with her
fingers; the tiniest gesture of tenderness between friends. She
had seen her own reflection swim on Molly's brown irises and
enjoyed the way her likeness blended with the reflected oil
lamps to become a collage of patterns flecked with gold. To
Lottie's own expert eyes, Molly had definitely been crying.
Much as she had tried to downplay what happened, there was
something in her expression that spoke of a colossal sadness.
The cold, unforgiving blackness of grief. She seemed to have
reached a decision that Meda was not coming home, and that
had been reinforced when Hilda told her about their grim
discovery while retracing Meda's steps. A police constable
had been indiscreet with the little information that he had.
A tramp's body had been found wedged beneath a riverboat
in the canal that cuts through Bethnal Green Gardens. His dog
had been making a nuisance of himself on the bank, yapping
and howling for days on end. He'd tried to bite the wardens
when they came to take him. Eventually the owner of the canal
boat had decided to fix the problem by mooring elsewhere.
As the barge took off, the bloated, alabaster-white body had
bobbed to the surface and the dog had let out a howl that sent
great shivers down the spines of the wardens. They had called
the police.

'Back up,' says Jay, excitedly. 'Good in ten?'

Lottie closes her eyes and thinks about what she is about
to say. She expects it to be popular with her hard-core fans.
She calls them her die-hards, which they love. More than
that, she hopes to attract in some of the floating viewers who
have yet to allow their interest in the art of death to become
a full-blown hobby. She knows they will be made welcome.
Most of her followers feel a little out of place in mainstream

society. When they attend her museum and feast on specially made cupcakes in the shape of ulcerated eyeballs, and listen to her lectures about the best way to make plaster stick to human skin, they seem much more at home.

'Maz_morbid wants to know if you ever found out what happened to the saw you were raving about.'

Lottie cocks her head, hawkish. She had ranted in a recent interview about the ghoulish collectors who were buying up anatomical specimens for private collections instead of scientific research or public display. She had just failed in a month-long attempt to purchase an important sample for the pathology museum. Heine's osteotome saw, made in 1850, was a beautiful specimen. Made by Charriere and terrifyingly beautiful in appearance, the object was an imbroglio of blades and spikes, including one spear used to fix the instrument to the bone prior to the grinding amputation. She had tracked down the seller only to learn that an anonymous private collector had already made a cash offer. The seller had refused to divulge the buyer's details and Lottie had still been in a frustrated bad mood when she gave a live lecture about such people. She had attracted the usual combination of sympathy and sneering. She has no shortage of online detractors who accuse her of turning death into soft pornography, but she has never felt compelled to defend herself. She has enough people to do that for her. Whenever a viewer leaves a critical comment, dozens of her die-harders leap on them like wolves upon an injured fawn. She feels lucky to have such a resource. She is half tempted to tell her viewers about Meda's disappearance. She fancies she would know everything she needs to within the hour.

'Lottie, can I read this please? Oh sorry, you're on . . .'

Hilda appears behind Jay. She hasn't been to school today. When she learned that the men in the East End did not have Meda, her face had crumpled into tears. She and Molly had held each other in a bloody embrace as they tried to comfort each other and Lottie and Karol had looked awkwardly away. They told each other the same things. Meda would still be OK. It didn't mean anything. The police would get things done properly now. They had both spouted the same lies and felt better for telling them than for hearing them. Molly had told Hilda she could stay off the next day and Lottie, asleep on the sofa, had said she was welcome to come with her to work. Together they have spent a pleasant enough few hours, cleaning up samples and dealing with interview and filming requests. Hilda has been a help. She shows no distaste at touching the specimens and shares Lottie's fascination for the stories behind each bobbing chunk of flesh. Lottie left her to clean the sample jar that contained a particularly ulcerated gall bladder from 1860, and had come back to discover that Hilda had invented an entire life story for the man who had once been wrapped around the painful organ.

'He was called Thomas,' said Hilda, lifting the gall bladder from its temporary home in a Tupperware jar and reverently tying it to the fine string that would dangle from the jar's lid when replaced in situ. 'He was tall and liked music and used to get a painful left ankle on cold days where he had fallen while running away from a butcher he had stolen some sausages from when he was little. He had scars on his back from the beating he got from the authorities. After he had his operation he told people the scar was from a bayonet wound and sometimes people bought him drinks for being a brave soldier.'

Lottie had looked at the girl and seen herself. Had entertained again the idea that the child belongs to herself and Molly. That they are family. Parents. Together. She did not let her thoughts linger on the mental images. She is confused enough already about her feelings.

'Come on, quick,' says Lottie, impulsively. She reaches out a hand and urges Hilda to join her by the chair. 'Do you want to be my assistant?'

Hilda looks taken aback but reservation quickly gives way to excitement. 'Do I look OK?'

'Brilliant. Quick. We're live in a moment.'

'Will Mum mind?'

'Why would she mind? She'll be thrilled. She might even be watching. She often does.'

Hilda grins and looks like herself again for a moment. She walks noisily across the wooden floor and stands next to

Lottie, facing the camera. Jay does not seem displeased by the alteration of the picture and raises a hand, silently, to indicate they will be live in three, two, one . . .

'Hello there, my ghoulish guys and gals. Welcome to the latest Dead Pretty video blog. Are you sitting comfortably? Probably not if you were the owner of this particular haemor-rhoid. Hilda, if you will? Excellent. Now, floating in this specimen jar is an infected haemorrhoid which, at its peak, was three inches across and which eventually ruptured and caused a bleed that had to be cauterized using hot pincers, then surgically removed. If you're descended from the poor gentleman in question, I would urge you to be grateful for every hot bath. Now, viewers, you'll notice that I'm joined by a rather glamorous assistant. This is Hilda, one of the best children in the universe, ever. Hilda, say hello.'

'Hi,' says Hilda, shyly.

'And can we safely assume that there is more than a touch of the peculiar about you?'

'Probably. I like weird stuff.'

'Weird stuff is what we're all about. Do you think you might like to work with the dead some day?'

'I don't know. Maybe. I'm not sure I'd like seeing bodies. Not sad bodies, like old people or little girls.'

Lottie nods, understanding. 'All you can do in those circum-stances is to honour the poor victim. To do what's best for them. Those are the days when you need two showers when you get home. The days you can taste death on your tongue even after the second glass of wine. But a body does not contain the soul, and I am happy to talk about souls while still thinking of myself as a scientist. I see that's already getting you all Tweeting like mad. Who's this? LuckyTiger wants to know how I would cope doing an autopsy on a baby. I suppose I would simply go into autopilot. It has to be done. It can be done tenderly. After death the body is just a machine, after all. Now, if you'll hold your horses, I will tell you about the most kissed corpse in the world. Did you know that the doll we all practice artificial respiration upon is based on the death mask of a teenage girl pulled from the River Seine, whose serenity so enchanted artists in her time that she led to a whole artistic movement that glorified the beauty of the corpse?'

Lottie reaches behind her and retrieves the box containing the grey face. It shows a beautiful girl, eyes closed, mouth curled into a soft and accepting smile. It has an angelic quality.

'Quite the looker, wasn't she, Hilda?'

Hilda is looking at the face that Lottie holds in her hands. Her chest is heaving and her bottom lip starts to tremble. Lottie could curse herself. What was she thinking?

'I'm not sure they'll do this with me when my time comes,' says Lottie, trying to make light of it. 'Maybe I'll be stuffed. Or turned into a rug. Just my head and my bum left as they are . . .'

'I'm sorry,' says Hilda, and she walks out of shot. For a moment, Lottie doesn't know what to do. She is live. She has thousands of viewers waiting and watching. But in this instant, death seems unimportant. It is Hilda's tears that matter to her. She shakes her head, just once, then tells Jay to cut the feed. She stands and runs after Hilda.

She does not stop to read the messages that scroll through on the laptop as it reflects back the endless rows of gleaming jars and scorching lights and the collage of excised organs that float like corpses in the clear preserving fluid. She does not see the insane stream of words flowing from the fingers of one viewer who has just looked upon perfection.

Does not see the line, repeated, over and over.

'Blood of my blood, beautiful child, sleeping cica, *slumbering angel, my blood, my blood, my blood . . .'*

MOLLY

'What were you thinking, you silly cow?' Molly is slamming the heel of her hand into her forehead. It causes the gash above her eye to throb but she is in too much of a temper to pay it any heed.

'I wasn't thinking,' says Lottie, her head dropping. She is breathing heavily, fanning her face with her fingertips. 'I thought it would be fun. I got carried away . . .'

Molly isn't paying any attention. She is kneading her forehead with her fingertips as if it were unbaked bread. 'Make her feel better, you said. Distract her. Perk her up. I thought you would take her to a toy shop and get a pizza. You've had her labelling spleen samples and put her online holding a death mask!'

Lottie looks appalled with herself. She has never been told off by Molly before and is clearly holding back tears.

'You watched it then,' says Hilda, brightly. She has been told off by her mum plenty of times and knows that this is the worst it will get. She is sitting at the end of the bar, using an orange felt-tip pen to illustrate a black-and-white wizard in her colouring book. She has been better since she got home. Ate a bowl of Irish stew with soda bread then road-tested the chef's peach and pineapple crumble and custard. The colour is back in her face. That is one relief. Had Molly been here when Lottie brought Hilda back, she would have presumed the child's features were already eclipsed beneath the mask that had so upset her.

'Yes, I watched it,' snaps Molly. She is wearing a short fur cape around her bare shoulders and her red lace top is tucked into a high-waisted pleated skirt. With a tricorn hat and a cutlass she would look like a pirate.

'Did I look OK?' asks Hilda. 'Before I got upset, I mean? Just Sienna at school, she always watches Lottie's programme and I don't want to have had a bogey or something in my teeth . . .'

Molly cannot help herself. The smile takes over her whole face and a moment later she gives Lottie an exasperated look. 'I'm supposed to be the hopeless one. You've got a degree. You're clever. I'm a numpty from Scunthorpe.'

'I'm a numpty from Reading,' says Lottie, giving a little gasp of relief. She had expected a much worse telling-off.

Molly takes a breath and decides to finish the remonstration with a few salient points. 'You put her online, Lottie. Without asking! Remember that thing we talked about? The *situation*, as we shall refer to it. The family ties that are so complicated you'd get a migraine just trying to work out who's related to who. And now there's a video of her in a pathology museum. Holding a haemorrhoid in a jar!' The absurdity of the sentence undoes the last of Molly's resolve and she creases into laughter. 'How can I have given her a life where it's possible to say a sentence like that!'

'She was really helpful with the specimens,' says Lottie, laughing too.

'I bet. You're bringing out the weird in her. I can see her now, going to parties when she's a teenager, sitting in the corner holding her samples. A tongue in a matchbox, maybe, or a liver, sitting in her hands like a frog. She's going to be quite the catch when it's boyfriend time.'

'The weirdos always become the sexy ones, in time,' says Lottie. 'Look at you.'

'I'm not weird.'

'Weird is a side-effect of awesome,' says Hilda, looking up. 'I was fine until I thought about Meda. I just got upset.'

Molly looks at her daughter and her face softens. She wants to make this all better. Something ugly seems to have drifted into their lives. She has witnessed blood and threats and violence and has felt these past two days as though the cold fingers of something sinister are tickling her skin. She feels at once energized and despairing. She has fought hard to keep such feelings contained since coming to London. Her night-mares have become tolerable and the things that she sees in her dark moments have become less real; more cartoonish; less visceral. But she is feeling the familiar sensation of mounting mania. There is a hyperactive quality to her thoughts, her actions. She is buzzing. Wired. She has a bizarre but overpowering desire to jump through the front window and sprint down the street. She wants to do something chaotic and remarkable. Were she in a car she would not trust herself to stop at red lights. She wants to stretch her limbs beyond comfort. She feels as though her blood is all flame and fizz and has a horrible suspicion that when the crash comes, she will descend into a sadness from which she will not know how to emerge. She keeps waiting to hear that a body has been found. The body of a girl. A girl who could have been saved if friends had only reported their suspicions sooner . . .

Lottie leans forward in her seat. Lowers her voice, conspiratorially. 'It was straight back here, was it? After Karol had the bust-up. No pulling into a layby for a bit of hide-the-ghoulash?'

'He had a dislocated elbow and we were both bleeding,' says Molly, sticking out her tongue.

'Sounds perfect. Sex is a great painkiller.'

'You know what else is a good painkiller? A painkiller. I took three of them and went to bed after you patched me up.'

'So you haven't seen him since?'

'No. I don't know why you think I would have done.'

Lottie sips her Belgian beer and Molly searches her face for further accusation or disbelief. She does not even remember Karol leaving. She has spent much of today waiting for her phone to ring and looking up, startled, each time the door has swung open. She has heard nothing from him. All day she has thought about whether or not to call the police and report her suspicions and every time she has resisted for fear that it would cause problems for the surly Lithuanian. She cannot understand herself. Were she told of the exact circumstances affecting somebody else, she would think ill of anybody who declined to contact the authorities. But she feels as though she is within this storm and is horribly aware of how different it feels to be carried by the hurricane rather than stand and watch.

'Do you think it will be a problem?' asks Lottie, brooding. She is tearing a beer mat into the shape of a human heart. 'Leaving the show like that . . . walking out when there were people watching.'

Molly starts rearranging the glasses on the shelf, all bustling energy and needless activity. She is feeling snappy. She tries not to let her face give away her lack of enthusiasm for Lottie's current woes.

'It's your own programme,' says Molly. 'You made it. You run it. There's no boss or backer to worry about so the only person who could be pissed off with you is yourself, and unless you're going to give yourself a verbal warning, I wouldn't worry about it.'

'But it's unprofessional. I don't want word getting around that I'm flighty or something.'

'You went to see if a little girl was OK. That's the right thing to do.'

'I'm not a little girl,' says Hilda, looking up. 'Lottie, your phone's ringing.'

Lottie plucks her phone from her bra and looks at the screen. Her eyes light up and she nods at Molly who instantly raises a hand to her face. It's warm and cosy in the back room but Molly still feels a chill down her back. She seems too tall for her skin, somehow, as though her skeleton is being squashed. She feels like a foot pressed into too-tight shoes. She feels bound. Her corset is suddenly rope; her chest constricting as she imagines the bones in her bodice slowly closing in. In her mind, her clothes become the gullet of a huge snake. She feels as though she is being digested. She reaches out to grab for the bar and sees Hilda moving to her side, face full of concern.

'Have you had your pill, Mum?' she asks, quietly, and she puts an arm around Molly's waist. 'Are you OK? Do you need me to get anything?'

A surge of emotion fills Molly as she looks into her daughter's wide, earnest eyes. She hates herself for cheapening her daughter's childhood with her selfish problems. No child should know of depression. No child should know that their mother takes medication to control their hyperactivity and hallucinations. She has always tried to be completely honest with her daughter but there are times she regrets it. Hilda knows about the times her mother has spent in hospital, mending her fractured mind and soul. She talks about her mum's issues as if they are any other illness – says that she is 'just poorly'. But Molly remains beset by a sense of guilt and shame and wants to claw great welts in her own wrists every time she thinks about the impact her occasional disorders have upon those who love her.

'It's OK, I'm just a bit funny in the head,' says Molly weakly. She blinks, hard. There is a smell of blood in her nostrils and her fingernails are digging into her palm. She cannot stop the strobing, flickering images that are melding with the scene in front of her in a dizzying spectroscope of grisly pictures. She is back in the interview room, watching the blood pour from a killer's scalp. She is answering the phone to her mother and folding in upon herself at the sound of her accusations and tears. She is lolling, rubbery and naked, in six inches of tepid water and spilled vodka as her child cries and bangs upon the bathroom door. She is watching the imposters beat upon Karol with the tyre iron and blinking blood from her eyes. She is watching Meda struggle for air beneath a mask of loose earth . . .

'No!' gasps Molly, and raises a hand to her face as though there are birds attacking her eyes.

'Mum, it's OK. Ssh, Mum, don't . . .'

Molly has screwed up her eyes and wrapped her arms around her head. She is suddenly childlike in her movements.

'Darling, what's wrong? Please, Molly, don't get sad. Should we get you sat down maybe? Tell me what to do.'

Molly hears Lottie's voice close to her left ear and the nearness of her makes her shudder. She sees herself as a hedgehog, folding in on herself, all prickles and vulnerable fleshy parts, and the vision suddenly becomes comical. Her gasping breath becomes a giggle and she opens her tear-filled eyes to stare into the worried expressions of her daughter and best friend.

'Mum?'

Molly feels exhausted. She could drop her head to the bar and sleep for days. She suddenly craves sunlight. Her skin feels clammy and pale, as though she has been living underground. She wonders how long it has been since she felt real light upon her skin. She feels as though the miasma of London's complicated air is somehow clothing her skin and blocking

her pores. She feels like she is suffocating. Suffocating like
the child whose pain suddenly feels colossal and real inside
her chest.

'It's OK, it's OK,' says Molly, half to herself. 'I'm fine.
Honestly, I'm fine.' She holds her elbows in to her waist, trying
to make herself small. She doesn't want anybody touching her.
She needs space to breathe.

'Should we go home, Mum?'

'No, no, it's fine. I'm fine.' She takes the glass of water that
Hilda has fetched and takes three deep gulps. Goose pimples
immediately rise upon her skin.

'What happened?' asks Lottie, quietly. 'I was on the phone
and the next thing you were staring at nothing and acting like
you were watching a horror movie. Did you take your pills?'

Molly flashes her friend an angry glance. 'They're not
magic bloody pills, you know. They're not miracle workers.
Sometimes I still get a bit overwhelmed, that's all. And this
is all a bit overwhelming. What's that thing Alice says in
Wonderland? I felt like I knew who I was this morning but
I've changed a lot since then. I thought I was on top of things.'
She stops, jerking her head away from Lottie as if trying to
slip a noose. 'I am fine. It's just all squeezing my brain.'

'We should stop,' says Lottie. 'Looking into it all, I mean.'

'We're not looking into anything,' says Molly, waving a
hand. 'What are we doing? Just getting in a mess and upsetting ourselves. We're witnesses to something that might not
have happened. I wish I'd never met the bloody family. I wish
I didn't care. Maybe I don't care. Maybe I'm just a nosey cow
who sees a chance for a bit of drama.'

The three of them stay silent for a time. Lottie starts picking
at the skin around her fingernail. Hilda has picked up the
cardboard heart Lottie had been playing with while on
the phone.

'What's *occipital*?' asks Hilda, reading the blue ink on the
ragged beermat.

Lottie reaches out and takes her makeshift notepad, shaking
her head. 'Not now, eh?'

'You may as well just tell us,' says Molly, shrugging. 'That
was your mate, I presume. The one who did the exam?'

'Yes, but I don't think it will help . . .'

'Maybe it won't, but I still want to know.'

Lottie looks from mother to daughter. They look suddenly very similar; big eyes and full lips and a solemnity in the way they hold themselves and each other.

'Throat cut,' says Lottie, looking down at the cardboard heart. 'Left to right. My colleague got the basics from the investigating officer, and the water has definitely taken most of his secrets. He was very bloated. But victim was a Benjamin Kinnealy. Thirty-seven years old. State of poor health and evidence of sustained substance abuse. Had been living rough for some years after being released from HMP Belmarsh where he had served time for benefits fraud and supplying amphetamine. Had drunk a large quantity of strong cider and eaten some packet chicken and tinned rice pudding in the hours before his death. Blood alcohol showed he was extremely intoxicated, though whether that would have shown in his manner is anybody's guess. Historic bruises on his elbows and knees. Recent injury to left occipital bone. The throat was cut so deeply there was little more than a flap of skin holding it in place. Virtually no blood in the body . . .'

'No more,' says Molly, shaking her head and looking at Hilda.

'Meda said he was a nice man. His dog was friendly. She brought him food . . .'

'Have they dredged the canal?' asks Molly, quickly. 'Why was he down there? Doesn't he sleep in the doorway of the bank? Isn't that why she called him Banky?'

'He's just the pathologist,' says Lottie, wishing she could offer more help. 'Tell me where your thoughts are, Molly.'

Molly clears her throat and feels a pain in her chest. It seems that the air is pressing in upon her. She is aware of the history of this place. Aware of all the suffering that the ground beneath her feet has witnessed. Is suddenly aware how much blood has seeped into the earth in this swathe of East London. Feels a sudden rush of revulsion at being a part of the ghoulish industry that has glorified such acts of violence. She forces herself to take control of her own thoughts. Tries to make it clear in her own mind. What does she believe? What does she fear?

'I don't think somebody has taken Meda as part of a ransom,' says Molly, quietly. 'I don't think they want money for her safe return. Karol's people have made an assumption because that's what has happened before. But what if the cases where the victim has ended up dead were committed by somebody else? There are people out there who will use any opportunity to make money. Look at last night. Those bastards said they had Meda because they'd heard she was missing and they saw a chance to cash in. They didn't care about anything else. How many times might that have happened? What if children have been going missing for years and nobody has been reporting it because they all think it's something else – something financial, a concept people can get their heads around. And that's been allowing something to occur which is so very much worse.'

'Like a very bad man?' asks Hilda, and she seems to get a little smaller as she says it.

'You've got no basis for that thought,' says Lottie, gently. 'That's just an irrational fear, and with what you've been through, that's hardly surprising . . .'

'Meda bought a tin of tuna for the homeless man's dog,' says Molly, ignoring the interruption. 'That means she must have seen him on her way to the shops. So she bought the animal a treat while there and went back to give it to him. She wasn't seen after that. The homeless man is found dead in the canal with his throat cut. Don't you think that maybe somebody planned this? Took Banky's place in the doorway? I can almost see it. Meda, all happy with herself, going to do a kind thing for the nice man in the doorway. He would have been in his sleeping bag, keeping warm. She tries to get his attention, in that dark doorway, and then . . .' She stops, closing her eyes.

'But Molly, that's just paranoia and darkness.' Lottie is shaking her head, looking confused. 'A bad thing has happened to a poor homeless man and that's awful. A girl has gone missing and that's awful too. But what you're saying is just some bleak imagining. There's nothing else to suggest that and, even if by some chance you were right, what would you do about it?'

'You've got police contacts,' says Molly, chewing her lip and thinking. 'The officer investigating Banky's death. He would be the logical one to speak to.'

'About Meda? But I thought you couldn't talk about Meda. Karol's orders.'

Molly gives a low growl. She wants a drink. Wants to fill herself with gin. 'I don't know what to do,' she says, and it sounds pitiful to her own ears.

'We should tell,' says Hilda, softly. 'Tell the police.'

Molly nods. She has known it since she started talking. She reaches under the bar for her phone. Three missed calls and a multi-media message. She gives a sharp intake of breath and feels the floor tilt beneath her boots as she opens the video clip that has been sent from a number she does not recognize.

A figure hangs from a hook in a dark, poorly lit and featureless room. He has been stripped down to his pale, flabby skin. His head rests upon his chest. Blood drips from his bare toes. A man in clear plastic overalls is standing behind him, holding a coiled hose in gloved hands. Without speaking, the man in the overalls points the hose at the hanging figure and water gushes out to soak the man's back. Steam rises. The man's head snaps up as the scalding liquid scorches his flesh. The video contains no sound, but there is no disguising the scream of agony that emerges from the victim's open mouth as his skin begins to blister and pop like burning jam.

The man on the hook is unmistakably the ringleader from last night's attack: the youngster who tried to profit from Meda's disappearance with a bogus ransom demand.

The man who points the hose is unmistakably Karol.

The message contains no words but its meaning is clear.

Molly realizes she is breathing hard. Realizes she has played the video four times before forcing herself to look up and acknowledge the others. She feels heat upon her skin. Cold within her bones. Feels a great swell of something raw and primal flood through her. A protective instinct wrapped inside something she cannot explain. It is a desire to see more. To watch and understand. To stand beside Karol and watch the dispassionate way he tortures the man who dislocated his elbow. This is a bad man holding the hose.

She looks at her daughter. Makes up her mind. Replies to the message with a simple communication of her own.

I'M GOING TO THE POLICE. IF YOU WANT TO STOP ME, MEET ME WHERE THE TRAMP'S THROAT WAS CUT. I KNOW YOU KNOW.

'I'm going out,' says Molly, announcing it to nobody in particular. 'Lottie . . .'

'Of course.'

'Mum, what are you doing?' asks Hilda, and there is a true fear in her voice.

'I'm going to sort it out,' says Molly, and she reaches to the shelf behind the bar for the knife she uses to slice lemons. She slips it into the pocket of her coat as she wraps herself in its great black folds. She feels none of her earlier disquiet. She feels anger. A sort of mania. Feels an urge to hurt or be hurt. 'Fuck them,' she adds, and her face is stone. 'Fuck the lot of them.'

A slug of gin from the optic on the wall.

Out the door and into the rain.

Into a night as bleak and pitiless as the figure who watches her leave.

HILDA

We could have done without the Ripperettes that night. The Bonnet was a magnet for anybody who liked their music to be written on the black keys. If you were ever called a weirdo at school or had owned a pencil case with a picture of a wolf or a unicorn on it, chances are you would have downed a cocktail and troughed through a pickled egg in our pub. Mum had no problem catering for the kind of clientele who spent their money on quills and potion bottles and replica Stoker goggles. They were our bread and butter, though Mum did once say that it would be more apt to refer to the Ripperettes as our bread and lard. Their love of all things Victorian didn't extend to their diets. There were four of them and none of them were wasting away on a diet of porridge and stale bread. Their appetite for big dinners was on a par with their hunger for any experience or artefact with even a nodding acquaintanceship with the Ripper, his victims, or the streets in which they bled. They were regulars on the Whitechapel Walks and could debate long into the night about which of the latest Ripper theories had the most holes. They also seemed dedicated to disproving the assumption that 'fat' always came with a side order of 'jolly'. They could complain to an Olympic standard and anybody with the misfortune to sit within earshot would soon find themselves uncomfortably familiar with their litany of medical concerns, career obstacles and the failings of the men who had let them down with their ceaseless disobedience. They dressed in a lot of black, though their boots had been ordered from specialists in wide-fittings and the raven necklaces that should have hung in their cleavages were dangerously close to becoming chokers. They were in their thirties and didn't appear to like each other more than they liked anybody else. They each read Edgar Allan Poe verses when we had a Halloween night and you could tell that they got off on the gruesome bits. Mum suspected that each saw themselves as exact replicas of the women who plied their trade in our neighbourhood a century and a half before. She said that this implied the only mirror that any of them owned was the back of a spoon. Then she felt bad for saying it and said there was nothing wrong with being a little on the chubby side – provided you didn't become a bitch or a total cow-bag at the same time. Personally, I think that deep down, they really wanted to kill somebody. I should know. I've looked into such eyes.

'They're in,' said Katriona, rolling her eyes. She was bar manager in Mum's absence and had been enjoying a quiet night until the murder squad bustled in out of the rain and plonked themselves down at the table in the window. Lottie and I were still in the back. She was reading some textbook and I was playing a game on her laptop. We hadn't spoken much since Mum left. We were both trying not to let our thoughts run away with us. We just wanted her home. Wanted everything to be better than it was.

'Who is?' I asked, looking at Katriona. She was Scottish and had blonde hair and pale skin and in her pure white shift dress and dark eye make-up, she sometimes looked a lot like a ghost. She swore more than Mum and always called me 'chicken'.

'Fucking ghouls. The Sisters of Perpetual Premenstrual Tension. Sixty stone of twat.'

'The Ripperettes?'

'Aye. Moody bitches.' She looked at Lottie, relishing the pained look on her face. 'They'll be creaming their granny-panties when they see you. No doubt they'll have a theory needs your attention. You should run, chicken. Save yourself.'

'Don't tell them I'm here,' said Lottie, urgently. 'I'll hide up the chimney or something.'

'They'll find you. There's a rumour that the Ripper carved his name on the fifteenth brick up the flue. They'll be in here staring up your skirt in no time.'

'Is that true?'

'No. But I might start the rumour, chicken . . .'

'Oh my goodness, you're the lady from the Dead Pretty podcasts! We saw you walk off. I must say it was very disappointing. We'd ordered pizza and planned to watch it right through. Rather shoddy to leave people in the lurch. And oh, you're the glamorous assistant. Rather a sexist thing to say, wasn't it? Still, I won't make a fuss. I hadn't put two and two together. Of course, you're the boss's daughter, aren't you? Do you drink here, Lottie? Do you mind if I call you Lottie? Of course you don't – it's people like me who give people like you an audience. I've got lost looking for the toilet. I don't know why there can't be signs. And no doubt they will be in a terrible state when I find them. Not much better than animals, some people. You have to come and meet my friends. They might want your professional opinion on something. I'm sure you don't mind . . .'

Half an hour later we were still in the front bar. The only other clients were old Connie, busy flashing angry daggers at the newcomers and saying 'Gordon Facking Bennett' under her breath, and Brendan, who had just wandered in from the street and who had clearly been drinking since breakfast.

I looked at Lottie, who had a pained expression on her face. She kept glancing at her phone.

'Anything from Mum?'

She shook her head.

'And where might the good lady of unceasing virtue be upon this detestable eve? Her hostelry is impoverished by her absence.'

In Mum's absence, it fell to me. 'Would you give it a rest please, Brendan? Just for tonight.'

He placed a hand upon his chest and mimed offence. He changed his accent and became a Southern belle. 'Well, I do declare . . .'

'Please, Brendan, my brain is going a bit. Mum says you don't mean any harm and I'm sure she's right, but sometimes you're a walking migraine.'

I don't know how Connie's geriatric ears picked up our conversation but she let out a peal of laughter at that. 'You tell him, girl. By Christ I only come in this pub because it's near enough the flat but there are times I wonder if I'm in the nuthouse. Time was you could go and have a half of stout without feeling like you'd gone to a freak show.'

'I hope you're not talking about me,' said the plumpest of the Ripperettes. She was wearing a red cape and looked how Red Riding Hood might have appeared if she had killed the wolf and had him deep fried.

'Not you, lovey,' said Connie, breezily. 'You're proper down to earth, I can see that.'

'I should hope so.'

Lottie was scratching at the back of her hand. She seemed agitated. I could tell she was worrying about her earlier argument with Mum. They'd never had a set-to before and it seemed to make Lottie feel a perfect schoolgirl who had just been summoned to the Headmaster's office for a caning. She wasn't herself. Normally when we were left alone I would use the situation to my advantage, but on that night I was feeling too peculiar to do much other than kick my feet against the bar stool and try not to get too agitated. It was taking all my effort not to think about the only thing my brain wanted me to think about. I was forcing myself not to let Meda pop up in my imagination. I knew that if she did, I would quickly grab hold of the picture as if it were a horse on a carousel and I would ride it around and around until I was sick and dizzy and Meda was dead or dying.

'Does your mother really say that?' asked Brendan, and his voice had lost the flamboyance. I gave him a smile, the way Mum always did whenever one of her hopeless drunks said something endearing.

'She'd sell you that thingy if she could,' I said, nodding at the scarificator in its case above the bar. 'She doesn't mind you.'

Brendan beamed. It may have been the best compliment of his life.

'It's me that you have to worry about,' said Lottie, looking up from her phone to pull a face. 'I know how to get rid of your body.'

'Food for the pigs, is it?' asked Brendan, and he sipped his wine. The bottle was on the bar in front of him. He chose his own tipples from the supplier each week and paid for his drinks by the measure instead of by the bottle. It cost him much more than it should have done but he never asked Mum to change the system.

'More unreliable than you would think, pigs,' said Lottie, and she put her phone away with a groan. 'Sea creatures would be my bet. Wrap you in wire, weigh you down, drop you in the ocean and let the tides and the crabs and all the microscopic organisms munch you into nothing.'

'Would I be nude?' asked Brendan, grinning at the prospect. 'I would take it all for a fulsome undraping at your exquisite hands.'

'You'd be dead.'

'That wouldn't stop me. I've been pronounced dead twice before and woke up both times after some careful chest pummelling. Decided not to head towards the light just yet. Too many things to do.'

'Like what, Brendan?'

'Complete my collection, of course. I have heard a whisper about a *statua humana* – a working human statue built in the seventeenth century. A working reproduction of the inside of a human being, created entirely from funnels and tubes and bellows. The male member is recreated by pushing on a balloon-like bladder and is said to still be able to become tumescent when pressed . . .'

'Can nobody have a proper facking conversation any more?'

'Sorry, Connie.'

We sat still for a while. The rain pattered against the glass like thousands of tiny hooves.

'How will the collection be complete?' asked Lottie, walking behind the bar to top up her gin and tonic. 'You want everything. You'd write me a cheque for every sample I possess if I let you.'

Brendan tucked his thumbs into the pockets of his waistcoat. 'I will always seek to possess that which fascinates me. I will stop when that impulse is no more.'

'How did you get into it, Brendan?'

'Oh facking hell, girl . . .'

Brendan seemed to light up with pride at being asked. Beside me I felt Lottie stiffen. Brendan could spend a whole evening giving an answer to a solitary question so enquiries about his life story were unlikely to be brief.

'Just the potted version,' Lottie jumped in. 'You know, the top line on the Wikipedia entry . . .'

'That dreadful thing is terribly inaccurate,' said Brendan, icily. 'I've requested it changed many times but without success.'

I paused. 'Have you really got an entry?'

'A reference or two. I'm habitually known as a "private collector", though it doesn't seem terribly private sometimes. The auction house in Durham made the most terrible fuss when I bought the Mary Ann letters, even though I was decent enough to make copies for public viewing. And yet they still won't furnish me with the name of my nemesis.'

Lottie gave a laugh. 'The Mary Ann letters? Mary Ann Cotton?'

'Yes, fascinating lady. Killed eight at least. Could be as many as twenty. The Black Widow, they called her, though from her words it seems she was no more evil than any of us. Concerned with money worries and bickering solicitors. The handwriting is so intriguing.'

'What's that got to do with scarificators and human statues?' I asked, confused.

'My dear child, I am a collector of the intriguing. The unusual. The fascinating. In all of its forms.'

'I'd love to see your house,' muttered Connie, coughing foully, and sounding as if she would like to spit out whatever her lungs had just given birth to.

'I will confess it is a little cramped, as are the storage units. But a fellow must have that which inspires him.'

'Inspires him to do what?' I asked.

Brendan looked at me as if I were simple. 'To collect more, of course. And I shall.'

'What have you got your eye on?' asked Lottie, drumming her fingers on the bar in an obvious attempt not to look at her phone. 'Found one of Jeremy Bentham's original toenails, have you? Honestly, you should put this stuff in a proper museum, properly curated and looked after.'

'You shall not have my artefacts,' said Brendan, and if he were a cat his back would have arched.

'I meant I could help you, though I don't know why I'm offering.'

'You could help me by finding out the name of that gazumping ragamuffin!'

At that, one of the Ripperettes pointedly cleared her throat. She had clearly not expected to hear the phrase 'gazumping ragamuffin' this evening.

'I told you, I don't know those people. Why would they tell me?'

'Because you are the great Dr Lottie! The blue-haired maiden of all that is corporeal.'

Lottie gave a low growl. She looked at me as if asking for suggestions and I gave a shrug. It didn't really matter. She wasn't busy and Brendan was a good customer and if she helped him he might shut up. 'Fine. Bloody fine.'

When Lottie's phone vibrated fifteen minutes later we both thought it might be Mum. It wasn't. Her contact at the auction house was replying in person to her email. Lottie put on her vlog voice when she answered and sat with her back straight and her lips pouted in the way that made Mum accuse her of setting feminism back by two centuries. I didn't pay much attention to the call. I was staring through the condensation on the window at the blackness and the rain behind Connie. I could see the familiar lights of passing cars and the gaudy neon of the shop across the street and suddenly everything felt cold and sad, as if I were looking at a dead duckling at the edge of a pond. I had a sudden vision of Banky, huddled up in his sleeping bag in his doorway and his dog all trembling and bony against his chest. And I thought of Meda, putting a smile on his face with a simple gift of a tin of tuna for them to share. I imagined what it would be like to shelter in a doorway, pulling the darkness about yourself like it was a blanket. I imagined that sense of utter vulnerability and exposure; the knowledge that you were laid out on cold stones and the only thing between yourself and death was the reluctance of people to waste their time by killing you. It made me feel all lonely inside, as if I was suddenly in a world where nobody cared about anybody and it was all for nothing.

I wasn't really focusing on what I was looking at, if that makes any sense. It was all just shapes and vague patterns.

But I became aware that I had been looking at the shape across the road for some time. I don't know why it had caused some part of my brain to take notice but as soon as I realized I was staring, I blinked and turned away. An instant later I questioned myself, as if I had blithely accepted a truth. I looked again and saw the figure. Tall, long-limbed and wrapped in black. They were standing perfectly still and as I watched I thought of the ravens at the tower; blacker than midnight and somehow wrapped in a kind of eeriness that always gave me goose bumps. They always seemed to look through you. That's how the figure seemed to be looking at me. But could they see me through the condensation and the rain? I almost felt as if I were having a staring match with a statue.

'Still bloody there,' muttered Connie. 'Bloody freak.'

'I looked at her, in her red coat and her gold jewellery and her white hair. She softened her face a little as I cocked my head and asked her what she meant.

'Another freak, working up the courage to join the show. Don't know what it is about the Ripper but he gets under your skin if you're an outsider. If you're from here you just think it's all a bit of drama over nothing. He did horrible things to those poor ladies, but do you think that was a one-off? Their lives were bloody awful. People chopping each other up were almost a blessing, you ask me. My grandmother didn't speak of it often but you got a hot toddy in her on a cold night and she'd give you chapter and verse. Tore through those women like they were made of paper, so he did. Real thirst for blood. All these theories about who did it and who was where and who wrote the letters. None of it matters. What does it say about us that all these years later we're still trying to work him out? We're still trying to understand what made him tick. Whatever was running in the veins of the women back then – it still runs in ours. We're no different. No better. Horrible people doing horrible things. You ask me, the Ripper was a woman. Taking it out on herself by chopping up people like her. But that all sounds like psychobabble and I'm supposed to hate all that.'

I must have looked a bit upset by her words and she

immediately changed her expression. 'Don't listen to my blather,' she said, smacking her lips together. 'Your friend's gone without the courage to pop in and join the show.' She gestured at the window. The figure across the street had gone. 'Won't look so sinister when a bunch of skinheads are kicking him in.'

I suddenly wanted a hug. Lottie had hung up the phone and was deep in conversation with Brendan. She had that zeal in her eyes – the sparkle that always got her viewers to send in badly spelled messages with lots of capital letters.

'. . . all this time – under my nose! And not so much as an apology. And they really said "expert", did they? I'm not one to sing my own praises but the man has no right. It's not . . . it's not decent. Not British!'

Brendan was in full flow. A smell of damp carpets was coming off him. I wanted him to stop talking to Lottie. Wanted her to myself.

'It would be silly not to,' said Lottie, more to herself. 'I think I will. It couldn't be more convenient, if you think about it. Could you do it? Drop a note? Or should I?'

Brendan poured himself another glass and Lottie turned to me, all excited and warm. 'Will you be OK for a little while? It's an opportunity. Honestly, I never thought . . .'

I didn't say anything important. Just gave her a smile that I knew she was after and took a kiss on the forehead as she pulled on her coat. She grabbed a notepad from behind the bar and scribbled down a few lines of blue ink. She tore the sheet off and looked at me with genuine glee. 'It would be amazing if he agreed, don't you think? I won't be long. Honestly. Under my nose!'

Lottie banged out of the bar and turned left past the glass. She was walking fast and an instant later I was alone in the front bar with Brendan, Katriona, Connie and the Ripperettes. I felt horribly dejected. Horribly alone.

'I feel betrayed,' said Brendan, and stuck a finger into his nostril, in a way that suggested an inventive and elaborate suicide may be on the agenda. 'Never once asked me. Never once.'

'Where is she going?' I asked, confused.

'To see my nemesis,' said Brendan, disgusted. 'To see Autolycus.'

I barely heard his final words, but they have resonated with me through the years; a whisper full of grim prophesy.

'She's gone to see his blood.'

MOLLY

A bright yellow sign has been tied to the railings outside the little courtyard garden beside the Baptist church on Globe Road. It asks witnesses to an 'incident' to come forward. The Metropolitan Police would appreciate any assistance to a 'violent' occurrence. The notice gives a three-day window in which the unnamed incident could have occurred. Molly suppresses a shudder as she stands in the teeming rain and reads this last line. Banky's body must have been so repulsive and bloated by his time in the water as to be forensically hard to read. The police cannot tie down a time of death. His corpse must have spilled its secrets into the murky waters. She wonders how people like Lottie can stand the sheer grotesqueness of sliding a scalpel into such horrid specimens, with their purple lips and blue-tinged skin and puffy, waterlogged flesh. She remembers sitting in a patrol car, years before, waiting for a Detective Superintendent to come back from telling the husband of a suicide that his wife's body had been found in a little tributary of the river they had been dredging. No, he would not be able to view the body. The police told him this was for 'procedural reasons'. In truth, she was so pulped and engorged from her time in the water that her flesh slid off the bone as the police divers slid her from the water. Most of her identifiable features slipped off the divers' gloves like soggy tissue paper.

Molly looks through the railings. By the light of the street-lamp she can make out traces of the activity that has gone on in the neat little garden. She sees footprints in the soggy ground. A scrap of forensic overall clinging to a spiky bush like tinsel to a Christmas tree. The absence of any kind of litter is also revealing. Any can of drink, any cigarette packet, any food wrapper, will all have been bagged up and taken away for examination by the forensics team contracted in by the investigations team. Everything will be tested. Every

database will be cross-checked. She doubts that such pains-
taking meticulousness is the result of any desperate need to
see justice done by the dead man. She knows from experience
that such things are done so that in the event of a cock-up,
nobody can accuse them of negligence. She does not believe
that whoever killed Banky would have been fool enough to
stop and share a can of cider with him first.

Molly sniffs, hard, and manages to inhale the rain that has
been pouring down her face. It catches in her throat and she
starts to cough. She feels weak. The ceaseless rain is extinguishing the urgency that propelled her out of the door of her
pub. Suddenly she feels ludicrous. She is a barmaid in fancy
dress, leaning against the railings of a murder site and waiting
for a meeting with a torturer. She wants to ball her hands into
fists and punch something solid.

'What are you bloody doing?' she mutters. 'Just go. You're
not in too deep. Listen to yourself . . .'

Molly realizes her teeth are chattering. She pulls her coat
around herself and shudders at the touch of wet fur. She
turns at a sound behind her and looks into the face of Karol.
In this poor light it's hard to make out the expression on his
face, but he is not smiling. She looks him up and down.
Black boots. Black jeans. Waxed jacket and exposed throat.
He must have a car nearby but she did not hear it pull up.

Molly feels a surge of emotion, as if she is flooding with
different chemicals. Her mind is aflame with flickering
images. She sees him hurting the men who came to her door.
Sees him smiling at her from the end of the bar. Sees his
face in profile, driving through the East End. Sees him
looking down at her and their blood mingling upon her face.
Sees him as he was in the video clip, doling out brutality
as a warning. She lets a burst of pure temper show in her
expression.

'I got the video,' she snaps. 'Proud of yourself, are you?
Needed to warn me off, did you? Thought you'd show me what
I'd get if I went to the police? Who do you think you are?
Where do you get off? I'm not some scared little woman . . .'

Karol gives a shake of his head. Water sprays from his dark
hair. There is almost no colour in his eyes and the way he is

staring at her causes Molly to slide a hand into her pocket and unconsciously close her grip on her keys. There is a prickling upon her skin and she fails to suppress the judder that suddenly wracks her. She shivers and grows angry with herself for looking so vulnerable; so feeble.

'You didn't go to where they found him,' she says, through gritted, chattering teeth. 'Didn't go to the water. You came here. Must have known. What else have you beaten out of your suspects, eh? What else could you have told me if you'd had the guts to just trust me?'

Karol looks almost amused. There is a tiny smile on his face and he continues to look at her face. His eyes are upon her lips and the shadow where her jaw becomes her neck. She remembers that look from before and feels a blush start to rise. She curses herself and her disloyal skin.

'You just came here to stare, did you? Probably tired after a hard night of steaming some poor kid's skin off.'

'Be quiet,' he says, so quietly she can barely hear it. A car goes slowly over the speedbump behind him and he turns to track its progress. Across the road is a graffiti-covered wooden screen, covered in advertisements for the new apartment block being built behind. None of the pictures of the futuristic construction show the railway bridge to its right, or the murder scene across the way.

'You don't tell me what I can do,' says Molly, stepping forward. She wants to slap his face. She feels betrayed, somehow, as though he has let her down. Were she not so irritated and uncomfortable she would start remonstrating with herself for making any of this about her. She barely knows him. She has no right to expect anything of a man who is clearly a criminal to his bones.

'I said to stop talking. Fuck, you English, it's like the radio. Just talk and talk and noise and noise. Stop. Listen.'

Molly opens her mouth fully, as if taking a huge bite of something. Her expressions have always been childlike. She looks like an infant who has just been told to go fuck herself by another pupil.

'I just want to know she is safe,' says Molly, and her cheeks and her eyes suddenly feel hot as pure frustrated helplessness becomes as heavy and sodden around her limbs as the soggy fur coat that drips dirty water on to her boots.

Through a veil of tears, Molly sees Karol extend his hand. She jerks her head back instinctively, as though he is about to hurt her, but instead the cool rough skin of his palm touches her damp cheeks. She flinches but does not pull away. She forces herself to keep her eyes open. Tears spill and run on to his tattooed fingers. She stares at him, defiant, looking like a beaten boxer who will not fall until their heart gives out. She sees an intensity in Karol's stare. He is breathing heavily. For an instant she feels his thumb stroke her cheekbone and brush the corner of her mouth. She shivers, and almost gives in to the mischievous, girlish smile that twitches her lips. The movement causes her to pucker her mouth and her lower lip brushes Karol's thumb. He leans forward, slowly. She raises her face, expecting his kiss, but instead he slides his face past hers and breathes in deeply, taking the scent of her into his nostrils and throat. Her skin raises in goose pimples as he draws her musk inside himself; her miasma of rain and gin, of crushed peaches and old clothes. She breathes him in too. Cigarettes. Leather. Something spicy and unidentifiable but which makes her think of sawn wood and new pennies.

She hears the clank of metal upon metal and realizes he is opening the metal gate to the park. A sudden flutter of panic rises in her chest but she forces herself not to give in to it. And then his hand is closing around hers and he is pulling her behind him into the darkness of the little park where a homeless man had his throat cut for trying to protect a little girl.

'Can we?' she asks, and curses herself for speaking. 'Is it OK . . .?'

Her boots squelch into wet grass as Karol pulls her into the dark space. She looks up, shivering. A billion raindrops are tumbling from a blue-black sky and the trees that edge the park look like angry slashes of charcoal. She feels thorns pull at her skirt and curses. Gives a nervous giggle as he pulls her, firmly, beneath the canopy of a tree she would not be able to name.

Suddenly her feet are sliding in mud she cannot see and

her back is against hard brick and Karol's mouth is upon hers. She feels his tongue sliding between her lips and is astonished by the fire with which she returns his kiss. She wants to bite him. Wants to pull at his hair and scratch at his skin. Her passion enflames his own. She feels his hands grabbing at her skin, pulling open her coat, seeking her out. Feels his hardness through his jeans as she pulls up his coat and runs her cold, soaking hands upon his skin.

There is barely any light but she catches a glimpse of the whites of his eyes and his pale skin and feels herself give in completely to the sensation of wanton, desperate need. She slides her hand inside his jeans and tugs at his fly and he gasps as she closes her hands around him. She feels him fumbling at her skirt, trying to turn her, to press her face into the brick, but she stands firm and shakes her head and pushes him back, forcing him down on to the carpet of thick mud. She lands heavily on top of him and is surprised to hear a sound midway between a gasp and a giggle but she cannot tell which of them made the utterance. And then she is lifting her skirt and pulling aside her knickers and she feels the heat of herself and smells her own need and he says something in Lithuanian as she takes him inside her and her boots squelch into the cloying mud as she rocks back and forth; raising her face; feeling the rain upon her hot skin, and gives herself utterly to the feeling that floods her; reaching down to force her fingers into his mouth as she lets out a wail of pure pleasure that fills her with a feeling that is all honey and flame.

They stay as they fell for a time. Karol moves before Molly does. His hands are still in her hair and he is careful as he disentangles them. He tries to direct her face so she is looking at him but she holds herself still, embarrassed and sated and unsure if she can stand. She finally slides him out of herself and collapses on to her back, staring upwards and feeling the rain upon her face. Her hands make fists in the mud and she wonders what kind of mess they have both made of themselves. She finds herself laughing though she cannot explain it, and then Karol's weight is upon her and he is looking down, concerned. 'Are you crying? Did I hurt you? You wanted to, yes? I thought you wanted to . . .'

She raises her hand to his face and pulls him down, kissing him tenderly, and he seems reassured. He slides off her and tucks himself away before reaching down and taking Molly's hand. He pulls her up and she is amazed at the strength in him. She has an absurd fantasy in which he lifts her like a princess bride and carries her home and then she is telling herself off for being so giddy and silly and the wave of guilt begins to wash in upon her good feeling. It is Karol who breaks the spell, his voice almost apologetic as he tells her a truth that she is not sure she would have been so similarly able to share.

'It was here,' he says, and he squeezes her hand before he releases it. He reaches into the pocket of his coat and finds his cigarettes have been crushed by her knees. He finds a smokeable, crooked cigarette and lights it. He holds in the smoke as he had held in her scent.

'Here?'

'The tramp. The homeless man. This is where he slept. Where his blood was spilled. Where she was taken.'

It takes Molly a moment to readjust. Suddenly she is aware of herself. Of the cold sweat upon her skin and the smell of desire and churned dirt in her nostrils. She looks at the patch of earth and the imprint their desire has made and is not sure how to feel as she considers the similarly animalistic act that took place here. A man died. Blood spilled. Human essence spilled into the ground . . .

'I did not want the clip to be sent you,' he says, like a child apologizing for eating the last of the biscuits. 'My patron. He was concerned. He thought you might be foolish.'

'Foolish?' asks Molly, and she stares at him without really understanding. She feels empty and yet full of flame.

'He knows you are clever. Ex-police. You saw what happened when those fools decided to try and make cash from Meda's disappearance. He wishes things to be done his way. He does not want the police to be involved. He thought that if you saw how his people could behave – what he could make his people do . . .'

'I understand.'

He looks at her and raises his hand to her face. His eyes are earnest. Searching. 'Do you?'

'I'm not stupid enough to think I understand your world,' she says, and she did not realize the truth of her words until she spoke them. 'I don't know who or what I am. But I didn't need the threat. I wouldn't have told. I just want her safe. Meda.'

'I see this when I look at you. You seem to feel her pain as if it were that of your own child. And yet you knew her so little. Why is this your concern, Molly?'

She looks around, as if hoping the answer will be written on the troubled ground. 'It's just so horrible. I know bad things happen to good people. That's the way of the world. But I knew her. I met her. It brought my daughter pain . . .'

'That is what my patron said,' mutters Karol, breathing out cigarette smoke. 'He says you don't care for Meda. You care for your child's sadness. He does not say this with anger or accusation. He understands this kind of mind.'

Molly shakes her head. 'You can't imagine just caring about somebody? They have to be yours to care about, do they? Are you saying Meda doesn't matter to you? She's just a pay-day? I saw what you did to those men who tried to capitalize on her going missing. You feel this, I know you do.'

Karol considers the glowing tip of his cigarette. He shrugs. 'I want her home. I want them all home. I want nothing bad to happen to innocents. I want to go the rest of my life without hitting or being hit. But life is not like that.'

They stand in silence and listen to the rain. 'You're keeping something back,' says Molly, at last. 'Please, whatever it is – trust me.'

Karol pinches out his cigarette and puts the stub in his pocket. He looks at the woman who just fucked him on the wet ground and slips his hand into hers.

'His throat was cut with a specific type of blade. Curved, with a rounded tip. It looks a little like a sickle. It was pushed in below the jawbone and great force was exerted. There was a microscopic trace of rust in the wound.'

'Shit . . .'

'More,' says Karol. 'There was a substance in his system.'

'Drugs?'

'Of a sort. A chemical. Chloroform.'

Molly stands perfectly still, unsure if she has heard correctly. 'Chloroform? That's not something you can buy. That's like, from the olden days.'

'Olden days?'

'The past.'

'There was a bruise on his chest,' says Karol, and touches Molly's left breast. 'Here. Leaned on and cut. The blood spilled here,' he says, pointing at the ground.

'But we're five minutes from where he was found.'

'He slept here most nights. The priest at the church turned a blind eye. Left him food and blankets sometimes. Meda came here to give him food for his dog. She had done so before. Somebody took his place. Killed him. Took her.'

'Why?' asks Molly, and the single syllable is weighted with despair.

'People do bad things,' he says, shrugging. 'I think you were right in your suspicions. Somebody bad has been taking girls like Meda. I have asked questions. These past years, we have thought all such crimes the work of gangs. Of men like me. Of men who want money. I think we have made a mistake. Somebody has been taking girls for their own reasons. I want to find this man. I want to hurt him for the pain he has caused.'

'Why do you think that, all of a sudden?' asks Molly, and suddenly feels horribly English.

'We have friends in the police. There have been more disappearances than we thought. You remember I tell you about the girl in the lay-by? She is not alone. Many girls have been reported missing. Such reports have made the police poke their nose in to things they should not know. So money has been paid. Mothers have told the police their children have returned. But they have not returned.'

Molly realizes she is biting the flesh of her index finger. She suddenly hates the world and her place inside it. Finds herself damning her species as poison.

'What sort of mother . . .?'

'One with more children,' says Karol. 'One who is willing to think of her family rather than an individual. I am sorry, Molly. This world must seem so strange to you.'

Molly realizes she has pulled Karol close to herself and is pressing against him as if searching for warmth.

'Do you think she is alive?' asks Molly, looking into his eyes. 'Truly?'

Karol holds her gaze. 'If she is not, I wish she were. The man who has her is so much worse than me. The man who has her is worse than anybody. He seeks her flesh, Molly. He wants her skin and bones.'

Molly shudders, and pulls herself closer to Karol. She presses her cheek to his and feels bizarrely grateful for the hand that climbs up her coat and presses against her bare skin.

'What do we do?' she asks. 'How do we make this better?'

Karol tips her head back and kisses her softly. 'We thank God. And pray we are forgiven for the revenge we take.'

'You're religious?' asks Molly, surprised.

He gives a quick flash of smile. 'No. I'm a blasphemy.'

'I don't understand . . .'

'In my country, they call me the Angel of Vengeance.'

LOTTIE

ottie is too excited to keep her thoughts to herself. She pulls her phone from her pocket and flips the camera function so she is looking at her own image. She checks her teeth for lipstick and smooths down her feline eyebrows before flicking up her quiff. There isn't much light in the back of the cab so she engages the flash and coughs, hard, to clear her throat. She licks her lips and grins into the camera.

'News flash for the Coffin Club. I don't want to spoil the surprise but I've got a treat lined up for you if I can pull it off. Maybe it will make up for tonight's shambles, eh? If you were watching you'll be pleased to know my glamorous assistant is feeling much better. Note to self – never hand an arse-in-a-jar to anybody under the age of thirteen until you have checked their gag reflex. And that sounds a lot grubbier than I meant it to. Anyways, I'm wittering on now because I'm on my way to try and sniff out an exhibit I've been fascinated by for years! Takes me right back to my university days when I was just a weird little odd-bod with a morbid thirst for blood and bones. Not much has changed! Check out a piece I wrote on the blog a year or so back if you're looking for clues. Jean Denys, Richard Lower and the Blood of the Lamb. If it doesn't give you goose pimples then check your pulse and I'll see you on my slab. Take care, you weirdoes.'

Lottie stops recording and glances up. The cab driver is looking at her with an expression of mild interest. 'You on the telly?' he asks, his accent East London.

'Now and again,' says Lottie, and tries to sound like a self-deprecating big deal. 'Internet mostly. Irons in the fire.'

'What was that about an arse-in-a-jar?'

Lottie grins and shifts her position to better see the driver. He's middle-aged and plump and there's a smell of cigarettes and spicy food coming off him. She finds herself picturing his arteries and the thickness of the subcutaneous fat around his belly. 'I'm a pathologist,' she says. 'I run a web show and blog for people interested in death.'

'Blimey,' says the cabbie. 'You and my missus would get on. Obsessed with it, she is. Always wanting to tell me about somebody she went to school with who's got this or that wrong with them. Wants me to get my things in order. Buried or cremated, buried or cremated. Always on at me. I've told her she can have me fly-tipped for all I care. Dump me down a lane. Put me out with the recycling if you like, couldn't give a shit. I'm only fifty-seven.'

'What does she fancy?' asks Lottie.

'She's read that you can have your ashes mixed in with paint and be used in a portrait. Reckons you can have yourself turned into a diamond ring if you want. Why would you want it? I wouldn't mind being put in a cannon and fired, I suppose, but when you're dead you're dead so it's not as though I'll know anything about it.'

Lottie rubs her chin and considers his perspective. She spends most of her time with the dead and those fascinated by mortality and occasionally it does her good to speak to relatively normal people about their views on the great beyond. 'You've got no hope of an afterlife, have you? Nothing at all?'

The cab driver shrugs. 'I reckon after you die you go to the same place you were before you were born. No-bloody-where. I hope that's the case, any road. Sounds nice to me. Nothing at all. You think Heaven would be any kind of a place for a man like me? I get bored ten minutes into Midnight Mass. Wings and hymns and praise for all eternity? Do me a favour.'

Lottie laughs, enjoying his perspective. She glances down at her phone. The video has not yet uploaded and she is almost at the address that Brendan would give an arm and a leg to acquire. She puts her phone away. She'll try again later, when the signal improves.

'This is about right,' says Lottie, and the cab slows to a halt at the kerb.

'You want me to wait?' asks the cabbie, and Lottie opens the door and steps into the darkness and rain. 'Dropped a fella off this way earlier on. Done up like a dog's dinner he was.

Cape and a hat and skin hanging off him like he'd just been dug up. Makes you wonder how people afford it, doesn't it?'

'I'll hopefully be more than a few minutes,' says Lottie, shaking her head and handing over a £10 note. 'Keep the change. And if you want my advice, burial is the way to go. But do something interesting. Have your head cut off and put between your legs so you can confuse the archaeologists of the future.'

'What you got planned?' asks the cabbie, lighting a cigarette.

'I want to be a rug,' she says, raising an arm to protect herself from the rain that blows in sideways. 'Just leave my head and my backside on and use the rest of me as a decorative throw.'

'You're mental,' laughs the cabbie. 'Love the hair, by the way. Best of luck with your arsehole collector or whatever he is.'

Lottie gives a nod of thanks and turns away as the cab moves off. She stands for a moment on the sodden kerb and checks the address she has written down on a Jolly Bonnet bar mat. She looks up at the dilapidated property before her and feels a shiver of excitement. For all of her bravado and desire to stand out, Lottie still feels like the same awkward teenager who spent most of her school life being picked on for wearing Doc Martens instead of trainers and preferring The Cure to Westlife. She knows that if she were to see her old schoolmates again, they would recall her as the weirdo who used to keep dead butterflies in a jar and who stole a frozen rat from the biology lab freezer and opened its skull with a rock hammer so she could look at the wrinkles in its brain.

The house is a towering five-storey affair, clinging to the edge of a terrace of better-kept but similarly ancient homes. All have the same shuttered windows and wooden front doors and none of these Georgian townhouses looks particularly British. To Lottie's eye they have a Dutch look about them. She can imagine such properties looking down on the canal in Amsterdam. But they sit at the heart of Spitalfields and sell for millions on the rare occasions they become available. She had assumed that the address she had unearthed for the man she seeks would be a more humble apartment, but when she peers closer at the number hanging lopsided on the soaking pinkish brick, she realizes her quarry owns the entire house. She wonders how many years she will have to work before she could even afford a bed in the basement and stops the thought before she gets upset.

There is something unsettling about the property. Lottie is only a couple of minutes from the bustle and laughter of the Ten Bells and she can see the outline of Christchurch at the end of the road. But there is something sinister about this old street. These houses have looked down upon violence. The pavements on which she stands have been replaced countless times since the homes were built but she finds herself wondering how much blood has soaked into the ground beneath. She feels oddly vulnerable, as if she might turn around to find the street filled with horses and carts and mud-soaked drunken men. She keeps glancing at the Fiat 500 parked to her right but it seems like an anachronism – a futuristic visitor.

Lottie breathes out and gives three sharp raps on the wet door. Unlike the neighbouring properties, this one shows no signs of habitation. Others on the street have been converted into offices by accountancy and architectural firms but there remain some private residences and in each, at least one light is burning. She can see the yellow outline around the shutters. At the house where the collector is listed as residing, there is no sign of life.

'Come on, come on . . .'

The man inside is rumoured to possess the actual journals of the surgeon whose experiments in blood transfusion altered humanity's perceptions of itself forever. In the same year that the Great Fire was devouring the streets upon which she stands, physician Jean Denys was transfusing the blood of animals into human beings, having successfully completed the practice with animals. The collector's specimens would make for a fascinating episode, but for purely personal reasons, she is eager to look upon the equipment which the maverick physician had crafted and honed.

Lottie gives an exasperated sigh, banging again upon the wood. She crouches down and lifts the letterbox, peering into the darkness beyond. A breeze tickles her eye lashes as she stares into the darkened space and then she catches the whiff of something rotten; a pungent tang that is as familiar to her as warm loaves to a baker. She smells decay. Corruption. Blood.

Lottie stands up straight. The rain is still coming down hard and the only sound she can hear over the endless patter of water on stone is the distant swish of car tyres on the damp road. She wonders if she imagined the smell. Worse, whether she has carried it with her from the morgue. She does not know whether there is a protocol for such a situation. Should she knock on a neighbour's door and alert them to the smell of death wafting out of their neighbour's letterbox? Perhaps the collector is away and a pet has perished. Perhaps one of his specimens has been improperly packaged and has leaked its contents on the hallway carpet. She finds herself torn. She is only standing on this step because she wants something from the man inside. She turns around, hoping somebody will be passing that she might be able to ask for counsel, then grows cross with herself for requiring it. *You're a grown woman*, she tells herself. *Make a decision.*

After a moment, Lottie reaches into her bag and pulls out a notebook embossed with a poison bottle and a raven. She scribbles a note, her address and phone number, and pushes it through the letterbox. She keeps her head back in case the smell should do something to her conscience.

Cursing, Lottie stomps down the steps and back on to the road. Her pace quickens as she heads up the street towards Christchurch. With every step she has the strange feeling that she is heading back to her own time and putting something dark and unpleasant behind her. By the time she passes the lights of the Ten Bells and raises her arm to hail a cab, it is all she can do not to break into a run.

MR FARKAS

Mr Farkas sits in the dark. He is resting in a high-backed chair and his lower half is wrapped in a red blanket. He has an old laptop computer upon his knee. His thumbs are leaving semi-circular grooves in his cheekbones as he rhythmically pushes his head back and forth along the sharp surface of his fingernails. He has scored eight trenches into his wrinkled forehead. There is a little blood upon the index finger of his left hand and three hairs have adhered themselves to one slender knuckle. He does not remember taking this position. He cannot remember drinking the acrid liquid that he can taste upon his tongue. He is unsure which room within his great house he has deposited himself within. He thinks he may be able to hear a knocking on the door but the sound could just as easily be the creak of the settling timbers or the rattle of the casters on the wooden floor. He can smell blood. A soft whisper of metal and earth. He knows there should be a stinging sensation upon his grazed skin and yet he feels no pain. He has taken his medicine. Nothing hurts him when it is in his system. He does not truly feel as though he has any form of physical presence. He sees himself as somebody else's vision; an apparition drifting upon the cold and murky air of his big and drafty home.

There was a time when such a thought would have provoked a burst of philosophical study. How would it feel to be the object of another person's imagination? Would a person be aware if they had been called into being by the creative whimsy of another? Are we all the unwitting fiction of something greater? He would have written long into the night. Querying. Questing. Seeking after truth. Would humanity even know if it were just God's daydream? Perhaps the whole of man's history could be reduced to a bizarre and orderless reverie within the cerebral cortex of some greater force. He does not write down such thoughts any longer. He finds that he tires too quickly. There is a noticeable shake in his right hand and he struggles to read back his own barely legible scribbles. He is little better on the occasions he brings himself to use a computer. It took him a Herculean effort of concentration to tell the blue-haired girl that there had been a terrible misunderstanding. She had his child. Somehow, she had his child.

Mr Farkas is only an occasional viewer of the little shows that the pathologist has been broadcasting over the last few months. He does not recall the first time he stumbled upon the programme or quite what he had been seeking at the time, but he does recall being transfixed by the attractive presenter and mesmerized by the samples which she held up to the camera and explained in explicit and grisly detail. In another time, in another life, Mr Farkas had been an expert in specimens of mortality and morbidity. He wrote academic papers and provided guidance and advice for auction houses, museums and private collectors. He ran a website for collectors of medical antiques, detailing the finest and rarest artefacts from the world of medical, surgical, apothecary and quack collectibles. Such work paid well. He had been fortunate to purchase his home while still a young man and paid off his mortgage around the same time Beatrix fell ill. That was a blessing. Her care has been extraordinarily expensive and he doubts he would have found the funds without resorting to murder had he still been paying for the house. As it is, he does not know how much money he has left. There are great gaps in his memory. At times he sees his mind as a complex lace; a web with more holes than fabric. He feels constantly as though he is in some garish hinterland between sleep and wakefulness. As a young man he would laugh when he would enter a room then forget why he had gone in there. But he feels as though he lives in such a sensation all the time. He forgets to wear a watch so is never sure whether the darkness precedes sunrise or follows sunset. In such moments of uncertainty he knows only that he is being a poor nurse. His daughter relies upon routine. She needs her own medicine at precise times. Sometimes he fears that he has forgotten to feed her or to hold the water glass to her lips. There are times he nearly forgets she is there. He wonders why he moved her to the basement in the first place. He must have had his reasons. Perhaps it was to spare his knees. There are four flights of stairs between the parlour and her room on the top floor. He must have decided the air in the basement was more beneficial to her lungs. If so, he has yet to see the benefits. If anything, she is getting worse. There is a clamminess to her skin that makes him think of rotting pork and a low, pitiful sobbing keeps erupting from her mouth. She did not enjoy the story book he had chosen for her. She had hurt his feelings. He had not raised her to be so ungrateful. He made allowances for her illness but had been harsh with her in his chastisements. Beatrix sometimes acts as though she has a right to her luxuries. There is an air of entitlement about her that sometimes makes Mr Farkas angry. His own father would have discouraged such behaviour with physical remonstration. There are still welts upon Mr Farkas's back from the studded belt with which his father would beat his shoulders, thighs and buttocks whenever he had misbehaved. Mr Farkas's wife, God rest her soul, used to run her fingertips along the wounds and press her damp cheeks to each of the places he had been hurt. He misses that closeness. He does not believe he will know it again. Within his confusion, the pain of her passing remains a constant. He has to keep reminding himself that she is gone. Too dead to save.

There is a sudden blast of colour and light as Mr Farkas leans upon the computer in his lap. He almost pushes it away from himself. He cannot recall placing it here. Cannot understand what forced him here, into this cold and creaking room. He should be with her. With his daughter. Why had he left her? He feels panic flare inside him and then just as suddenly he is shrinking back inside himself as the screen fills with the image of the pathologist.

He remembers. He had needed to see it again. Needed to confirm his fears. Though his fingers shake he manages to operate the pad on the computer and then he is recoiling like a vampire shying from the light as the woman gives way to the young girl with the plump face and unkempt hair and the bright but baleful eyes of a pure and beautiful soul.

Her child.

His child.

The recollection floods him. How could his child be both there and in her bed? How could his perfect *cica* be out so late with this strange and colourful woman? Through the fog he had typed out a demand for answers and a desperate plea for help. He had begged. *Please. My blood. My blood!* And the child had heard him. She had glanced at the screen and she had walked off camera. She was coming home. Back to her bed, where she would be safe and protected and under the umbrella of her father's perfect love . . .

Mr Farkas feels a sudden burning terror inside his chest. With Beatrix coming home, who is the girl who has tried to deceive him? Who is the pestilent figure who sweats and fits in his daughter's bed? He fears consequences. He has made a mistake. In his delirium, his confusion, he knows he must have picked up the wrong child from school or the hospital or her mother's grave. Yes, that is it. A mistake. An honest mistake. But even after so many years he is a foreigner in this country. A rich foreigner. A quiet, reclusive man. He has no friends. Nobody to speak for him. Would the authorities forgive such an act? He feels a creeping horror prickling inside his skin. He has a sudden memory of such a mistake occurring before. He remembers the feel of cold and clammy skin upon his own. The ugly thud as body met hard, unforgiving ground. He could not be forgiven again. And even if he were, would such actions not alert those who would take his child away from him? He has fought such battles before.

Her condition makes it unfeasible for her to be cared for at home, Mr Farkas. She needs constant medical attention. We have the best facilities and will take care of her. You cannot do it all yourself . . .

He rises. There is a voice in his head, talking of shattered metatarsals and a filleting knife. He realizes he is moving. The wall and the door are closer. Clearer. But the darkness is clawing at his vision and he feels as though he is half submerged in tar as he stumbles into the kitchen and hauls at the door in the floor. The smell hits him. Decay. Fever. An ugly fog of corrupting skin. He feels terror and rage and shame. This person, this *almost-daughter*, is dying in his daughter's bed. He remembers Beatrix's sister. Remembers her laid out like this, beneath a tight blanket and with nothing but spilled ink upon the whites of her eyes. She needs help. Needs to survive. He has done a terrible thing. A terrible, terrible thing . . .

As Mr Farkas closes his arms around the girl on the bed, the mask slips and for a moment, the burning skin of the real girl beneath the prosthetic touches his own fragile flesh. Their tears pool upon their connected skin.

'I'm so sorry, my child. Hush. Hush. I will help you. I'm so sorry . . .'

He starts to drag the child from the bed. As one arm flops loose, he sees the quilled hypodermic protruding from the crook of her arm. Blood drips into the black shadows below.

He scoops her into arms that can barely take her weight and begins to stagger towards the door. He will take her to hospital. He will save her. He will do things right.

The note from Lottie catches his eye as he drags the child out of the kitchen hatch and down the hall. Among the island of unopened letters and spilled papers it is a square of perfect white. It has unfolded itself and in the near blackness he is barely able to make out the words.

Through the fear and the guilt and the horror at himself, something like hope flares in Mr Farkas. The pathologist has come to his door. She has sought him out. Beatrix must have given her his address. She must be on her way home. He has so little time. He must make things nice for her. Must make sure her bed is ready and her storybook is where it should be. There is no time to take the imposter child all the way to the hospital. No time for kindness.

Later, he has little memory of loading the girl into his car. Does not remember the drive down Wilkes Street or the bustle and neon of the busy street by Christchurch. The next time he is aware of himself he is opening the passenger door as he drives along the flyover off Mile End Road at 50mph and kicks the child's body on to the soaking tarmac. He drives away without looking back. He never sees what he has done.

Never sees the girl in the nightdress staring sightlessly up at the tumbling, teeming sky.

To: DCI Trevor Granger
From: Dr Mal
Subject: Idiot's Guide to Blood
Date: 04/03/2015

Hi Trev,

Not quite sure if this is what you're after as you were kind of vague when you asked and I'd definitely had more than the daily recommended dose of shiraz! But I think it might help fill in some of the gaps. Is this what the Met pays you for? Seriously, sounds a sad one. Did I understand correctly? It was a young girl? Needle tracks in her arms and an open wound in her thigh? Sounds barbaric. Hope you catch these butchers. But you're right, there is a real market out there for donor organs and plasma and I can't say with hand on heart that it wasn't some former bloody classmate who was responsible for botching the operation. Did you say you'd heard whispers of other cases? Hope you throw away the key, my friend.

So, the basic science here is to do with blood groups and ABO compatibility – or, more importantly, incompatibility. We all have various antigens, little proteins, on the surface of our red blood cells (RBCs). There are two main types of antigens in this context: A and B. You can have one, both, or none. That means your blood type can be A, B, AB or O (the ones with no antigens).

In addition, you can be rhesus positive or negative. This matters because it determines who you can get blood from without getting a reaction. A quick immune lesson – if the body gets exposed to anything 'antigen' that is not part of the body already then it will treat it as an intruder and try to kill its ass. That, of course, is what antibodies do. They are the henchmen.

AB pos person

If you are AB pos then you are golden – you have all the antigens already so you can receive any kind of blood of anyone. (At least for the major blood groups – there is always room around the fringes for this stuff to get more complicated.) These people are known as UNIVERSAL RECIPIENTS.

O neg person

If you are O neg then you are completely screwed if you are given any blood other than O neg – your body will immediately start fighting off the 'bad' blood cells.

However, because they have no antigens then their blood doesn't offend anyone. They are the UNIVERSAL DONORS. Blood banks have plenty of stocks of O neg blood. It takes a bit of time to get someone's blood type and when someone is hosing out the claret then there is not a moment to be wasted – you'll be given O neg blood as an immediate response until they get a proper blood typing.

Reactions and transfusion problems

Allergy
You can have an allergic/anaphylactic reaction. These tend to happen quickly (though not always) and include things like feelings of impending doom, shortness of breath/wheeze and swelling of face/tongue. Never actually seen this – rare!

Haemolysis
More commonly, you can get a haemolytic complication. Haemolysis basically means the breakdown of RBCs. The body clocks the unwanted antigens on the surface of the RBCs – these are attacked and the whole RBC gets destroyed in the process. This tends to be slower

but is bad news – you want those RBCs or you are in
trouble. Usually patients given blood transfusions
are monitored carefully for reactions – pulse (would go
up), blood pressure (down) and temperature (people
having reactions can spike a fever). Patients would
be clammy, pale, sweaty and nauseated/vomiting maybe,
feeling fairly ropy.

Fluid overload
Sometimes people are given transfusions because they
are anaemic – not actually because they have low blood
volume (from bleeding for instance). That means they
can get overloaded. Young healthy people can usually
cope with this – their kidneys just work harder and pee
it all out. Older folk or those with rubbish kidneys
sometimes don't – and fluid starts building in lungs
etc. They get short of breath and can die from that –
pulmonary oedema.

Anyways, if you do end up looking into it more
officially do please give me a shout and I'd be glad to
help. The goose feathers thing sounds really weird. Did
you know they used them as syringes back in the old
days?

Love to the family and let's meet up to hole a few
birdies some time soon.

Dr George Malcom.

MOLLY

Three days have passed since Meda Stauskas was pushed from a moving car on to the hard, damp road. She was found by a taxi driver who slammed his car to a desperate halt just millimetres from her unmoving form. He believed to his very bones that he had somehow struck her with his car. He was on his knees and weeping when the paramedics and the police arrived. He'd wrapped her in his coat and was cradling her in his lap, sitting there in the inside lane of the dual carriageway with his black cab blocking the road. It took two police officers to prise his grip from the sad, pale shape in the nightgown. He was arrested and breathalysed and kept saying he was sorry. It was only when his solicitor arrived at the station that the cabbie learned he was in no way responsible for the injuries to the girl. He was, if anything, a hero, though he was about to be charged for being slightly over the drink-drive limit and for being in possession of a vehicle that had a broken brake light.

Meda is in a critical condition at the Royal Hospital on Whitechapel Road. Her body has been shutting down. She is suffering an intense allergic reaction and shows signs of having been systematically drained of blood and then transfused with an unidentified plasma. There is writing on her stomach: flashes of black ink among the ugly red welts. She is delirious most of the time. She has a high temperature and the doctors fear that her organs are shutting down. She is sweating and shaking and the consultant responsible for her care has warned her family that he can make no promises that she will survive.

Molly and Hilda only learned of her whereabouts this morning when Lottie burst in to the Bonnet and told them she had seen Karol leaving the hospital with a pale and weeping woman she took to be Meda's mother. He had seen Lottie and given her a virtually imperceptible nod.

Yes, it said. *The girl is alive . . .*

Lottie had gone straight to the children's ward and spoken to a colleague and been appraised of the story doing the rounds on the ward. Meda had been abducted by a maniac. She had been drugged and drained of blood. She had been brutalized and starved then dumped on a busy road. Her family were doing all they could to keep the police at arm's length but a unit at Whitechapel station were trying to get a court order demanding the family oblige them in their investigations. They have consented to an intimate examination which mercifully shows no signs of rape.

Molly and Hilda had listened to Lottie's revelations in a maelstrom of emotions. Hilda had been in tears the moment Lottie said her friend was alive. She soon drifted into horror and rage and then despair as she learned that Meda's chances of recovery were no better than 50/50. Molly had held herself very still as Lottie spoke. She had spent two days awaiting a call or a text or any of the means of communication that she and Karol had promised to employ upon their parting. For two days, she had heard nothing. And now she was discovering why.

It is a little after 8 p.m. and Molly is hurrying down Turner Street. She looks so unlike herself that she has passed by three regular customers from the Bonnet without causing any of them to look up. She is dressed in blue jeans and battered trainers, a mustard-coloured jumper and a black leather coat. Her hair is pulled back in a short ponytail and her face is not made up. There is a rash of spots upon her jawline and the whites of her eyes have lost their gleam. She has bitten the red polish from her nails.

A mizzling rain is blowing in from the east on a biting wind. The pedestrians are hunching into scarves and pulled-up collars and the drivers who slide by, nose-to-tail, cannot seem to find the right setting to keep the rain and the steam off their windscreens and windows.

Molly chews her lip as she hurries towards the great turquoise-blue mass of the hospital. She passes nurses and cleaners in groups of twos and threes. Watches as a delivery van nudges a parked BMW while performing a tight three-point turn in front of the parking barrier. Hears a voice, sweet and lyrical, muttering some West African language into a mobile phone and looks up to see a pleasant, round-faced woman, who blesses her and apologizes for getting in her way. Molly steps to her right and again stumbles into the large lady, who smiles and apologizes afresh.

'I'm sorry,' says Molly, flustered. 'I'll go this way, you go that . . .'

Molly rubs a hand through her hair and shivers in her coat as she manages to get past. Turns back to give a nod and sees him. Sees Karol. He is sitting beneath an ugly beige awning outside the pub on the corner of the road. He is leaning back in a metal chair, smoking a cigarette. He is the only smoker braving the conditions. He has wedged himself up against an industrial bin. Anybody approaching him must do so from the front.

Molly is halfway across the road before she realizes she has started walking towards him. She does not know what she wants to happen. There is a pain in her chest and her skin feels sore. As she changes direction, the wind and rain assault the other side of her face and she winces as if she is being slapped.

Karol narrows his eyes. His stubble has become a beard and he looks pale and tired. He stiffens in his seat at Molly's approach and she realizes, aghast, that he does not recognise her. She lets her temper show in her expression and puts both her hands down on the wet metal table and leans forward to glare into his eyes.

'Nice to see you too, dick face. Were you going to tell me? No phone call? No text? I'd have settled for a bloody WhatsApp message and I can barely use that. How dare you? And don't go thinking I'm some jealous little woman who thinks every shag is going to turn into a great romance! This isn't about what happened on the grass. You know what Meda means to Hilda and you know what we've been going through and what I've been trying to do and I have to find out she's alive because Lottie happens to spy you with Meda's mum . . .'

Karol raises his hands, patting gently at the air. He closes his eyes and the tip of his cigarette glows bright red as he inhales.

'Please,' he says, softly. 'Sit. Take a drink. Drink mine, if you wish. It's not as good as the ale at the Jolly Bonnet but it is passable. I believe they serve desserts here too. Would you like cake?'

Molly's face drops open into a wide O of indignation. She feels certain he is making fun of her.

'No I don't want fucking cake! I came here to find out if she's OK! I came here to get some answers. I've earned that, don't you think?'

Karol stubs out his cigarette in a puddle on the table top. He sucks his teeth and looks at her without expression. 'Why you deserve that?' he asks, candidly. 'What you do to deserve answers?'

Molly looks murderous. Were she to look at a snapshot of her face in this moment she would think herself ready to do murder.

'This has been eating us up!' she splutters. 'Hilda hasn't been sleeping! What I saw . . . What you told me . . .'

'You've had a bad week,' shrugs Karol. 'So what? You think Meda's family have had a fun time? They know her. Love her. Feed and clothe her. You are the mother of a girl that Meda sees once a week. You are nobody's priority right now.'

The words sting like the cold air. Molly realizes she has been pushing her knuckles into her cheekbones as Karol talked. She stops herself and chews on her lip instead.

'That's not fair,' she says, quietly.

'I didn't ask you to come here and start shouting in my face. I didn't know your silly friend with the big tits and blue hair would see me. I didn't know you would walk down this street. You think maybe I wanted to have some answers before we spoke? You think maybe I have other things to do for the family?'

There is a blare of loud music from the open window of a white van that is cruising past on the wet road. Molly winces, suddenly aware of the headache that is clustering at her temples and sinuses. She feels some of the temper drain from her. Suddenly she just feels sad and cold and empty.

'Is she OK?' Molly asks, and she lowers herself into the chair opposite Karol. It is soaked with rain and she shivers as the water seeps through her jeans. She doesn't care about the discomfort. She feels as though she has earned it, somehow.

'OK?' asks Karol. He pulls another cigarette from his jacket. He fails to light it with his cheap lighter. Curses in his native tongue as the wheel on the orange device fails to turn.

'Meda,' says Molly, and she reaches out to take the lighter from him. It sparks as she rolls her thumb over the wheel and as he leans forward to take the flame she looks into his dark eyes and wonders what she actually wants from this man. 'Lottie says she is very poorly. Said things had been done to her . . .'

'Bad things,' says Karol, and he wrinkles his nose as if something tastes bad. 'Steppen will have answers soon.'

'Her uncle,' says Molly, to show she has remembered. 'How is he? Her family? What do they know?'

Karol says nothing. He picks up his half-empty pint glass and puts it back on the table without taking a sip. He seems less vital than the man Molly thinks she knows. He seems to have been wrung out by the events of recent days. He seems to have had the juice squeezed from him.

Molly sits forward and tries to get her face into his eye line. 'Karol, I'm sorry for shouting. I'm upset. I've no right to take it out on you. This is a horrible thing. I've been through horrible things and this has maybe brought it back. I don't know. I just want to know she's OK and then I can go and tell Hilda that all of this is over and that the bad person isn't somebody to worry about.'

Karol rolls his head from side to side and there is a crack as the bones in his neck give under the pressure of the movement.

'Sounds sore,' says Molly.

'Not much sleep,' says Karol. 'Think I slept upside down.'

Molly gives a tiny smile and something seems to thaw between them. She feels absurdly relieved, then reminds herself of what she has witnessed and what this man is capable of. She feels unsure how to behave. Doesn't know quite who or what she is.

'Please, Karol,' she says, and hates herself for the pleading. 'I'm not a reporter. I'm not police. I'm not after anything other than some answers. Is it all done? Have you . . . sorted it out?'

Karol stares at the end of his cigarette for a time. 'Sorted it?'

'Whoever did this . . .' Molly hisses, and she realizes how many questions she has been asking in her head without finding a way to articulate. She is suddenly aware of the decisions she has unconsciously made. Suddenly aware what she knows Karol to be. 'Are they dead? Have you hurt them? What else did they do? How many people?'

Karol looks at Molly with something like sadness in his eyes. 'What you think of me, Molly? You think I'm like Google? Think I know it all and that you just ask and I tell? You know nothing about my life. About the paths we all choose. You think because we shared some times that I'm going to tell a fucking ex-cop all the truths that Steppen is paying money to hide? Why I do that?'

Molly wants to shake him. Wants to grind her fist into his face and force him to stop seeing her the wrong way.

'Check me,' says Molly, gesturing at herself. 'You think I'm wearing a wire, is that it? Or maybe my phone's trans-mitting right now. Maybe some of the old colleagues from the good old days have brought me in to get a confession from the big bad gangster about all the terrible things that he and Uncle Steppen have been getting up to. Yeah? Well, how about if I say some things for the benefit of the tape? Things to show you that I'm past fucking caring about all the rights and wrongs and cops and robbers shit? How about if I tell anybody listening that I fucked the suspect in the mud three nights ago and we both came so hard I thought my bones were going to shatter? How about that? Or how about I tell them that I saw the suspect torturing the little wanker who tried to profit from Meda's disappearance and that instead of phoning the police I felt glad to my soul? That help you feel better?'

Karol is pushing his tongue against his lower teeth. Molly's voice has risen as she speaks and two young men who are hurrying by turn to look at the angry exchange. Karol blows them a kiss and they continue on their way. Karol gives Molly a hard glare, and then purses his lips into an approximation of something softer. 'Came so hard your bones were going to shatter? You write that down for me? Put on my CV?'

Molly reaches over and back-hands him on the chest. 'Wanker!'

Karol pushes himself forward in his seat. He tilts his head and his manner becomes gentle. 'I believe you, Molly. I believe you are all that you say. You got involved in something you were not meant to. You continued to nose around because it mattered and because you wanted answers for your daughter. I admire you. I like you. But I am here at the request of a powerful man, and that man does not know you, or care about you. He has already done what he must. The family will not remain here for long. Meda may wake, she may not, but I promise you that her parents and her siblings and her uncle will soon be somewhere else. There will be no publicity. No arrest. No trial. Things will be done as they have always been done and you will never hear the outcome. I do not say this to distress you or to make you feel unimportant. I say this because you have waded out far enough. We are beyond the shallows. Any deeper and you will be swimming in the kind of waters where it is all blood and sharks and I cannot protect you from them all.'

'Protect me? I don't need protecting!'

Karol sighs, as if tired to his bones. 'We all need protecting. You do. I do. Your friend does. Steppen is *vor y zakone* and his niece was stolen by a madman. Those men I hurt? They thought they were strong and powerful and then I made them bleed. I know that when the end comes for me I will not think myself at risk. That is what it is to be human. We all believe ourselves somehow immortal. We all believe we will be the one to escape. None of us will. Nobody gets out alive.'

Molly feels as though she is running out of whatever has been powering her. The headache is becoming more intense. She turns to stare into the rain and for an instant it feels as though everything is dissolving and fragmenting. Each drop of rain is a pixel of the picture before her and each is being blown away by the gale from the river.

'Who took her?' she asks, weakly. 'Hilda is with Lottie. I'll go straight there. I won't go into the hospital. I just want to have an answer for her when she asks if everything is OK.'

Karol rubs his eyebrows with his forefinger and thumb. The

action causes his jacket to open slightly at the chest and Molly glimpses a yellow document, rolled into a tube. Karol sees the direction of her gaze and sits back.

'That's Metropolitan,' says Molly, quietly. 'Case files. Not a photocopy. An original . . .'

'Do not ask any more,' says Karol, urgently. 'Stop.'

'Karol, please . . .'

Karol curses, biting down on his lower lip. Slowly, he reaches into his coat and removes the sheaf of papers. He closes his eyes and unrolls the top page. It shows a series of stills from CCTV footage, dated and marked with the time. Molly looks at the page. The images were all taken on different cameras. The earliest is dated almost four years ago. The most recent was the night of Meda's disappearance.

'This man,' says Karol, quietly. 'This is who did it.'

Molly looks at a shape that seems more shadow than anything else. She blinks several times, trying to make sense of the pictures. Each is of a quiet street. Each is taken in darkness. The only light is from a solitary streetlamp. Each shows a figure in a cloak and hat, a cut-out of absolute black.

'Are you taking the piss?' asks Molly, recoiling. 'That's a Ripper actor. Somebody from a Whitechapel tour. It's a silhouette, at best. Where were they taken? Are you serious? Karol, I don't . . .'

'The girls I told you about,' he says, and his voice is not more than a whisper. 'Steppen has been asking questions. People have been very helpful. We know times and dates and places. We know more than the police. We know that this man, this thing, was nearby each time a child was taken.'

'How . . .?'

'We know, Molly,' says Karol, as if explaining to a child. 'Not who he is, but what he has done. The police have done their tests. There was dead skin on her face, as if she had worn a mask made of skin. Those skin cells are being tested for DNA at a private facility at this moment. Those results will come to us, Molly. We will take vengeance. This man took Meda's blood. He pumped her full of his own. Her body is rejecting it. She is dying. The quills that punctured her skin – they were needles. Syringes. They were used for this man's madness. We will find him, Molly. But you will never hear of it. And I ask you to settle for this.'

Molly's hand is on her mouth. She can feel her heart beating hard. She does not know whether she wants to know more or to cleanse her mind of the ugly thoughts with which it is full to bursting.

'You can't know all this,' says Molly, desperately. 'Not for certain. Not some old Russian gangster in a little flat in Stepney. It's guesswork. It's insane . . .'

'Ask no more,' says Karol, and he reaches forward to put his hand on Molly's. 'Please, wade no deeper.'

Molly yanks her hand away and knocks the glass, which topples from the table and splashes her front. She curses and jumps back and as she does so her mobile phone falls from her jacket pocket and clatters on to the table. Raindrops immediately pattern the surface and the feather-light touch causes the screen to illuminate.

Molly stops still as she looks at the image. Feels the ground tilt as she looks at the photograph of her daughter. Tall. Long-limbed and clumsy. Bushy-haired and red-faced. Beautiful and ungainly. She scrabbles with the display and starts pawing at the screen. She reaches out and closes her fist around Karol's arm. She suddenly knows, to her bones, that her child needs her. It is as though her blood has found its voice and is screaming her name. She feels it in the centre of her bones; the utter certainty that her little girl, the girl who could serve as a mask for Meda, is in danger.

'The other children,' says Molly, urgently. 'Did they look like her? The mask, you see. The dead skin on Meda's face . . .'

Karol looks down at the table. 'I can tell you no more.'

'Karol! Did they look like her? Did they look like this?'

Karol glances at Molly's phone as she shoves it in his face. He gives the slightest of nods.

'Fuck. Fuck!'

The chair clatters to the ground as she pushes away from the table and sprints through the rain, feet thudding on the wet road like the heart that hammers in her chest.

HILDA

ottie was drumming her fingers on her teeth and pulling faces; sighs and raspberries and all sorts of expressions that made her look as though she was battling with something difficult. It was getting on my nerves a bit. She'd been jittery all night. I understood what she was going through but I thought she was being a bit selfish. After all, Meda was my friend, not hers. I was the one who had got people asking questions and got Mum and Karol involved in looking for her. It was probably because of their digging around that the bad man let her go. That meant I was the one who had saved her, in a way. But Lottie was acting like it was her best friend who was in the hospital bed, not mine. She'd given me her phone to play with but she had no decent games and her music was all gloomy and whenever I tried to talk to her she told me to just give her a moment. She was bashing away at her laptop as if it was a piano and she was trying to see how loud she could play. She'd been like this ever since she arrived. Tara was working the bar and she had always been nice to me, so if Lottie had better things to do she could get off and do them. I was on the verge of telling her so. It wasn't my fault that Mum had gone to the hospital without her. I was as angry about it as Lottie was. I should have been there. Should have been kneeling at the hospital bed and holding Meda's hand and getting thank yous from her family. I should have been the first thing she saw when she woke up.

'That's kind of annoying,' I said, nodding at Lottie's hands as she lifted them from the keyboard to rap out a rhythm on her front teeth.

'Sorry?' she asked, not looking up.

'The teeth thing.'

'Oh, right,' said Lottie, and glared at the computer screen. 'Soz.'

We sat side by side at the bar. My glass of lemonade was half full on the bar top. Lottie was sampling the new cocktail that Mum had chalked up on the specials board this morning. The Whore's Drawers. It smelled of geraniums and the glass it was served in was bound with a lacy garter. It looked pretty.

'What is it you're doing?' I asked, properly bored with myself. I was dipping my fingers in my lemonade to draw stick men on the bar and couldn't even be bothered to give them all heads. I just wanted Mum to ring. Wanted her to get in touch and say it was all fine and that I was going to see my friend again soon. I wanted Lottie to hug me and say something daft. It was all too serious. There weren't even any other customers to entertain me.

'Sorry?' asked Lottie, and she gave me a look like she was cross with me, then went back to her computer. She didn't even look like herself. Her hair was flat and she had less make-up on than I'd seen her wear before.

'I'm bored, Lottie. Could we play?'

'Can't you play something on my phone?' she asked, seemingly exasperated.

'Like what? I don't know your account password so I can't buy new games.'

'There's books on there. Read a book. Or ask Tara for some paper or something. Do a drawing for your mum . . .' She stopped, halfway through a word. Read something on the screen. Looked up with big, wet eyes. 'I'm so sorry, Hilda . . .'

My friend was dead. They'd managed to restart her heart but it had given out again. The emergency transfusion had come too late.

Lottie moved a little closer and I got that smell of her. Hospitals and perfume, cigarettes and fried onions. I put my head on her shoulder and she angled the screen of the laptop towards me. She was on her own website, rattling about some posting under the headline 'Bad Blood'.

'What's that all about?' I asked, and as I looked at her it felt like I was looking at the world through a porthole on an old steamship, the horizon shifting up and down as the waves rolled beneath and around me.

Lottie looked as though I had caught her doing something naughty. She gave me this tight little grin, then hunched her shoulders like she was doing an impression of a miser and put her arms around the laptop. 'Mine,' she said. 'All mine.'

'What is? What's the blood stuff?'

Lottie sipped her drink and checked around behind us. The bar was still empty. Tara was busy loading glasses into the dishwasher. I think they'd already been through twice but she didn't have anything else to do.

'The blood stuff, as you put it, is a webisode you're going to love. I sometimes think I have the luck of the Irish.'

'You're Irish?' I asked, unsure what she was so giddy about.

'No, you turnip, I mean sometimes good fortune just comes along. Like, who would have thought Brendan, with his horrible pony tail and all that mad talk – who'd have thought he would give me something useful. And Christine! Who'd have thought that the mousy little thing would actually have something up her sleeve that could really get the serious telly bods taking notice?'

I didn't have a clue what she was talking about. I think she realized, because she started talking in a baby voice, as if I was an idiot. She didn't seem to know how to talk to me about Meda. She dealt with death all her life but she couldn't communicate any of it to me. I'd have been happy if she'd lied. I'd have settled for a cuddle and a promise that I would see my friend again, one day, in whatever passed for an afterlife. She couldn't bring herself to do it. Just tried to make things normal between us. To talk like she always had done. I wanted Mum. Wanted her so much it was like a toothache all over my body and the air around it.

'You know Brendan?' she asked, and I tried to focus on what Lottie was saying.

'Of course. He collects stuff. He puts eyeballs on the bar and wants to buy the scarificator.'

'Yes – and congratulations on your pronunciation, by the way,' Lottie remarked.

'What about him?' I asked.

'He goes to auctions to buy weird stuff. Medical implements. Collectors' items.'

'Like you do,' I said, nodding.

'I'm a medical professional,' she said, bristling. 'I'm not a collector. I'm a curator of a museum and a clinical pathologist.'

I had nothing to offer in response so just let her get back on track without any nudging.

'Anyway, Brendan is always getting beaten at auction by a collector who goes by the name of Autolycus. That's what the auctioneers call him. Do you read Shakespeare?'

'I've seen some films,' I shrugged, remembering an evening watching Mum cry in front of *Romeo and Juliet*. It all seemed a little far-fetched to me.

'There's a character in *The Winter's Tale* called Autolycus. He's a pickpocket. He snaps up unconsidered trifles. It's a very scholarly joke.'

'Oh,' I said, shrugging. 'I don't get it.'

'No, neither did I,' admitted Lottie. 'But Christine . . .'

'The fat one?'

'She's not fat, that's mean. But yeah, the little odd one who gets nervous when somebody sneezes. Well, she's a bit of a collector too. She's really into this transfusionist from the seventeenth century. She wrote papers on him and has mentioned him in blogs and stuff. He put animal blood into humans and vice versa and nearly got executed for murder when one of his patients died. It's really interesting.'

'Right. Well, what?'

'Christine did some digging about for me so Brendan would stop bugging me and she rang one of the auction houses. Spun some yarn about Dr Lottie being desperate to speak to the buyer with a view to using him on my web show. Auction house couldn't give any details about him but they took her number and promised to pass it on to the buyer.'

'And he rang?' I asked, trying to work out when this would get interesting.

'No,' said Lottie, sighing. 'But, when she spoke to the auctioneer again she asked if Autolycus had bought any other items of interest and he was happy to give her a full list from the recent catalogues of all the things he had been after.'

I waited, hoping more would be forthcoming. Lottie made fists with her hands and gave a big smile.

'Christine recognized one of the pieces he had bought. So did Brendan when I showed him. A Lister spray. Beautiful thing. Brass and wood. It puffed out the carbolic spray that was introduced by the great Lister in 1870 to purify the atmosphere during surgery. Amazing piece, owned by Lister himself and still in working order. Brendan had tried to buy it a few years earlier when it was being sold as part of a private collection. It had belonged to a specialist dealer that Brendan knew pretty well. It had sold to an anonymous buyer. Brendan called the dealer and asked if he knew who had bought it, or whether the piece was back on the market. He told Brendan that he had been contacted three or four years back by somebody trying to track it down. Said he wanted to own it and didn't mind the cost. Brendan hadn't been able to persuade the new owner to sell but he had taken the potential buyer's name and details. Turns out he was under Brendan's nose. A writer and teacher by the name of Farkas or Firkas. Had written books on philosophy and science and taught at half a dozen universities.'

I looked at her and realized she wanted me to show some excitement. I gave her a thumbs-up. 'OK. And?'

'And he just lives ten minutes from here. Somebody with the biggest collection of medical curiosities you can imagine is just a few streets away. I went to see him the other night and there was no answer but he contacted me by letter this morning. Can you believe that? By letter?'

'That's nice,' I said, and felt my attention starting to drift.

'He said he would be interested to talk with me and even said he was a fan of my show. I've Googled him and he's quite important. Real expert in his field though no shortage of sadness and drama by the looks of things. He said he was watching when you were on!'

'Me?' I asked, embarrassed.

'Mentioned it specifically. Said you were a great helper and that you reminded him of his daughter.'

I pulled a face. 'That's a bit weird.'

'No it's not, it's nice. People used to say nice things like that in the old days.'

'Whatever.'

'So, I'm doing a blog to whet people's appetites. A special on Jean Denys, just like Christine wanted. Honestly, I feel bad. If I'd read her emails I might have had the idea ages ago. Never mind. He's game, that's the thing. I was really giddy about it all earlier on, but then with all the stuff happening . . .'

I patted her arm, the way you're supposed to. She put her warm hand on the back of mine and looked at me the way you do when you're trying to be likeable.

'He might still pull out, of course. Or be really funny about how the show deals with his collection. I really don't want him backing out. It was all I could do to stop Brendan burgling him.'

'I'm sure it will be fine,' I said, shrugging.

'It's just, well, it's not far. And he said how ace you are. And maybe it might be fun and educational.'

I realized what she was saying. I could be helpful. Valuable, even. But I was broken in two inside. My friend was dead, and it was a school night and my mum would kill us both if we made poor decisions. Lottie needed it to be my idea. I thought about it for a moment then shrugged. 'If you want to go see him now I don't mind. There's nobody in and you have your phone. Mum will be ages.'

Lottie grinned and squeezed my forearm. She had colour back in her cheeks. She swallowed down her Whore's Drawers in a gulp.

'Get your coat. We'll run.'

I finished my lemonade and realized I felt happy. This was normal. This was my life. An adventure in the rain with crazy Aunt Lottie. A chat with a collector of blood and steel. I found my coat and Lottie zipped it up for me.

'You sure this is all right?' she asked, as she slipped her laptop in her rucksack then hung it on the peg at the end of the bar. 'Look after this please, Tara. We won't be long.'

As we left the Jolly Bonnet, a gust of wind screamed in

our faces. It sounded like somebody shrieking in fright and it made the hair on my neck stand up. Somehow, it had sounded like my own voice; like a screech of pain and fear. I didn't like it, though Lottie was too excited to notice. I gripped her hand tight and we jogged in the direction of Fournier Street and the great shape of Christchurch. The only thing I knew about the building is that the funerals of the Ripper's victims had been held there and that its bells sounded pretty in summer and scary in winter. That night, as they chimed the hour, the noise was swallowed up by the grey clouds and tumbling sky.

We were damp and pale-faced by the time we reached the house. On the way, Lottie had told me her ideas for the web show. She'd even asked me whether I thought people would want to see a re-creation of the famous experiment. Whether there would be any problems with transfusing the blood of a calf into a willing participant. She reckoned students would do anything for money. When I didn't laugh she told me I was sick and we both giggled at that.

She stopped talking so much once we got to Fournier Street. She might work with bodies and bones and blood but she could still get that creepy feeling like anybody else and the house we were visiting certainly looked pretty unwelcoming. It might have been the rain or the dark skies of the nearly full moon, but I got a little goose-pimply as we walked up the steps and knocked on the door. 'Sort yourself out,' said Lottie, quietly, and tucked my hair behind my ear. 'Be nice. Be helpful.'

There was no sound from inside the darkened house. No footsteps or creaking of the door handle. Lottie knocked again. Lifted the letterbox and shouted his name.

'It's Dr Lottie! I got your letter. I'd love to chat. I've brought my glamorous assistant with me!'

She smiled as she said that. Then she pushed her hand through the letterbox. She turned to me, her eyes all bright and with raindrops on her face, and I was about to say something funny, when suddenly she seemed to lunge forward. She threw herself at the wood, smacking her face on the damp door. She gave a startled cry and then winced as if she had been bitten. She stared at her arm, wedged in the letterbox, and she didn't seem able to compute what was going on. Then I heard a sound like a branch breaking and Lottie's face twisted in agony and her eyes went glassy, like a doll's, and rolled back in her head as she flopped forward and slumped against the door.

It had all happened too quickly for me to say or do anything. I just stood there, frozen to the spot, staring at Lottie as she slithered down the door.

There was the sound of a key turning in an old, creaky lock. Lottie moved like a spirit as the door opened, slowly, and the sweet, sticky smell of rotting meat spilled out on the great wave of darkness that seemed to roll out from within.

'Come in, *cica*,' said the darkness, and I felt cold, bony hands close around my wrist. 'Let us put you back to bed . . .'

I jerked as if stung. Tried to turn away from the black shape in the black hat and black cloak; tried to run . . .

And then the mask was on my face and I was breathing in something that stunk like whisky and petrol and I was sinking to the floor, tumbling into darkness, listening to the desperate song of my own blood as it screamed into the cold night air.

MR FARKAS

Mr Farkas cannot remember entering this bedroom at the end of the long corridor on the second floor of the house. He cannot recall the walk up the stairs but he knows from the tightness in his chest that he has exerted himself. He looks down at himself and sees that he has dressed himself peculiarly today. He wears a long white apron that reaches down to his bare feet and as he moves his head this way and that he feels his scrawny throat rub against a stiff, starched collar. He pushes his hand through his thin hair and as his wrist passes his nostrils he inhales a scent of deep, floral perfume. He looks at his wrist as though his hand belongs to a stranger. Why does he smell of such a scent? Who has he touched? He immediately thinks of his wife, but then discounts the notion. She has never been one for perfume. Her scent is of the home; baked bread and furniture polish. His daughter, then. Beatrix. *Cica*. He knows at once that his little girl would never wear such an ostentatious aroma. She is a child. A princess. A cherub. She smells of fresh laundry and autumn. The girl, then. The one who helps him. Her latest fad, no doubt. A waste of her grant money and a blatant advertisement of her charms. He scowls at his hand. He will need to scold her when she returns this evening. After supper, perhaps. No, it would not do to spoil the evening by reprimanding her as soon as she returns from the auction house. She works hard, even if she is too headstrong for her own good. Too emotional by half. Can't take a castigating without bursting into tears or losing her temper in return.

The blood does not lie.

Mr Farkas shivers and realizes he is cold. There is no heating in this empty bedroom and the wind blows in through the gaps around the window frames. He wonders when his wife began to let the house fall into such disrepair. Probably around the same time *cica* fell ill. No time to clean. Too many blood tests and plate counts and specialists and treatments. Too many trips to old Victorian buildings that stank of disinfectant and boiled vegetables. The house had not seemed important. Not when their *cica* was dying. Not when his cherub, the blood of his blood, was fading beneath her white sheet; the colour leeching from her skin to blend into the snowy linens in which she withered and shrank before him.

Mr Farkas sniffs his wrist again. The girl? He cannot recall having touched her. Theirs has not been an easy union these past months. He knows that he is largely to blame for their fractious relationship. He demands much of her. Too much. Has expected an almost slavish level of dutiful obedience since Beatrix fell ill. He tells himself daily that he should treat her with more affection, more as he would his youngest child, but his good intentions never seem to turn into action. He reaches inside his apron and withdraws his pocket watch. The yellow light that spills in through the window allows him to see the ornate face and he has to force himself not to gasp aloud as he sees how late it is. Why is he alone? Where are his children? His wife? Why does he smell so? Why is he dressed this way? What did he enter the empty room to retrieve?

He is growing used to this feeling of displacement; of having been picked up and manoeuvred by an outside element. In recent months he has become increasingly accustomed to this sensation of returning to himself. He often finds himself blinking eyes that ache with tiredness and staring into surroundings that are alien to him. He finds stains upon his clothes that he has no recollection of creating. Sometimes he can smell foulness upon his skin or taste something bitter and chemical at the back of his throat. He feels as though whole pages of his life are being turned over two at a time. He has begun to see his body as a vessel or vehicle into which he occasionally seats his conscious self. At other times it serves as a carriage for something else.

Mr Farkas rubs at his forehead. There is dried blood upon his brow. He winces as a scab tears and as he looks at the teardrop of inky black blood upon the tips of his pale fingers, he has a sudden recollection of having seen something similar before. Blood on skin; ink upon the page; quills scratching

upon fine white paper; blood and ink, melding into one vision
. . . quills, feathers, goose feathers full of blood; precious blood,
spilling on to his skin as the syringe punctured vein . . .

'Cica . . .'

Mr Farkas breathes the word and then his legs seem to
buckle as the weight of recent memory crashes into his
consciousness. He reels as though the bare floor is the deck
of a trawler in heavy seas. His daughters. His wife. Those
months. Those terrible, terrible months, when he did those
terrible things.

Mr Farkas staggers back and touches the bare wall. This
was her room. His child. His darling. His gift. His fingers
fumble at the light switch but the room continues to bathe in
darkness. There is no bulb at the end of the electric cable that
hangs high overhead like a severed noose. Did he rid his
house of her possessions when the doctors said there was no
hope? He cannot recall. Did his wife take them? Sell them?
Give them away? He was too busy. Too busy trying to keep
their child in his world. Busy with his needles and his cats
and his dogs and goose-feather hypodermics. Busy honouring
and worshipping and cherishing the blood that flowed in her
veins, even as he drained it from her and into the chalice in
his trembling hands . . .

He slides down the wall. Crouches in the dark, pressing
his knuckles to his head. He wants to remember. Needs to
better understand those final days. When did his mind betray
him? Where is his wife? His daughter? The stolen child. The
one who called herself a cuckoo and held his hand steady as
he placed the leeches upon her belly and began to pray.

Memory thumps into Mr Farkas's mind afresh. Blue hair
and big lips, glass jars and smooth stones. The sensation of
bone cracking beneath the weight of his knee. The feel of her
as he dragged her inside. And her! His *cica*! He remembers.
His spirits begin to lift as though a sun is rising inside him.
He saw her. Saw his child. He had made a terrible mistake.
The child in his cellar had been an imposter. He had freed
her and sought out his true blood. And she came, willingly,
to his door. The blue-haired woman had responded to his
simple letter and brought his child home. She has been so ill.

Been through so much. She needs her rest. He had put her to bed. Helped her on her way. Changed her into a simple nightdress and smoothed down the blankets over her slumbering shape. He had come upstairs to find a storybook. He wanted to read to her. This was his pleasure. To comfort her as she lay dying. To forever exist in this moment of perpetual goodbye; her blood in his veins and his in hers, and everything perfect and peaceful as it was meant to be.

Mr Farkas wipes his face. He feels better. His *cica* lives. He has vague recollections of having done this before. Of recreating his dying daughter over and over. Of filling the veins of other children with her blood and covering their faces with her death mask, but he dismisses such a notion. To do so would surely be the actions of a madman.

He leaves his dead daughter's bedroom. Retreats down the darkened corridor and begins to walk down the stairs. On impulse, he visits his own bedroom. He switches on the light and allows himself a moment of utter delight as he considers his collection. It is a dazzling display; floor-to-ceiling shelves filled with preserved body parts. He lingers for a moment in front of a display case before reaching out and selecting a bone-handled scalpel fleam. Made in 1850, with a rounded, tapering tip, it is, like all of his curiosities, a splendid thing. He enjoys the weight of it. It cost him a lot of money to secure it but he has never been frugal when it comes to securing the specimens that speak to him. He looks at the implement as though it were a lover, then switches off the light and leaves the room. He whistles as he walks down the corridor and the bottom flight of stairs. He steps over the form of the woman with the blue hair. Her arm is broken and twisted at a hideous angle. The shock alone would be enough to keep her unconscious but he had plunged a hypodermic full of morphine and laudanum into the back of her hand as she reached through his letterbox and he will not have to consider her for some time. She did well to drag herself this far.

Mr Farkas feels a thrill as he crouches down in the kitchen and pulls up the hatch in the floor. The smell of her is already flooding the house. The smell of his child. His *cica*. His blood. He knows he will enjoy this evening. He will read to her. Tell her stories of his childhood. Tell her about the great philosophers and scientists and pioneers who advanced the world. He will wipe her brow and kiss her cheek and when the pain becomes too much, he will give her something to help her sleep.

As he descends into the darkness of the cellar, he wonders if this is how animals feel. Whether they can smell one another's blood. Whether fathers in the wild have a natural disinclination to procreate with their own offspring. He would like to write a paper about such an issue. Would like to transfuse the blood of Lion A into Lion B to see which partner Lion A's father would prefer to mate with.

Mr Farkas begins to descend.

As he feels the stone and the mud upon his bare feet, a sensation of peace enters Mr Farkas's bones. This is his place of sanctuary. His place of remembrance and rebirth.

The girl in the bed looks out through the eye holes in the death mask. Beneath the unmoving lips, her own mouth has been bound shut with muslin. The image which Mr Farkas looks down upon is one of radiant peace; a beatific immortality. It is the face of his daughter, preserved in the hours before she died. He leans down and kisses the hard, unyielding cheek. As he does so, he feels a moment's annoyance. Beatrix's eyes should be blue. She must have changed them. Contact lenses, perhaps. A modern affectation. Yes, that is the sort of thing she would do.

Mr Farkas shrugs as he sits down in the rocking chair and turns up the oil lamp. He will not worry about such things now. Will not allow it to spoil this moment. Glancing at the array of medical equipment upon the shelves at the foot of the wrought-iron bed, he knows only too well that such imperfections can be fixed.

He clears his throat and begins to read. When the muffled sound of screaming reaches his ears, he merely raises his voice.

MOLLY

A s she runs past the Blind Beggar, Molly tries Lottie's phone again. It continues to go to voicemail. She gives a little squeal of frustration and it is echoed by the shriek of brakes as she runs out from between two cars and a black cab has to slam on its brakes. Unheeding, she sprints across the road, finding gaps in the slow-moving traffic, staring at her phone and desperately thumbing through the list of most-called numbers to seek out a familiar contact. Were anybody to ask why she is so convinced that her child is in danger, Molly would not be able to answer. She has had her tarot cards read and her tea leaves analysed but has never truly believed in anything paranormal or psychic. She simply knows, deep inside her core, that there is something deeply significant about Hilda's similarity to Meda. Something that had not struck her until Karol started to tell her what he had kept hidden.

Molly jabs her finger in her ear as the phone begins to ring. Tara answers on the fourth ring.

'Tara, it's Molly. I need to speak to Hilda please.'

'Sorry, she's not around at the moment. She's popped out with Lottie.'

Molly squeezes her hands into fists. She stops still, then reaches out a hand for support. Her palm touches damp brick. She feels dizzy and nauseous, as though her heart is trying to climb up her throat.

'Where has she gone? I'm trying Lottie's number. She's not answering. Why isn't she there? It's late . . .'

'Hang on, I'll see if she mentioned to anybody where they were off to.'

Molly can hear her blood rushing in her ears. Can feel each pulse beating against her skin like the beak of a bird trying to escape the egg.

'Brendan walked in just as they were leaving but he said they didn't have time to talk. I heard her going on about some broadcast they want to do. Blood transfusions, or something. Apparently Hilda could be a big help, or something. I'm sorry, is there something wrong?'

Molly ends the call and puts her hands to her face. She realizes she is crying. Her tears are warm amid the raindrops. She does not know whether to run for home or to the police station or back to the hospital. She feels utterly lost and does not know where to seek direction.

'Concentrate,' she tells herself. 'Focus.'

She screws up her eyes and promises herself that when she opens them she will know what to do. Counts down from five as her thoughts tumble over and against one another and her head fills with images of her child being skewered with feathers and masked with the flesh of the dead . . .

'Molly. Fuck. Get in.'

She opens her eyes and becomes aware of her surroundings. She is opposite the bagel shop on Vallance Road, blue lettering on chocolate-coloured brick and a huge painting of the original baker, all strongman moustache and starched collar. She feels a sudden loathing for the man she has never met. Feels a hatred for her obsession with nostalgia: with looking back. Hates her clothes and her style and her infatuations.

'Molly!'

She shakes the dust from her thoughts and focuses on the car that has pulled to a stop in the middle of the quiet side road. The driver has bleached blond hair. He is not looking at her. The voice comes from the far side of the vehicle. Karol is leaning across. His face is pale and his eyes dark.

'She's not there,' says Molly, and her voice breaks. 'I know she's in danger, Karol, I know it . . .'

Molly thrusts her hands into her hair and grinds her teeth as she forces herself not to dissolve into panic. She focuses on his words. Hears him, over the sound of the city. His repeated plea to get in the car. She finds herself walking across the road towards the vehicle before she has even made up her mind to do as he asks. She has only a moment's hesitation, hand upon the handle, one foot in the warmth of the vehicle. She pays the voice in her head no heed. It is the calling of her blood that she listens to. She drags herself inside and slumps into the back seat of the car. Karol immediately turns around. The driver does not even glance at her in the mirror. From where she sits, Molly can see that his jaw is locked tightly at the hinge. He is holding in anxiety, or temper. His whole body language screams with displeasure at the presence of the sodden, sobbing ex-cop in the back of his car.

'I tried to shout you back,' says Karol, urgently. 'You got up and ran when the call came through.'

Molly is shaking her head, not really hearing him over the din of her thoughts.

'Lottie has taken Hilda somewhere,' she says, shrill and desperate. 'She should be at the Bonnet. Or at home. Or here, with me. But I did this. Karol, I put her in this position. Tried to make life exciting and now look . . .'

'Molly, stop all that.' Karol's voice is not unkind but there is no doubting the firmness of the command. 'Molly. This is important. We know. We know, yes?'

Molly is pulling on her lower lip, squeezing it, misshaping it. She catches sight of her reflection in the dark window of the car and has to stop herself giggling as she notices that her lower lip looks exactly like a fortune cookie. She wants to show Hilda. And then she is wondering why her thoughts have taken her here. Wonders what she is doing here, in this strange car, with a man who steams the skin from those who displease his boss.

'What do you know?' she asks, as his words penetrate the fog. 'Karol, where is she? Please.'

There is a low muttering in a language Molly recognises as Lithuanian. The driver is grumbling. Karol snaps at him. His gestures are aggressive. Molly senses there is more than tension between them. There is something akin to a battle for dominance. She can smell impending violence as surely as she can feel her daughter's need for help. She wants to grab Karol by the hair and shake answers from him. Memories smash into her like a fist. She suddenly realizes how little of himself Karol has shared with her – how much his stilted accent has dropped to be replaced by near word-perfect English. She realizes that he is a lie.

'The company that tested the skin cells,' says Karol, quietly. 'They have a match.'

Molly sits forward in her seat. She can smell him. Lager and cigarettes and sweat. She tries to force the chaos from her mind. She was a copper once. She caught a killer. She has done things with her life. She has achieved things. She is clever and creative and is not this feeble thing in a mess of terror and tears. She takes a breath. Thinks of all that has come before. Of Meda. Of the conversation with Karol, just minutes ago. Of the sudden realization that the person who took her daughter's friend has targeted the girl who looks like her. That they have targeted Hilda. She glances out of the window and realizes they are heading away from the Bonnet. They are drifting towards Stepney. She suddenly understands and a wave of battling emotions floods her.

'You're going to tell him. To tell Steppen. Karol, it's gone far enough. The police need to know. You can't sort this all out. Not if he has her. What if Hilda is already there!'

Karol holds up a hand. 'We are only here for Steppen. What he wants is as it must be. I do not make the code, Molly, but if I do not follow it then I have no code at all. And to be without code is to be like all weak men.'

Molly bites back tears. She needs to understand. Needs to shake all of Karol's secrets from his skull and pick through them until she finds something that tells her that her daughter is safe.

'Lottie has been trying to get in touch with this private collector of surgical antiques. The other day Hilda was on Lottie's show. Tara says Lottie has taken Hilda with her for something to do with her web programme. What do you know? Do you know where she is . . .?'

Karol swears in his own language. He turns to his associate and bares his teeth, as if daring him to reprimand him. He spins back to Molly, looking grimly resigned.

'The skin cells on Meda's face have been analysed,' he says, flatly. He looks at his phone, reading from a document on the screen. 'The presence of plaster particles alongside the skin cells has led to speculation that a mask has recently been in place upon the victim's face. These are speculated to be in the form of a "death mask" – a *memento mori* that immortalizes the visage of the deceased . . .'

Karol scowls and flicks onwards with his thumb, seemingly refusing to look again at Molly, whose hand has gone to her mouth. She is chewing on her index finger, trying not to shake.

'. . . DNA extracted from the cells has been tested by specialist private sector company—'

'Karol, please!'

'There were no direct matches on the database but a familial match resulted in a hit. The cells are linked on the paternal side to a Domonkos Farkas. The sample was taken when Farkas was arrested four years ago for assaulting a doctor at a private medical facility in the Thames Valley Constabulary region . . .'

'Who is he, Karol? Does he have her?'

Karol turns angry eyes on her. 'Listen to me! His daughter had been receiving treatment there. The police report is clear. His daughter. Beatrix. Twelve years old. Tall. Big for her age. Suffering from acute myeloid leukaemia. She was dying. He wanted to take her home to die. Home for her final days. The doctor advised against it. Farkas lost his temper. Assaulted the doctor and two nurses. Police arrested him. No charges were brought because the doctor declined to cooperate further. Understood Farkas's emotional state. Let it slide.'

Molly bites her lip. Says nothing. Hopes to God there will be more.

'I've been looking him up, Molly. He was a university lecturer. A Ph-Fucking-D. Emeritus Professor of Health History. Published textbooks. Says on an old page at UCL that he was research supervisor on the history of the classical tradition in medicine, from antiquity to the present . . . Fuck, why am I telling you this shit? Look, his daughter got sick, yes? He couldn't take it. She died and now he's trying to – I don't know – somehow make her alive again. It's like fucking Frankenstein. But we know who he is. He owns different properties in London. Another overseas. Partner in a limited company set up to administer earnings from a side business concerned with the buying and selling of art and antiques. Partner, research student Selina Berry . . .'

'Enough!' The driver loses patience. Speaks in English, so

Molly can hear how much he disagrees with his partner's actions. 'Fuck man, tell her everything, yeah? Scream it out the window too. What you think Steppen's going to say?'

'She won't speak, I told you,' hisses Karol. 'She helped us. Keep your mouth shut and Steppen doesn't need to know he was second in line.'

'This from the man with the code, yeah? You're sworn, Karol. He's a fucking captain. He's killed people for less than this. I've seen it! His own two hands. I took the face and fingertips myself, Karol. Dumped him in a suitcase in the Grand Union Canal. You're getting her killed, Karol. It wasn't bad enough to fuck her, no? Not bad enough to—'

Molly feels the vehicle lurch to the left as Karol lunges at the driver. She topples against the glass and bangs her head, crying out in pain. Eyes wide, she sees Karol pushing the driver's face up against the window, shouting something she cannot make out, and then she is looking past him, at the rear of the blue van that grows suddenly huge as she opens her mouth and bellows a warning . . .

She hears tyres screech on the wet road; the crunch of metal on metal; of glass shattering and the incongruous whoomph of the airbag exploding.

Molly is thrown forward, head slamming into something solid, and she hears a crack and tastes iron and pewter and sees something black skewer directly through the centre of her vision like a lance and she is already blacking out as the smashed carcass of the vehicle comes to land on its side; sparks and terrible squeals emerging from its ruined shell as it grinds along the unyielding road.

There is silence for a moment. A silence filled with pain and bewilderment and a sense of being wrong way up then right way round, and then somebody is saying her name and a warm hand is holding hers and a nice policeman with a name like Barry or Scott is telling her that she is going to be OK.

Molly isn't sure whether she imagines the voice. She is only halfway sure of where she is. She tries to move her arms but they seem to be pinned to her sides, and when she manoeuvres her head, the scene in front of her stays still.

She half hears a voice she recognizes. She manages to inch her way left, and then she is looking into the dark eyes of Karol. Karol, who put them all in danger. Karol, who was on his way to see Steppen. To waste this information on revenge.

Hilda.

A gasp catches in Molly's throat and when she swallows she tastes the iron flavour again. She coughs, trying to clear the blockage, and hears her own voice, feeble and distorted.

'My daughter. He has my daughter!'

Karol is shaking his head. His eyes are softer now. He looks sad. His expression seems to ooze regret.

'Don't worry about this now, Molly. You've done so well. We've got him, do you understand? It will make sense, I promise.'

Molly feels firm hands tugging at her neck. Somebody is trying to put a tube into her throat. She swats with her hand and the movement pains her.

'The man who took Meda?' she gasps. 'You have him?'

'You will understand,' urges Karol. 'It was an operational decision. It was an opportunity. Anything unearthed in this investigation will be shared with the Major Incident Team when the investigation into the missing immigrants is given over to a particular team . . .'

'The missing immigrants?' gasps Molly. She is starting to understand. Through the pain, through the gathering darkness, she is putting it together. 'Farkas?'

'He's a viable suspect,' says Karol, lightly. 'Steppen won't get to him, either way. There's time to build a case.'

'My daughter. What about Hilda?' She begins to thrash at the arms that hold her. She rolls left and tumbles with a painful thud on to the road. A woman in a yellow coat is bending over her, trying to help her back on to the stretcher, but she lashes left and right with arms that have recovered their strength and then she is dragging herself upright, battered and cold, and reaching out for Karol's throat as the full weight of it all hits her like a fist. Strong arms grab her by the waist and she swings wildly, fists and feet, hissing at anybody coming near her.

'Molly, please, we'll get him.' Karol is patting the air, trying to calm her. 'I've told you more than I should. I needed to keep him talking. Needed the confession. We have it now. We'll start building a case against Farkas. Do it properly. There's some compelling evidence . . .'

'You bastard!' She screams it, turning her face up and into the moonlight and rain. 'You fucking bastard! You'd let a girl die to catch a gangster? You have to knock on his door. Find out where he is. I know he has her!'

Karol turns at the sound of running feet. Molly sees uniformed officers arriving alongside plain clothes. She hears curses in English and Lithuanian. Hears a crackle of static from a police radio. Imagines the platoon of officers who will be smashing in the doors of Steppen's home and arresting him for murder and participation in organized crime based upon the recordings of an undercover operative who used his niece's abduction as a way to ingratiate himself into the organization.

'We can't knock on his door or we lose all the evidence,' says Karol, as if explaining to a child. 'There's no investigation team. We don't know if it's what you think.'

'But the cells! The blood. Farkas . . .!'

'We will examine it all,' says Karol, and Molly can see how much it hurts him to repeat the words of senior officers who had overcome his own misgivings with the self-same speech.

'You must have been watching the Bonnet,' gasps Molly. 'Where did they go? Are they really going to see him? Why have you told me this?'

'Why is she asking about Farkas?'

Molly starts at the sound of the new voice. She traces it to the tall, shaven-headed man to her right, standing in the glare of a flashing blue light that turns the rain into a million daggers. He is staring at Karol angrily, questions in his eyes, anger on his face.

'Please, Karol, just tell me you know where she is . . . I'll call Lottie, you can trace it, that's that . . . Why would you let her go and see him? Why haven't you protected her?'

Karol glances at the senior officer who stands between them. She understands what is crackling, unsaid, between them. There are those up the chain of command who are unconvinced that there is even a case to investigate. It is not an operational priority. All that is known is that a girl found on the ring road had come into contact with some dead cells that had belonged to a relative of a noted professor who had made a solitary mistake. There was no need to keep tabs on the child of an ex-cop whom the undercover operative had come into contact with.

'Where is she now?' begs Molly. She rubs her forehead and her hand comes away bloody. She stares at the crimson stain on her pale skin. She lets her feelings bubble up and is suddenly awash with understanding. For an instant she can feel the anguish that must have throbbed within Farkas's heart as he prepared to say goodbye to his child. She understands it. Can imagine the brutal insistence deep within himself; the command that he keep her alive, somehow. To keep a part of her. To let there be more . . .

Karol steps forward. 'You're bleeding. Here. Let me . . .'

She freezes as he puts the paper to her head. Feels heat coming off him. Feels wave after wave of some magnetic force, urging her to keep her mouth shut. She puts her hand upon his and the paper upon her brow feels wrong. It is printer paper. A document, not a handkerchief or napkin. She catches his eye as she steps back. Pain shooting down her side as she pushes aside the girl in the yellow coat.

'They don't care,' whispers Karol. 'I don't know if she's there, but try. Push me. Run.'

It only takes an instant. A burst of adrenaline and a shove in the chest, and then she is pushing through paramedics and skipping past the open door of a police van, and now she is running back towards home, pulling the paper from the open wound. She reads the name through a veil of blotted blood. Reaches into her pocket for her phone and realizes she has left it in the ruins of the car. She does not stop. Puts her head down and feels warmth run down her cheek. She tastes it again. Her blood. The blood that beats in her daughter's veins. The blood that cries out for her.

HILDA

There was pain, of a sort. More a brutal sort of numbness, the way your fingers go a little after you've slammed them in a door. It was an emptiness, too. As if I was a half-made thing. I had the sensation of being a vessel, somehow. Through the blur of ripped-up memories I saw myself as a suit of skin. A costume; a wetsuit hanging on a peg, waiting to be unzipped and worn. I don't remember fear. It felt like coming round after an operation – that sensation of being wrapped too tight in thick damp wool. I remember fragments. Tangled ribbons of something intangible.

'Do you remember the car with the bubbly leather seats, *cica*? You said they always made you want to eat chocolate. Perfect lines, stitched so intricately. You used to run your finger over the seams, stroking the stitches, stroking, stroking, so softly, so rhythmically. I would see your little fingers, pale, like twigs stripped of their bark; the little sea shells of your fingernails, and I would glance at your face and wonder where your mind had gone – which great adventures you were having behind your eyelids. You were so brave, my love. You never allowed the pain to win. Your cries were tiny things – an animal trapped behind glass. I never knew whether it was better to let you find your own peace, or to hold you and give you my strength. So many times I got it wrong. I woke you from nightmares only to pitch you into a world of pain. Or I would let you rest only to learn at daybreak that you had fought demons in your sleep. We have both fought so hard, my darling. We deserve these moments of peace. These times of bliss, when it is just you and I, alone in the quiet; safe in our cave, father and daughter, blood of my blood . . .'

I couldn't breathe. The thing on my face was too heavy. It felt like there was a hand on the bridge of my nose. When I opened my mouth my lips touched something hard and brittle, like the bottom of a baking dish. I poked out my tongue and explored the ridges. I tasted dust. Clay. A foulness, like water left still for too long. There was a dampness at the crook of my arm and a precise, silver-coloured point of pain somewhere near my belly button. I couldn't move. My limbs seemed to belong to somebody else. I could feel myself shaking though there was a heat within me that was so intense I fancied I could burst into flames.

'You will need more medicine, *cica*. This is our time. Our special time. Father and daughter, blood of blood. Please, try and hush. Should I tell you a story? A favourite? Do you remember the Musicians of Bremen, my love? How you would laugh at the different animal voices. If people had seen what I became in your presence! I, fusty, dusty – the grump of the halls. I simply saved my smiles for you. I became a clown for you. I would do anything to make you smile. Still, that is all I seek. Though I love these moments of peace, these quiet moments of togetherness, I yearn for your resurgence. I long to hear you laugh. Long to hear you call my name. I want to hear your feet upon the stairs above my office. I wish to scold you, then melt as you scolded me with your big sad eyes. We have lost much, my love, but we will regain it. You will find your strength.'

I didn't hear him move but he was suddenly there in the dark space above me. I had never seen him before. He was thin. Gaunt. There were hollows in his cheeks and his eyes were sunk deep. It was like looking at a skull over which insufficient skin had been stretched. I smelled him, too. Sweat and lotion, mothballs and detergent. I was already shaking but the tremble became a shiver as I saw his hand come down upon my eyes like a huge spider lowering itself on a web.

'Please, Beatrix. Hush now, be calm. Find yourself. Find your way . . .'

I have a memory of something I cannot truly explain. For a moment it felt as if I was two people. For an instant my whole body felt flushed with a kind of tingling ecstasy, as though all the blood in my veins had been somehow carbonated and thickened. Everything felt sensual and elegant. I lost sense of what I could see and what I could only feel. Memories rippled in and out of my peripheral vision; imaginings becoming real and reality flickering into a haze. I felt as though vines were tugging at my skin. I saw tendrils and tongues and wreaths of smoke, wrapping me, mummifying me, as something else, something other, probed and prodded at my flesh as if seeking a doorway. I heard my name, and yet it was not my name, and as I grabbed for something familiar amid the flotsam of disappearing memory, I had the sensation of being invaded. I thought of wasps, laying their eggs in the skull of another creature; parasites forcing their will on to a living thing that had become their carrier and sustenance. I told myself to fight it. To push back against the sensation that flooded me, bathed me, rushed into my arteries and veins like pure crystal water through bare riverbeds.

'Please. Come back to me. All will be well. All will be so perfect . . .'

I think I may have seen her. Somewhere, between the jumble of sputtering pictures, I saw a girl who looked like me. Saw flushed cheeks and brown eyes and a big ungainly frame. She was not much more than shadow; a dirtied oil painting hidden behind layer upon layer of grime. She was searching for something. She was a child seeking a favourite toy; her gestures manic and desperate, urgent in her jerky movements, and then she was lost to me as the man leaned back into my vision and smiled. He opened my eyes between a finger and thumb that I could not feel. And then he grinned; a knife-wound in rotten fruit.

'There,' he said, and his voice was a prayer. 'I see you, *cica*. I see you . . .'

And I knew that if I screamed, the voice that erupted from my mouth would not be my own.

MOLLY

A plump man in a grey cardigan is leaning out of an upstairs window. The glass is frosted and refracts the light from the flickering fairy lights that are strung across the pergola in the garden below. From where she crouches in the rear of the neighbouring garden, Molly cannot see the lights. From her vantage point, it seems as though the fat man is a robot; his torso a circuit board of blinking reds and yellows. He cannot see her. He is smoking a pipe. Blowing out a steady lungful of grey. Molly has a sudden urge to tell Hilda a story. She will tell her of this man, with his round head and his glasses and his pleasant fleshy face. Who leans out of the window of his house on Fournier Street and exhales all the clouds in the world. She will call him The Rainmaker. Hilda will grin, and tell her how the story could be improved. She will hold her hand, like she did when she was young and scared, and Molly will breathe her in; inhaling as if she were a breeze that carried the first sunlight of spring.

The thought causes Molly to shake her head with such ferocity that she almost loses her footing. She is angry with herself for this hesitation. She is so used to drifting off; to following her fantasies on their meandering courses, that she has let go of herself for a moment. Drifted away from her child. From this place. This now. She bites her cheek. Munches down hard with her molars on the soft peach-flesh of her inner cheek. She needs all of herself.

It is perfectly dark in the garden of Mr Farkas's house. The long, thin space is a mess of broken-down walls and tangled grass. As she had clambered over the high wall at the rear she had hurt her leg on a rusted piece of metal that had once formed the frame of a miniature trampoline. She had lost her footing treading on the head of a broken ornament; the concrete cranium of a regal-looking woman with sleek hair

and upturned nose. The wound across the neck of the bust
was clean, as if it had been cleaved with an executioner's
blade.

Molly's breath comes in staggered bursts, as if she has
cried herself into a state of neutered hysteria. She hears herself
and forces herself to be quiet, then reaches her hand to her
mouth and bites upon the skin of her index finger, screaming
at herself for her indecision. She does not know whether she
wants to be seen. As she sprinted here she kept asking herself
whether or not she should make all the noise and disruption
it is possible to make. She wants noise. Chaos. Mania. For
that could stop the man who has her daughter from hurting
her. But to alert the neighbours would be to cause Farkas to
panic. He could finish what he has begun. The thought makes
her gorge rise and hot acid burns her throat. She wants to
shout out. To beg for help.

'Sort yourself out,' she hisses, cat-like, as she moves quietly
towards the glass. 'He's got your fucking daughter . . .'

Molly tastes iron as she licks the rain and the tears from
her lips. Blood has dripped into her mouth. Sucking in a breath
she darts forward. The glass is dark, curtains shut. She puts
out her hands and touches the wet glass. Moves sideways. Her
eyes have grown accustomed to the darkness now and she can
see that she is in front of a bay window. She moves left,
reaching out, searching her way around the rear of the big old
house. Her hands close upon a door handle but the wood stays
stuck in the frame as she pushes. She steps back, tears of
frustration in her eyes. Her feet squelch in mud and she glances
down. She is standing in a long trench of turned earth. Every
part of her wants to fall to the ground and begin scrabbling
at the earth like a dog. She forces herself to fight it.

Could be nothing.

Doesn't matter.

Get in the house, just get in, get in . . .

She edges back along the window. Stops at the drapes.
Looks up and sees the softest chink of grey light lancing
through the blackness. She puts her hand on the rotten wooden
sill. Feels pain. Looks at her palm and sees blood. Ignores it
and reaches up to wrap her fingers around the frame of the

smaller windows. She hauls herself upright, stretches up on her toes, and looks through the tiny gap, two inches long, above the Venn diagram of the conjoining curtains.

A light spills into the kitchen from the hall. It illuminates a big, square kitchen. It looks as if it has been ransacked or used by somebody living rough. The table is awash with dirty dishes and discarded boxes. Discarded paper covers the floor. Exposed wires protrude from walls on to which the maelstrom of words have been scrawled over and over: a lacework of spiralling, intersecting text scribbled so deeply that in places they have gouged into the plaster beneath.

Blood of my blood
Blood of my blood
Blood of my blood . . .

There is a hatch in the floor, the trapdoor raised like a sail. Along the wall stand three large refrigerator units, each as tall as a man and wide enough for two.

Molly gasps, her thoughts a hard slap. Realizes at what she has been looking.

Lottie. Laid in the doorway. Not moving. Arm bent the wrong way.

Molly leaps down from the sill. There is no longer a question of making up her mind. She senses that she is leaving herself. That for whatever comes next, she will be mere passenger.

Then she runs into the garden. Turns and looks up at the startled smoker in the neighbouring house.

'Call nine-nine-nine right now. Police officer needs assistance. Mother and child, immediate risk to life. Suspect still on premises, I repeat, suspect still on premises!'

Before she can register the response, Molly bends down and picks up the head of the broken statue. It has a pleasing heft. She puts it under her arm like a rugby ball and runs back to the house. She grips the rocky skull in her hands and slams it into the wood above the lock. The door bursts open and Molly stumbles inside. She hauls herself up, dropping the rock on to a cracked mosaic floor. She stands up and the smell of it hits her. The smell of bad memories. Damp walls. Rotten carpets. Spilled blood.

Molly pushes forward, tripping over a cardboard box that has been casually discarded. In the half light of the corridor, she can make out the words upon the packaging. Can see the medical symbols and the official-looking symbols that have declared the medical paraphernalia within to be transported.

Molly wrenches open the inner door and pitches forward into the hallway. The light is coming from a solitary bulb hanging high overhead. A sensation of vertigo flows through her as she stares up and up through the centre of the tall staircase which winds up three floors to a distant skylight. She screws up her eyes, seeking control, and then she feels herself bumbling down the corridor, arm upon the wall, biting her tongue to stop from shouting her daughter's name.

On the floor before her, Lottie is a pitiful thing. She is unmoving and her arm looks as though it has been snapped completely at the elbow. Both hands lie face-up on the floor, even as her face is pressed against the broken tiles of the floor. Molly crouches down and gently moves her friend's head. Her lips pull for a second; her lip gloss and spit momentarily gluing her to the floor. Breathing slow, forcing herself to stay calm, Molly puts her fingers under her friend's nose. She gasps with relief as she feels a faint, warm breath upon her skin.

Molly is about to speak when she hears it. Hears the low, hushed, lullaby voice. She lowers Lottie's head back to the floor and slowly turns. The void below the open door is a perfect square but to Molly's perception, it is a mouth, open and screaming for her. She stands. She does not want to know what is there, in the dark, beneath the house. And yet she cannot stop herself from moving towards it. Cannot help but suck in a breath of air laced with the copper and chemical tang of the mortuary room. Cannot help but step inside, down, deeper, deeper . . . She half imagines that she is lowering herself into shimmering black oil. And then she sees the flickering light. Hears the soft voice. The gentle pleas. The carillon sound of something between laughter and weeping and the soft hum of a generator whirring in the space beyond.

Molly hears the words. Feels them thud into her very centre and pitch shards of flint through her every nerve.

'You are a beautiful girl, *cica*. I see you. See you looking out at me. Oh my child, my child . . .'

She steps down.

Ducks into the light.

Sees . . .

MR FARKAS

It sounds to Mr Farkas as though somebody has shouted his name or lightly slapped his face. He experiences a sudden burst of waking; of having emerged from beneath packed earth.

He blinks, rapidly, until the thing before him comes into view.

It is his daughter. His daughter, as if viewed through cracked glass. A lifeless mask, amateurishly daubed in lipstick and paint. He feels himself twitch where he stands and he is overcome by a feeling of weakness. He looks down at his arm; bare below his rolled-up shirtsleeve. His skin is white and clammy and there is an open wound in the crook of his arm. Blood leaks from the ugly fissure as he slowly turns the limb and he watches with fascination as it trickles down his wrist. He continues his gaze downwards. Looks at the starched white sheet pulled tight over the still body. A red stain is spreading on the sheet, blooming like damp, and Mr Farkas looks at the clear tube that leaks blood from a thick, blunted syringe.

Mr Farkas fights to control his breathing. Looks back up at the caricature of his child. At this ghoulish imitation, made more grotesque by the realistic quality of the eyes that twitch, frantic, and fill with tears as they rove back and forth beneath the mask.

Mr Farkas rears back as if a hand has reached out for him from a grave. There is a child! A child, in this bed, in this place, wearing the face of his daughter . . . here, in this terrible place . . .

Images flash before him; explosions of memory and understanding; a vile stream of lurid snapshots that burst as cannon-fire in his vision. He feels himself lose the power of his legs. He pitches forward and lands upon the child, the girl . . .

Body-blows of recollection slam into him. He sees himself

and all that he has done. Recalls tastes. Touches. The tensions in their bodies as he drained them to make room for his girl.

He staggers back, knife in hand, raising his hands to his temple.

Stops, suddenly completely still.

A woman is standing in front of him. She is pretty, with red hair. There is blood on her face and her palm and she is looking at him with murder in her eyes.

'Is that my daughter?'

Her voice is raw. Hysterical. Unhinged. Mr Farkas feels fear. Who is this person, to have come into his home and look at him so? To address him so. He is here with his child, sharing stories, laughing, making up silly voices, and she strolls in and dares look at him . . .

'I said, is that my fucking daughter! What have you done? Get off her. Get off her!'

And Mr Farkas looks down at the child and sees the perfect lips and rosy cheeks and tousled hair of the child that he adores, and he is suddenly very cross indeed. He remembers. He had been giving her some medicine. Giving her the blood she needs to stay well. Doctors didn't care, he remembers, suddenly furious. Gave up on her too soon. *My blood cannot end with me. It will not. She is blood of my blood. I will make her well* . . .

And he had. Had he not extended her life? Given her more and more precious time. He had emptied himself for her. Drained her own bad blood and gladly poured his own into her veins. He had followed the teachings of the men he admired. Visionary thinkers past. Surgeons. Scientists. Philosophers. It had always been transfusion that fascinated him. The true pioneers. Men who sought to align spirit with science. Men like Denys. He had succeeded, had he not? Altered the natures of both beast and man before cruel fortune forced him to cease his work. Beatrix's illness had allowed him to become pupil to an ancient master. He followed Denys's experiments to the letter. Recreated all that the great transfusionist decreed. The results were extraordinary. Bad dogs became good. Hysterical animals were pacified by the blood of the meek. He had discovered what he had long suspected. That nature, the very soul, was not in the skin and bone. It was in the blood. And that was what he would keep. His blood would flourish. Would thrive. And he would forever have his beloved daughter at his side, listening to a heart beat with the same blood that ran in his own veins. His wife had protested, had she not? Finally spoken up after decades as a timid, mousy little crinkle of a thing. Stopped spending money long enough to scold him for his obsession. The obsession that bought them everything. That had made him rich enough to buy her whatever she wanted. To finally afford the treatment which allowed their child to be born. Her egg fertilized, mortifyingly, in a laboratory far from home, three days after he had emptied himself into a plastic pot and wept for the shame of it. The girl had been more help. His student. The loyal one. Eve. Loved Denys like he did. Got his little jokes. Looked up to him with a look that he had never seen outside of films and said she would be honoured to help him in his pioneering work. She had been crucial. Helped source the specimens. Brought in the dogs and cats. Even sourced two lambs. Had a friend in a slaughterhouse who brought true calf blood. She believed in the work. Better, she believed in him. It was his wife who spoiled things. Lost her temper. Said she could stand losing him to their dying daughter but not to a failed research assistant. It had become heated. Mr Farkas had been embarrassed and angry. He had been forced to strike his wife. He struck her harder than he intended to. Struck her again and again and again. And when he was finished striking her, there was not much left to hit. The girl said nothing. Just put her hand on his arm, her gesture sympathetic. Understanding. Later that night, when they made love, she told him that she wanted to volunteer. To use herself as a test subject in the same vein as the greats of science and philosophy. Though he had wanted a more markedly different test case, the opportunity was too great to turn down. He had agreed. He wanted to see what would happen. Would the girl's nature be softened or sweetened by his daughter's blood? He had been stockpiling it for weeks. Tapping her vein every few days to build up a refrigerated wine-rack of blood, thinned with the anti-clotting agent his assistant had sourced from overseas. He had not given up hopes of his daughter's recovery, but it was the blood that must take priority. She died while he was transfusing three pints of her blood into his assistant's thigh. There was no doubting the presence of Beatrix within her. Once the sweating and nausea and the headaches had passed, there was a playfulness, an other-worldliness, that caused his eyes to fill with tears. His assistant was delighted that she had pleased him. Happily volunteered to start draining herself as swiftly as her body could reproduce it. Each fresh beat of her heart brought more Beatrix into her veins. It was a pity when she fell sick. The heat of her. The sweat upon her skin. The fits of agony that sent her into rictus spasms. It had touched his heart to see her die. But the blood was safe. And it was not difficult to find new carriers. He knew from his own time as an immigrant that the world was full of disposable people. He targeted those he felt confident would not be sought. Hunted those with the right height, the right shape, the right bearing, to carry the blood of his daughter. It had all gone surprisingly well. His daughter took up residence within her. He read to her. Mopped her brow. Bathed and changed her. Told her that soon, she would be well. The girl lasted four weeks. It was a pity when she died. But by then, the blood was safe . . .

Mr Farkas realizes that this woman is here to break the chain. In a moment of weakness he had freed the last girl to carry his child's blood. Even now she is shivering and fitting in a hospital bed. All he has left is the few frozen sample bags that he cannot vouch for the condition of, and his own tainted blood. The child beneath the mask may die. And that will be the end of it. The end of her. Of his blood . . .

There is a flash of silver as the knife in Mr Farkas's hand slices through the air. The woman throws up a hand to cover her face and yells in pain as the blade jabs into the back of her hand. She lashes out with her foot and kicks Mr Farkas hard in the chest. He falls backwards, gasping and hurt, clutching at his ribs and the woman is on him, wrapped around his waist, pushing him to the floor and punching him, again and again, sobbing as she smashes her fist into his jaw.

And then she is standing. Sobbing. Gulping for air. She is saying a name, over and over.

Mr Farkas cannot see out of one eye. But through the other he watches the woman stumble forward, the dead weight of the child dragging down her arms.

Mr Farkas stands up. In the reflected surface of the brass antiseptic spray tank by the bed, he sees himself. Fine boots and breeches. Braces. Collar and cravat. Wing-tipped moustache, soaked in blood. Dressed the way his daughter likes. Dressed the way she told him to always dress so it would be like forever living in a story.

He sees the woman pushing at the barely moving body.

He looks for the dropped knife and finds it beside the girl's discarded clothes.

Painfully, holding his ribs, Mr Farkas hurries across the cellar floor. The woman is nearly at the top of the stairs. She is dragging the girl like a ragdoll. She is big for her age, his Beatrix. Solid. Fleshy.

Mr Farkas reaches up to grab the child's bare ankle. It is dragged out of his reach before his fingers can close upon it.

He growls, frustrated, and climbs the stairs, reaching out, grunting at the pain, listening to the woman's squeals of frustration as she hauls the child up the last two steps.

Mr Farkas does not hurry now. The woman cannot get the child out of the house. Not before he gets there. He imagines what it will be like to remember this story at bedtime. Whether she will still sleep well after he tells her the story of the bad woman who came to take her away.

He is about to emerge into the cool grey light of the kitchen when the trapdoor smashes into his head. The impact is like two boats colliding. Mr Farkas thinks only of black and purple and a sudden inexplicable white waterfall that folds in on itself and runs upside down . . .

Mr Farkas has fallen awkwardly. The wooden trapdoor is pinning his head, neck, shoulders and one arm to the floor. The rest of him hangs below, kicking against the stairs, scrabbling for purchase. The door is heavy, but a fit person could push it clear were they given enough time. Mr Farkas is not very fit. His body has been shutting down for weeks. He has septicaemia. But with enough time, his resolve could give him the strength to extricate himself from the painful trap.

Mr Farkas does not have time. He is pinioned and he cannot seem to work out which way is up and which is down. He can taste blood. His own. His daughter's. He cannot seem to focus on the pictures in front of him but he sees the shape of a woman. A black silhouette. A raven's shadow. Mr Farkas hears himself gurgling. Realizes he is pleading.

The woman looks inside the refrigerator. Stands there, bloodied and glowing in the light of the appliance, perfectly illuminated for his viewing. He sees her face perfectly. Sees the horror. The sheer, overwhelming revulsion at what she sees.

Mr Farkas drifts into unconsciousness for a moment. When he returns to himself, it is to the sound of squeaking. Of something heavy being pushed across the broken floor.

Mr Farkas opens his eyes in time to see darkness fall. His mouth does not utter a sound as the refrigerator topples forward and lands squarely on the angled trapdoor. His body emits a noise like the cracking of a tree trunk.

There is just light, then darkness, and the sense of true separation; of severing. A sound like a bag of meat falling on to stone.

Mr Farkas's brain ceases to function only moments after the disconnection of his upper torso from the rest of his body. They are very long moments for Mr Farkas's brain.

Then everything is nothing.

And Mr Farkas is dead.

HILDA

It's not the past any more. It's now. I'm not remembering it, I'm living it. I've had a birthday. They brought balloons and cake and ate it around the bed. They played music. Lottie joked about unplugging the life-support machine by accident so she could find a socket for the speaker. Mum laughed, though it was an effort for her, I could tell. She doesn't seem to find things funny the way she used to. When she reads to me I can hear the tears in her throat. Sometimes she will take my hand and press it to hers and she will beg me, literally beg me, to come back. And I'll try to squeeze her hand. Try to get my lips to cooperate. All I have managed is a tear. It ran from my left eye on to the knuckles of her left hand and though my eyes are closed, I sensed that she had held it to her face and breathed it in for a very long time.

I've only heard snippets of what came after. Lottie and Mum, talking in whispers. The neighbours had called 999 but the police were already on their way. Karol had phoned in an anonymous tip while he was driving himself to the house. He'd been the first to see what Mum had done. I was still half conscious at that point. I have memories of tears and screeches and Mum's desperate urging that he look inside the refrigerator. I don't know what happened next but Lottie has told Mum that Karol had done a good thing. He had made it right. He has some laurels to rest on, according to Lottie. Caught a killer.

It's blurry after that. Some of the voices I hear cannot really be there. I hear them in the centre of my brain, as though they come from within me. I sometimes feel as though I am being pulled apart; that I am a ragdoll built to be pulled apart.

Mum opens my eyes from time to time. When she does I can see how much weight she has lost. She has a grey tinge to her skin, as though she is a drawing. She does not dress like Mum any more. I will tell her off for that when I wake up. We will go shopping together and I will tell her to buy the wackiest, most totally insane ensemble she can find. And even if she looks like a dog's dinner in it, I'll tell her she looks great, because she's my mum and she's awesome and she saved me.

Complications is the word the consultant keeps using. An infection in my blood. The coma is intentional, apparently. They chose to do this to me. There is much room for optimism. When the swelling in my brain goes down they will know better. My body has been through a lot. He took pints of her blood. Pumped his own infected plasma straight into an open vein. She's fighting it. She's tough. Her blood is winning, we're sure . . .

Sometimes, in the dark hours, I am visited by something . . . other. I can't really describe it. It just feels as if something is scuttling about, inside me and over me and probing at the cracks in my shell with its long, spidery legs. Sometimes I hear a voice that I have never heard before. A child's cry; a sad little plea.

Let me in. Please. Let me in . . .

In such moments I hide within myself. I find the locked rooms in my mind where nobody can follow. I hear the locks being rattled, the handles being turned, but I stay motionless in the little pockets of shadow and the visitor eventually moves away. On such nights I feel my body shiver and fit and the machine beside my bed makes strange noises. Nurses and doctors gather around and there is chaos and shouting and my Mum cries, and that sound is enough to bring me from the locked room and back into my skin for a time.

I will wake up, in time. I will open my eyes and sit up straight and rip the tube out of my throat and I will make sense of the bits that are still all a jumble. I will sit in the back of the Bonnet and drink hot chocolate. Mum will help me with my homework and I will go to Believerz and stand at the back with Meda and get the steps wrong. I will get into mischief with Lottie. I will play with Ripper and listen to Connie's stories.

'Morning, fancy pants. Sleep well? Good dreams? Traffic was murder. Lottie would have come up but she managed to fall asleep in the bath and she's soaked her plaster cast and needs to go have it re-set. She's asking about doing a webcast. I've told her that if she doesn't wait until you're back on your feet then I will thumb her in the eye. How you doing? Hungry? You're looking bloody gorgeous.'

She opens my left eye with her thumb. Looms in front of me; light behind her like a halo.

'Please,' she says, quiet now, as if the brightness of her entrance has already drained her. 'I can bear it if I have you. I'll know what it was all for. I can't bear it alone. I can't.'

I turn and kick towards her. Try and force myself back to the surface; to break through into the familiar world of her kisses and hugs and her warm, safe smell.

And then I feel it again. Feel the cold, shadowy fingers gripping at the part of me that floats in the dark. The bitter chill, like being wrapped in metal and thorns; the feeling of being consumed from the inside out.

There, at the very back of my consciousness, a whisper; a breath . . . the voice in my blood.

'*Cica . . .*'

9 781780 296487